DEEP SLEEP

'The complete thriller, ingenious and engrossing, containing one of the most convincing field studies of grub-into-monster since *Malice Aforethought*, and handling the fissile stuff of human relationships with the depth and sensitivity of a first-rate novel.'   *Observer*

'Ruth Rendell is not the only one who can create frissons around mild-seeming people; and Fyfield has the further gift of pinning down with casual ease the often unregarded minutiae of love and other hazards.'   *Sunday Times*

'A dark mixture of human tension and nineties urban decay. Formidable Fyfield talent burgeons.'   *Guardian*

'Atmospheric, suspenseful, finely crafted . . . a cunning mix of domestic cliff-hanger and psychological thriller. Ignore the comparisons (Rendell, James, etc.), Fyfield is bound for the top, and in her own way.'   *Literary Review*

TRIAL BY FIRE

'In only her third novel, Frances Fyfield shows herself superbly in command of chills and ills. Her effortless wit and emotional perception establish her as one of our very best crime-and-punishment writers.' *Sunday Times*

'Fyfield gives us something that seems more authentic than a mere whodunnit, something more in accord with our experiences of the world . . . always readable and reliable and . . . as an honest attempt to depict the sordid pathos that must lie behind so many murders, *Trial by Fire* succeeds rather well.' *Independent*

'Fyfield stakes her claim to the year's laurels, home-grown variety. Coiled menace, wit, the human touch. Her third novel puts her firmly with the elect.' *Observer*

'Her deadly realism and wry psychological insight mark Frances Fyfield as an upcoming queen of crime. This tense page-turner is wonderfully astute on human nature.' *Company*

SHADOWS ON THE MIRROR

'Enthrallingly readable . . . a novel of menace . . . superbly threatening set-pieces . . . a fine feeling for the needling treacheries of married life.'   *Sunday Times*

'Fyfield is lethally intelligent but never chilly. There's a love story in this psychological thriller.'
Cosmopolitan

'Extraordinarily atmospheric tension sustained throughout. Anguished excellence.'   *The Times*

A QUESTION OF GUILT

'. . . authentic and riveting courtroom detail . . . an excellent debut . . . I'm looking forward to the next case.' *Options*

'. . . an intelligent first novel . . . legal detail is convincing . . . always interesting.' *Independent*

'Reminiscent of Ruth Rendell . . . her writing could win Fyfield a position as lady-in-waiting to just such a Queen of Crime.' *Evening Standard*

DEEP SLEEP

No murder suspect, no misadventure but the simple
and unacceptable fact of death. Chloroform, self-
administered, well, well. Twelve milligrammes, she
read, not lethal. How did anyone know, since no
modern doctor used the stuff any more? The arrogance of all this infuriated her. Why sniff chloroform
when you live upstairs from a stockpile of pills you
could drink in your tea?

. . . She jotted on the blotter, phone . . . retest
blood – for what? Chloroform in bathroom, body
in bed. How? I hate facts, she complained to herself.
I hate facts and smells.

Smells, obnoxious scents. She lived by visual
images, second to words heard and things smelled,
all of these senses acute and long-remembered. The
cough sweet tasted of eucalyptus, but alongside that
was another smell, reminiscent of a dentist, the mask
coming down over the face, a sickly smell inhaled
in mute protest. A little like the smell of the dry-
cleaning she had placed over the spare chair on the
other side of the desk, the polythene covering disturbed to release that waft of cutting scent, so
suggestive of aggressive cleanliness. The smells in a
pharmacy, as clear as a notice saying we have cleaned
everything twice. She jotted on the pad again, 'Dry
cleaning fluid: test . . . ' How weird was the association of smells, worse, oh far worse than the
association of words.

No, she did not believe. No one willingly dumped
such cloying smells over their faces simply to sleep.
Not if they had ever been to a dentist. Somewhere
this report contained a lie.

FRANCES FYFIELD

Deep Sleep

Mandarin

A Mandarin Paperback
DEEP SLEEP

First published in Great Britain 1991
by William Heinemann Ltd
This edition published 1992
by Mandarin Paperbacks
Michelin House, 81 Fulham Road, London SW3 6RB

Mandarin is an imprint of the Octopus Publishing Group,
a division of Reed International Books Limited

Copyright © Frances Fyfield 1991
The author has asserted her moral rights

A CIP catalogue record for this title
is available from the British Library

ISBN 0 7493 0891 5

Phototypeset by Intype, London
Printed and bound in Great Britain
by Cox & Wyman Ltd, Reading, Berks

For my father
Dr Andrew George Hegarty, D.Sc.
for all he was, and all he knew, with love

Acknowledgements

With thanks to Mr Franklyn Rosenfeld,
Rose Chemists, St Pauls Road, London,
who let me sit in his dispensary
and told me a thing or two.

All characters are fictional.
Liberties have been taken with the geography
of the East End, but not with the bomb,
defused in Ford Square, E1, in February 1989.

PROLOGUE

Since she had shut the window, the room was stuffy. She liked the central heating fierce, imagined the night air would infect her. Please, she said, I know you prefer it open, but ugh, winter cold out there, honestly. And all the dust from the building works, please . . . She had a way of drawing out the 'please' to make a whole sentence, a series of pleas which ascended to a whine. He should have been sorry for her; but all he could summon up was a rage as hot as heartburn, a furious discomfort which made him smaller and smaller until he felt he might disappear in the smoke of his own anger. One free weekend in a hotel, the chance to breathe and open his own window, but she had called him back, saying Pleeeas, come home, I'm frightened, don't leave me. I'm not leaving you, he had said down the phone; I'm simply staying here, talking, drinking, sleeping, at someone else's expense, for Christ's sake, I can come back tomorrow afternoon if you want, for an hour. I shan't half look a fool . . .

And even then, back across the city with his teeth gritted, very slightly sloshed, he did not think of how angry he could be. Thought of nothing but keeping the peace while she nagged him about the stock, told him how to run the place, and then finally on top of everything else, Will you please close the window?

He could not breathe. Mother had once bound him so closely into his bedclothes that he had lain like a swaddled baby, his face purple. Now Mother was dead and still he could not breathe.

She had settled herself in all right, his little wife. Drew clearly for him, with the blunt pencil of her voice, the extent of his reliance and her control. She had moved the settee, and an ugly cushion had been added to destroy the effect of the worn, Edwardian brocade; two of his favourite pictures had been removed; there was a coffee ring on his mahogany table. All of it so old-fashioned, she said. Why can't we ever get anything new? Like your waistcoats, precious one, light of my life, that make you look like a fella from *My Fair Lady*. I sometimes think you live in that age, hmm? But I do love you, sweet pea, oh, I do. Do you love me? Go on, tell me you do, 'cos I really love you.

And she did, of course. Couldn't live without him, neither he without her since she owned so much of the business. Though he never resented that since greed was not his weakness. Standards slipped, that was all, in the loneliness of relief after Mother's death, that vacuum filled by no one until this woman appeared, like a miracle, offering position, self respect, the chance of popularity and influence, all gifts Mama had denied. He had leapt into these skinny arms. Never mind the love; love grows like roses, don't you know, with desire blooming up among the weeds. Or not.

Oh, my love, my dear love. He closed his eyes to see that other womanly girl, standing in the shop all day, with her gorgeous, worried face; big in front, big behind; so fabulous from every angle he wished he could see each facet at once. Tight cotton shirts in summer, a scent he could smell from fifty paces: worse in winter when she wore bright sweaters stretched over a generous bosom. She never even saw him looking and never guessed how much she visited his dreams. Respectful, undemanding, an angel.

Oh my love . . . If I do not find out about love, I shall die. I shall never know it here.

Ostensibly, wife slept. Please, dear, please, go to sleep, wife, you've done enough damage for one day. Especially mentioning the window in the same breath as the plan to clear out his back room, the only place where he could exist alone, reigning supreme with his secret knowledge. No, not that. Please. Leave me alone, sometimes, please.

She had no idea what he had in mind as he brushed his teeth, looking in the old mirror. Finding her there alongside his own, tired reflection, a tiny, startling vision, scantily dressed in a translucent nylon negligée which gave a view of nothing, no hills, no valleys, but sagging muscles and a face made up with black eyebrows, dyed hair in curls and a very red mouth, smiling. Crimson lipstick disfiguring large teeth, the only things in that face she could call her own.

C'mon, she said. You're being so mumbly. I love you, sweety pie. Give us a kiss.

Not now, darling. Pleees. Had a bit too much to drink, see?

She was always ordering, even before the window was shut while he himself wanted to scream, and clutch his own throat in suffocation. Soundless, in case she awoke and asked silly, obvious questions such as, what's the matter? A man was not even allowed to claim a headache. She would talk; she was going to shame him. She talked too much, was bound to tell soon.

Oh, my love; wait for me. Let me know what love is.

'You awake, sweetheart?' A simpering, anxious voice in the dark. He kept his lips pursed shut, breathed in and out with less speed and more noise through his mouth, counting between each breath to keep the sound regular. She sighed, adjusted, breathed louder herself.

So many nights like these. Days in which work achieved for him those irresistible rewards of love and authority, trust and credibility, nights where that alternative manhood was crushed in this dreadful intimacy. Sweat began again. The negligée generated heat, and in his pretend sleep, clutching his own side of the bed, he realised she was crying, little snuffling sounds without dignity, pathetic as a puppy shown rejection. She could cry in this fashion

4

for hours, knew only the gross comfort she had anticipated when donning the nylon nightie. The reassurance of sex was what she wanted, that bloodless pleasure she mistook for love, and believed in, no matter what aid he employed. Making love fun for both of them, he had said, and she had laughed, immoderate but co-operative. A waft of sickly perfume filled his nostrils. Rage exploded like a quiet set of fireworks in his head, no noise, simply a terrible intimation, a crystal clear picture of what he was going to do.

'What's the matter?' he mumbled. The bird body lay rigid.

'That window's not properly shut. Please shut it. Like I said.'

He checked the window, but the unbearable sobbing continued and suddenly the idea was fully formed, plucked out of cold storage into the stuffy heat. The window was shut. No ventilation, no moving air as he returned to bed and took her stiff little body in his arms.

'Come on, sweetheart, there, there, there.' She clutched him so hard he could feel her long nails digging into his shoulders. His sweating had stopped and his skin to her touch felt as cold as ice.

'Come on, sweetheart, come on then. I'm here. Let's have a bit of fun, shall we? Come on, like last week, eh? You liked that, didn't you? You know what gets me going.' Her head, buried against his chest, nodded gratefully. As long as he loved her she would put up with all the incentives he seemed to need, and if his needs were insulting she did not mind. Do as your husband does: that way you keep him.

'There we are, sweetheart. Deep breath . . . Oh nice, nice . . . Hold me . . .'

When he opened the bedroom window some time later, there was a vague suggestion of light in the sky. Looking out over the back road, leaning right out in order to breathe long and deep, he watched the lamps on the watchman's hut in the building site glow weaker as a cloudy pink grew visible on the horizon behind the crane. Man-made city lights, a false dawn. He watched the buildings come into blurred focus, a hotch-potch of ugly styles, the view marred by experiment and the destruction of a global war which had coincided with the more important event of his birth. The site below lay empty, a vast muddy field, scratched out for a new square, new houses, new people, more customers; a brave new world. For once, this scene of desolation made him shiver with joy. Beneath a jungle of foundations and piecemeal plans, high rise in the distance, low rise next door, there might have been hell and destruction, but at that moment, he found the view perfectly beautiful.

Then, in strict accordance with his plan, he closed the window carefully as his wife would have done, seeing under his outstretched hand a brief hint of familiar movement in the street below: someone else stirring too early, even for market day, a shape in the distance which was disturbingly recognisable, shuffling along by the hoardings which protected road from mud. Let them crawl, let them shuffle like crabs: he did not care. He was jubilant, pushed the window back wider, tempted to shout greetings, then shut it quietly instead. He moved to the next room, where his clothes lay folded precisely over a chair, dressed carefully, exactly as he had been dressed the night before, taking nothing new from any cupboard. He crossed to the opposite window, tidying away all traces of the recent present, careful this time to remain out of view while he heard a familiar rumble in the street below. Market day; one old man beginning at five-thirty to drag out the wheeled stalls. A grand time to leave, the whole of London an empty shell and himself buoyant, brave and free. There was in these movements nothing of the small man schooled to perfection in all domestic tasks: he was a tiger, full of mysterious power. Rejoice, said the radio. Christmas cometh. Rejoice in rebirth.

Ice cold outside, but rejoice; the saviour is born; a tune bubbling out of his throat. The car was parked one whole street hence, near enough still for the building site dust to freeze on the screen. As he sat inside, turned on the lights, and leant forward to straighten his hair, he saw how his face was smiling serene, like a carol singer on the sleeve of a record, mischief still in the face. And also, fat, wet tears, stinging his cold cheeks and descending slowly and steadily into the mouth which smiled and smiled.

Oh my love. Wait for me.

CHAPTER ONE

Helen West lay in a big, high bed, slightly too wide for one: passenger on an institutional mattress which could perform contortions. Despite the ungainliness of her couch and in the haze of post-anaesthetic, she could envisage the stainless steel framework dancing across the floor, this way and that to the tune of a Strauss waltz, drawn by the company of other beds swishing in the corridor outside. Her own bed could be wheeled, raised, lowered in whole or part for anything but titillation; an expensive couch, but never sexy. The thought of the word, a very fleeting thought, made her shudder as she might at the mention of necrophilia. Helen found it very difficult indeed to see how a person could feel as bad as this without being dead; and if anyone entered now, it would have to be an undertaker. In which case, the bed would be able to spill her into a box and take her away, quietly.

The door opened on oiled hinges as she closed her eyes, denying the existence of anyone who might wish her to respond. But manners did not take wings, even in extremis. They remained buried in the bones, forcing her to follow some bloody-minded instinct for politeness even in the face of an impulse to tell the visitor to . . . She surely had the right to be rude? But, although resentful, Helen began to haul herself upwards, out of the fog and the imprisonment of the stiff sheets. Smiling.

'Well! Well! Well! And how are we feeling then? Fighting fit? Ho ho ho. Sorry about that. Had to do a little more than we intended. Oh dearie, dearie me. Nasty little cyst, left ovary. No, the other one. Had to take it off.'

'What, the ovary?'

He laughed as if he had been told an extraordinary joke. 'Oh, my dear me, no, only the cyst. Jolly good.'

The goodness of anything remained beyond Helen's comprehension, but she battled with the question of why she should be so protective about an unemployed ovary. Odd, the human response, and oh how painful intellect, in a subdued form, coming back, and why did they all talk like imbeciles? He was so loud, and why did he have to speak to her as if she were deaf, while the nurse towered above his shoulder with a face like a smiling but slightly apologetic sphinx, professionally concerned. The surgeon reminded her of the small boy at school who drilled holes from the boys' to the girls' lavatory out of curiosity, but the nurse leant forward with surprising tact.

'You'll feel better soon,' she said. 'You might not think so, but you will, believe me. Your husband called five minutes ago. I told him to go away.'

'Thank you,' said Helen. 'Thanks very much.'

For all small mercies. The one portion of brain which would appreciate her hand being held and her blankets tucked was absurdly disappointed, the rest enormously relieved, sinking, eyes closing, still smiling. 'Thank you.' For nothing. Push off, who-ever you are. Leave me alone.

Comforting darkness after they left. Nestling into it, descending slowly again into the mattress of that bed, all of her a strange feeling shape, tiny and large in silly proportions and nothing to do with real life. The buzz of distant traffic a comfort to the ear, warm in here, deliciously warm, almost comfortable as long as she did not move, and a smell, tugging at distaste. Something there was, scrabbling for entry, while somewhere, shortly after this descent, there was a dim memory of a kiss on her hair, soft steps, someone going away. I happen to love you, darling. Very much. You do look small.

Geoffrey Bailey, Detective Chief Superintendent, squeaked back down the polished corridor in what his sergeant called his brothel-creeping shoes, away from Helen's room, his heart thumping lightly. Of course she would survive; women were tough, but they looked so vulnerable when asleep he always wondered if they would wake or shrink away. All right, said the Sister, not proof against his second attempt to visit. But only for a minute, mind, and don't wake her, she won't like that. I have to go in, you see, he had said humbly. Seeing her unconscious brings such memories my sleep will disappear if I don't, and I must work tomorrow.

His long frame was bent charmingly, recognisably a copper for all his distinction, something of the watcher evident in the eyes and the lines, the accent perhaps, but not in the cut of the suit. Oh go on then, but mind you behave.

What exactly did Sister think he might do? Scream? Weep? Create a scene? But then strange things happened in hospitals, even private hospitals like this, an abnormal situation for the likes of Helen and him, except for the prudence of her almost forgotten insurance policy. The shiny efficiency of the place sniffed of privilege without any adornment and for once, Bailey approved. The sick should be fêted, although in his experience they rarely were, while all his own waiting behind screens for persons recovering from gunshot wounds, stab wounds, accidents or simply hiding, had rarely been in places like this. There was nothing here of the abattoir smell of the ordinary Casualty. A passing nurse caught his eye, smiled as he smiled back. He would have preferred sleep in the chair by Helen's bed: discomfort was second nature.

Out in the street, the cold struck like a cannon-shot to the chest. His car, indifferently parked, felt icy to the touch. Going home alone, he mused on the business of being referred to as Helen's husband and wondered how long it would be before she corrected that glib supposition. Wished, at the same time, that his borrowed status was real.

The precious sleep was short-lived. Helen surfaced like a diver from muddy water granted only a confused glimpse of light. Thrashing through a dream of being in a chemist's shop where music played while she searched for painkillers, finding nothing on the overcrowded shelves but cosmetics, hair-brushes, stockings, gift-wrapped powders. Moving to one side, the pain increased sharply and she was horribly aware of where she was. Four a.m., winter darkness seen through flimsy curtains, a face by the bed, her nostrils filled with the antiseptic hospital smell, but this time, a scent lightly flavoured with a different kind of alcohol and a whiff of nicotine which made her eyes open wide. Not a face poised to mouth clichés, but an old, disreputable face, quite different from the surgeon who looked as if he washed on the hour and shaved three times a day.

'God, you look awful, woman. If looks could kill, I'd be dead.' The face moved round the other side of the bed and examined the drip. 'I put you to sleep,' he went on. 'Like a baby. You wake up without any trace of nausea and then look at me as if I were a gibbon. Gratitude. This is your bloody anaesthetist, if you don't remember. Do you hurt?'

The head by the bed was grizzled and wrinkled, grey hair sticking out on end and large eyebrows arched in a permanent question.

'Well . . . A bit . . .'

'Don't sound so bloody apologetic; so you bloody should. Only surgeons say otherwise. Operations hurt, also dangerous to health, they don't seem to mention that either. Thank your God you're alive, but never mind. One more injection in a minute, but the longer we leave it, the longer it lasts. Hurt? That you should be so lucky. Want a cigarette?' There was a clipped Irish in the voice; platitudes were clearly anathema.

'Oh, please.' Despite herself and the ache, Helen grinned, full of that sense of the ridiculous which was never far from the surface. How idiotic to be thus, hung over, half alive and wanting nothing more than the cigarette proffered by a doctor, of all people. He read her mind and sighed.

'The very height and depth of foolishness, like all addiction. Plus life in general. Sister'll skin me; we'll open the window after. Here.' He passed her one lit cigarette. Helen knew why they used to be called gaspers. The right hand which took it felt spongy: the taste delicious.

'How do you feel?'

'I don't really know. Unwell. Disgustingly dis-embowelled. Lower end of me resembles an Easter egg wearing a goatee beard.'

He chuckled softly. 'I like that, now. Poetic description of post-laparotomy surgery as endured by the patient. Not a suicidal patient at the moment. I hope?'

'Earlier, yes, but not now. Her friends would shoot her if she so much as thought of it.' She gestured vaguely with the cigarette.

'Easier ways, are there not, to bring oneself to the door of heaven or hell? No point in suicide, really.' He did not sound entirely convinced. 'Now, let me tell you; there's a fellow down the corridor, poor bastard, had a circumcision earlier. Can't get his thing down lower than a flagpole for six hours.

And you think you females have problems. How's the cigarette?'

'Wonderful. Awful.'

'You'll be purified yet. Time for the needle. Then you're fit for heaven.'

'Oh no, not heaven. Hate white clothes.'

His chuckle, amazingly comforting and infectious, emerged from beyond the bed. Something signified the presence of a nurse, presenting a dish towards hands which now smelled of soap. After a split second's sharpness, the injection spread into a warm glow from behind her hip, pushing out pain, closing the eyes. The picture of the chemist's shop came back, unthreateningly, something in there teasing at her memory, the haunting smell of medicine. Dr Hazel looked down at the sallow and attractive features of his patient, distinguished by thick, dark hair, a faded scar to her forehead, then folded Helen's arms across her chest. He turned the strong face to one side to aid breathing, wondered objectively if he could describe her as beautiful, decided he could, uncrossed the ankles to aid circulation and pulled the single sheet to chest height, all with a swift economy of light movement at variance with his age.

'You'd make a good nurse, doctor,' said the voice of the acolyte nurse. He sighed and patted her shoulder.

'Pity I wasn't. All very well for a boy today, but in my own time, darling, it just wasn't the done thing.'

14

Four-thirty in the morning and this was certainly no task for a man. Geoffrey Bailey, without a single witness to his activities, felt silly, and because of the three whiskies he had used to dose his sleeplessness, slightly elated. The fact that Helen's persistent pain had proved curable, albeit by the savage means of surgery, made him enormously relieved. He was fiddling, far from efficiently, in the cheerful, chipped kitchen of her basement flat. On the draining board was a block of what he could only think of as flower-arranging foam, into which he understood he had only to stick stems of things in order to obtain a perfect result every time, according to the instructions. 'Destructions,' he corrected. Bailey had crept out to the garden like a thief, careful not to alarm the neighbours, found two large and frayed winter roses, but otherwise sparse foliage for his purpose, and the result was looking bare and crooked, jaunty in defiance of ever becoming elegant. He was only attempting to translate part of Helen's precious but untidy garden into her hospital ward, but this was pathetic; looked like the work of a person too mean to buy a bunch of proper flowers. Which, swathed in polythene, he would hate as much as she. Little failures loomed large and this was not his forte. Geoffrey crossed from kitchen to living-room in pursuit of the Irish whiskey.

Living in Helen's flat without Helen's presence was an odd sensation which he rather liked as long as he knew she was safe. They had keys to each other's apartments, his in the East London warehouse so very different from her own, an eyrie as light and bare as this was comfortably full of mahogany, pictures and colour. The fire in the living-room lit the red walls, casting shadows from the overflowing plant in a brass urn standing to one side as if needing the heat. Helen's daily books were stacked to one side where she sometimes worked; Archbold *Criminal Pleadings*, forty-fourth edition: Stone's *Justices' Manual*, Wilkinson on *Road Traffic Offences*, Cross on *Evidence*, referred to as necessary in preparation for the next day along with an untidy heap of law reports which he longed to straighten and give some sort of index, but he would never presume. Stock in trade to a criminal lawyer, perhaps more especially a prosecutor, although it was impossible to imagine her in that guise now, not quite stripped of the dignity she never quite lost, even playing the fool. Bailey liked this frail Helen as well as her strong counterpart, the one with a will of iron and a useful tongue, though he conceded liking was a weak description of their mutual condition. Why else would he be in her place in her absence, touching her things with such affection? He rarely expressed sentiment in her presence: but here alone he could feel as he pleased. They spent the weekends vacillating between their two abodes, half the week as well, but this was different. An unmarried married couple, he had often said, sometimes with more grace than others. There might have been a better formula, but for now there was not, since one year living together out of London had been no improvement on this status quo. He knew better than to question any arrangement which worked, most of the time.

Bailey stepped away from the fire, went into the bedroom where sleep had evaded him, sorted a few items into an overnight bag. She would need things, such as the clean nighties she did not possess, face cream, a dressing-gown and a couple of books. The selection of these he could manage, packing quickly, jealous of her privacy. Then he settled back by the fire with one of the hundreds of books, ready to wait for morning. No visitors a.m., Sister had said. To hell with that; he wasn't a policeman for nothing. Helen, darling, I may rarely say it, but I do love you; miss you like my right arm and I must not have any more of this whiskey. Thank God I believe you love me back, though there are times when I do wonder.

'Lerve . . . is a many splendoured thing . . .' Oh yeah? At six-fifteen, Duncan Perry, Detective Constable, Met Police, leered away from his own reflection in the cracked mirror of the tiny bathroom, avoiding an expression flushed by alcohol with eyes puffed from lack of sleep. The face was one of which he had once thoroughly approved, but he no longer thought it handsome as he pulled his chin into a better shape for the blunt razor. Overused blades were better for the early morning shave since there was less chance of small nicks to the skin covered with salmon pink toilet paper, adornments he tended to forget until reminded in public, but the current disposable left his chin feeling scraped. The place was overwarm, largely the result of his failure to turn off the gas oven in the kitchenette cheek by jowl with the bathroom. Inside the oven lay a desiccated steak and kidney pie, forgotten the night before.

Tiptoeing out of his flat although there was no need, the quiet steps a result of constant training and an endless sensation of defending his back, Duncan broke into a jerky sprint for his car, the slight sweat freezing on his forehead as he stuffed his hands in the pocket of his suit. He sat inside at the wheel for the few minutes it took for the windscreen to clear, conscious of the solidity of the car around him; it was one of his few remaining possessions, one of the few things which had not gone the same way as his wife, his family and his face, all of which were cheaper to maintain. Kim never asked for a bloody penny, and while that was a relief, it was also insulting. He would get used to living in one and a half rooms sooner or later, but he was not reconciled, not yet.

Six-forty-five, too early for early turn, parade at seven-thirty and not his first task. Duncan drove south from Highbury where he lived, skirting the emptiness of the City, through Shoreditch and into Whitechapel. Jack the Ripper country, now known as little Bengal, hit for the third time in a century by the newest wave of immigration. The first Chinatown, then the Jewish capital, and now dusky, full of spices, coronaries and striving poverty. Hit by a thousand bombs in the war, rebuilt and rebuilt again. Where did they all go when they moved on, he thought. Where am I supposed to go? Nowhere in particular but just Somewhere Else, where you won't be an embarrassment. Well he wouldn't. You didn't treat a dustbin like Kim had treated him, fuck it.

He turned the car into a service road behind a parade of shops, stopped and looked up expectantly. There were flats above the shops, nasty concrete structures of the boom-building sixties, at odds with the wider pre-war stuff, their only advantage the reasonable space inside that offset the stained exteriors and cumbersome balconies, the ugly steps from the street. He was looking for a light in the third one from the end, the unconscious early-morning signal of his wife's presence as she got ready for her own long day. If he could stay where he was until seven-thirty, he might just see the animal arrive, something supposed to be a childminder, a grunting, yawning, shambling man who, to Duncan's anxiety, seemed to take his effeminate child to school. Detective Constable Perry did not like any of the choices made by his wife, but there was nothing he could do.

OK, estranged wife as his solicitor so nicely put it, pompous bastard. Also estranged, one smallish package of truculent child named Tom, whose parentage Duncan had questioned in the course of a blazing row with Kim, a row that ended with her saying, yes, she was going now, leading to the door the boy who was Duncan's spitting image, as if he had ever seriously believed otherwise. The eyes, green eyes, remained with him still, in accusation, along with many other regrets.

Perry could see the shape of her head, or what he hoped was her head and not the skull of some unknown overnight visitor, framed against the frosted glass of the bathroom window. He clenched his fist on the wheel of the car, shut his eyes for an instant. A man in residence might just send him over the edge; the thought made him want to vomit, but she wouldn't, no she wouldn't. Not until she'd qualified, got what she wanted from that poxy shop where she started work so early. She wasn't half determined, he had to hand it to her, worked like she fought, no holds barred. Perry started the car and crept down the street, aggressive, holstering his energies and his jealousy by slanging her under his breath, ashamed.

Helen awoke by seven, not exactly refreshed but considering herself far from dead. Her customary gesture of pushing the hair out of her eyes with her left hand was defeated by the tube attached to the back of the wrist, such a surprise that she looked at it in consternation, swore softly. She also looked at the clock on the wall, remembered that today and on several succeeding days, she would not be in her office by nine o'clock. The thought was a mixed blessing. Work did not evaporate, it simply accumulated, but the hospital cocoon was suddenly appealing, all wrapped up like this and waiting for someone to bring tea. But then the nurse came with her whiff of antiseptic and Helen, remembering some of the files on her desk, groaned out loud.

'Sister's gone off,' the nurse hissed in conspiracy. 'So I'm letting your husband in for a second. OK?'

'He's not sterilised,' Helen said, 'not for dust, anyway, not in my place . . . And he's not my . . .' she began, ever a stickler for detail, but was stopped by her desire to laugh at the picture of Bailey being let into the room like a lion into a pen. There he was, sidling round the door almost shyly, a broad smile on a tired-looking face and in his hand two decadent winter roses.

CHAPTER TWO

'Oh come on, Tom, please, lovey. What's the matter with you?' Kimberley Perry knew her voice was sharp, and was sorry, without being able to do anything about the edge. Or about the fact that Tom was only ten years old, with a face far older, a large head on thin shoulders. Nothing ever fitted Tombo, even today's stained tracksuit which she privately considered too cold for December but which was de rigueur in his school, or so he insisted. The material bunched at the waist and hung over training shoes which had been the subject of intense pride when new: the exact make, the flashes on the side, the colour of the laces all of paramount importance and he had worn them as if they were silk shot with gold. And similar expense, his mother had considered wryly. Tombo knew more about the rules of dress and behaviour than he did about the school curriculum, she thought as she fought the impulse to empty pockets where the marbles and other invaluable detritus looked like twin hernias. She also yearned to brush his spiky hair for him, but both actions would have been insults. Tombo might look like a baby on more endearing days, or behave like one, flicking his toast across the table as if firing a gun, Kchoo! Kchoo! a bullet imitation noise which sounded like a sneeze, but he was not a baby in his needs. Kim's early morning glances were full of guilt, irritation and a very brusque love. She might have killed for him, but at the moment he was unlovely.

She got up, shoved the dishes in the sink, splashing the front of her sweater with hot soapy water, making Tombo giggle provocatively at her swearing. You should have better clothes, lovey, she was telling him under her breath; better school and better mummy. Only a month or two more till I'm qualified and I'll make it all up to you. Don't look so sulky, please. You little sod.

'Is Daddy coming today?'

'You know very well he isn't. Next weekend.' Sharp, again.

Kim smoothed her skirt. Maybe it was a little too tight for the shop but she could not resist that colour. Life was dull enough. Duncan had always laughed at her tight skirts, high heels, big bosom, big behind, but then he had laughed at everything. All her years of study met with nothing but scorn. 'A chemist, love? You? Oh, ha, ha, ha . . . Sorry about that, sweetheart, didn't mean to laugh, but ho, ho, ho; Kim the Chemist? See, it rhymes! Kim the Chemist who can't even take cough medicine.' So what if it was a big change from happy-go-lucky, down the disco Kimberley with punk hairdo and micro skirt, a person quite grateful to be pregnant, married and apparently out of it all by the age of nineteen. Until Tombo was two and she found herself bored out of her skull, the brain her teachers had despaired of idle and frustrated. Working part-time in a pharmacy, beginning to think, why not me, why shouldn't I learn how to do this? Duncan would have been forgiven anything (since she did not have high expectations of the married state) if he could have begun to understand her excitement. Kimberley from the East End, cheeky girl without an A level, ex school truant making good. Almost a proper pharmacist all these years later, a new kind of rebellion chanelled into hard, hard work, rewarded by the kind of love which tried to thwart her in case she should grow up and escape. Taunting all the time, always putting her down.

Great big handsome ape. So she snapped the leash between them, already frayed by argument. He thought her walk-out was spontaneous, but she had planned it. Don't ever laugh at me, she told him: I've got a place, a job. I mean what I bloody say. Don't you laugh at me.

'You'll turn that boy into a pansy,' he had shouted.

'Better than a pig,' she shouted back. Repeating that cold comfort in her mind as she watched him now.

'Don't want to go to school. Kchoo! Kchoo! Kchoo!' More crumbs flew into Tom's milk.

'Oh come on, yes you do, lovey. You like it really.'

He gave her a look of withering scorn and the silence was ominous. Then a noise on the stairs, a

24

groan announcing the arrival of Daniel. Daft Daniel was another worry with his empty morning face and that sickly pale skin. Duncan would kill her if he knew what Daniel was and it was only a matter of time before he found out from Tom. Just a bloke, this Daniel, she had informed Duncan. Just a man, helps in the shop with boxes and things, helps up and down the street, takes Tom to school and meets him sometimes when I can't; stop interfering. She did not say how Daniel was simply omnipresent in the Parade, calling in at all the shops in one endless perambulation, but invariably at the pharmacy for his daily prescription of methadone. Daniel was twenty-five going on sixty, sweet-natured, curious, argumentative about his drugs, but Duncan could not see any strange man, especially a stabilised drug addict, as harmless. Kim was defensive about Daniel, reacted to him as one lonely and truculent soul to another, even fed him sometimes (beans and chips, their favourite fare), and also reckoned that beggars could not be choosers. Daniel was big enough to stop Tom getting thumped and that alone made him better than nothing.

'How are you doing, Dan?'

'O.K.'

''Lo, Danny.' A surly greeting from Tom. Dan was a sort of a friend, but not much fun.

''Lo.'

Daniel was designed to sit without much movement, and take Tom to school with a tribe of others whose rude remarks passed over his head like clouds. Standing there now, puffing the cold out,

25

smiling a stupid smile while Kim snatched her bag, planted a kiss on the time bomb that was her son and hurried away, guilty, but relieved.

'Don't let him go on the site, will you? Or pick up rubbish, will you?'

'Nope.'

There was no direct access from the shops of Herringbone Parade to the flats above. Some of the shopkeepers owned the upstairs accommodation, including Philip Carlton the pharmacist who owned his own larger flat and the one next door, rented out to Kim. To get into the street, upstairs occupants had to descend their steps, turn left or right through the litter of the service road which served their own front doors and then turn back. In Kim's case, she arrived beneath her own bedroom windows. The Carltons had been generous in letting Kim rent the flat: she knew they could have got more, and while wages were low, the arrangement suited her well. She reminded herself not to think of 'the Carltons' plural. Since that frothy, bossy little Margaret had died in her sleep four weeks ago without anyone understanding why, there was only one. Kim tried to push this out of her mind along with the vision of dead Margaret in bed, not for lack of rough sympathy, but because she could not afford her concentration to be rocked. Life was far too complicated as it was: death and sentiment presented crises she could not afford.

As she clattered down the steps, knowing she would regret the high heels later in the day, a workman en route to the site whistled. Kim stuck her nose in the air, ignored the compliment, but her large backside wiggled as she walked, unconsciously, blissfully sexy. Gruff and irritated she may have been, but Kimberley Perry in the morning was a sight which glowed in winter.

Seven-forty-five, and only three lights glowed in Herringbone Parade. The view here was an improvement on what she saw from the back, a dirty service road, feeding the back of the shops and flanked by a building site. An improvement zone, old houses, left damaged since the war, finally coming down. You could hear the rumbling of a cement mixer creating filling for foundations, and, some time next year, there would be two dozen new homes which people in the Parade were unlikely to afford. Bitter for those who could remember the bombs which had put their neighbourhood into a twilight zone for two generations. Never mind, the Parade was proud. There were twenty small shops in one unbroken row, and, whenever she thought about anything not related to the minute she was in, Kim thought that was plenty. The lights which glowed so long before conventional opening hours were those of Carlton's Caring Chemist, while three doors down Mr Oza's newsagent and tobacconist was already doing trade. Five doors beyond was Cyril's Caff, renowned for bacon rolls and lorry drivers' breakfasts, the inside windows already steaming. Next to that, though not yet open, was Sylvie's Hair Salon, half-price to pensioners Thursdays only, hotbed of gossip. The other shops included a greengrocer, a butcher, two Indian takeaways open only at night and one slightly famous Chinese restaurant on the other side. There was also a baker's, an emporium of discount electrical goods run by Ahmed, and a toy shop which Tombo scorned as hopelessly untrendy. Alongside that was an off-licence and on the other side of the hardware store, the boutique and shoe shop, selling discontinued lines from shopping catalogues and a few other things besides. No shop was streamlined; there were socks in the hardware store, videos for hire in the off-licence, and everything under the sun on the two days a week when the street outside became a market. Herringbone Parade was an enclave against the world, providing all the urban soul could ever require, filling a gap wherever a gap was mentioned, ordering anything which might sell. Pip Carlton, the Caring Chemist, was easily the worst at this game. He could not bear to be found lacking and the shop burst at the seams in tribute to his passion for pleasing. No wonder Margaret had complained.

Kim closed the door behind her, blinking in the bright strip lighting which illuminated everything on display. Behind the corner at the far end lay Pip's dispensary, always in half light by contrast despite the close work they did in there. Here, stock ran wild, escaping from shelves to be thrust back hourly and even then Kim swore everything got up at night to change places. There were all the conventional shampoos, toothpastes, soaps, patent medicines as well as the homoeopathic range in one corner along with the vitamins, a perfume bar under lock and key, a section devoted to babies' bottoms, one to handcreams and festooned among it all, underwear, cheap jewellery and fourteen different brands of cosmetics. The underwear, nylon dreams of black lace, frills, suspenders, knickers and multi-coloured stockings, somehow spilled across the shop to lend it a raffish air. All this had been Margaret's sideline, while the rest of her strove to bring order into the chaos. She had wanted such changes, Margaret, such as less ordering and the closing of the back dispensary, a room beyond the room he shared with Kim and where Pip insisted, like a good, old-fashioned pharmacist, on making some of his own preparations. In strict privacy. Not commercial, Margaret had said loudly, get rid of it. God rest her soul, said Pip piously, forgetting the arguments.

'Morning, Pip. Are you winning?' Kim shouted as she edged her way through the crowded shelves which customers would rearrange and upset with their various bulks throughout the day as they made their way to the counter where Pip was endeavouring to hang a tinfoil sign bearing the legend 'A Happy Xmas to all our Customers'. Really, she thought, this shop was made for midgets, not someone of her statuesque build, a sharp contrast to Margaret who had been built like a pixie. Hence the nature of all Mrs Carlton's favourite underwear, best worn by persons of miniature proportions and chiefly bought for a joke. Kim loved it.

'Course I'm winning. I have winning ways.' Pip was perched on the counter, posed like a coquette, one hand spread fan-like in greeting. 'My, you're a sight for sore eyes. By which I don't mean an eye-sore, ha, ha, oh dear me, no. You look very pretty.' He scrambled down, the decoration trailing after him. Pip never quite finished most tasks, all of them started with boyish enthusiasm. 'Here, let me take your coat. How's Tombo?'

His puns and his civilities were engaging and irritating by turn, but Pip's energy was always infectious. He was a thin, sprightly man, forty with the bounce of twenty, kept trim by the lonely jogging which he undertook with obsessive zeal, the way he did almost everything. The old customers loved Pip; Kim said they would eat cat food if he told them it was good for them. This morning, after breakfast, she was disposed to like him, forget that undertone to his affectionate manner which was ever so slightly disturbing. The hand on her arm pressed the elbow unnecessarily as he removed the coat: she was not sure if she understood that or not.

'Tombo's fine,' she said hurriedly. 'Sulking, though.'

'Never mind,' he said. 'I'll send him home something nice. Health-giving lollipops, new order.'

'Oh, Pip,' she said, looking at an open box on the floor, full of sugar-free sweets, a new line when there was no room for the old, 'where on earth are we going to put them?'

'We'll find a place. We'll find places where we didn't know we had places. Tea?'

His glance was rather too intent in its admiration, but for once, she was buoyed by his artless optimism. He was such a kind man and you had to make allowances for grief. 'All right, Lord and Master,' she said grinning back. 'But I'll make it.'

'Ready to tee off, are we?' He roared at his own pun, ready for the day. Silly git, she thought with weary affection, ready for a day full of more of the same and a dozen cups of tea. Kim hung her coat on the hook Pip had placed too high. The red skirt rode up, revealing an acre of sheer-coated thigh. Only one of them noticed.

'Would you like tea, Dr Hazel?' the nurse asked, reconciled to the doctor staying longer than anyone usually did with a patient.

'No, I would not. I'd like an extra large belt of whisky, but I doubt if you could arrange it, darling. Then I'll go on and breathe my glorious fumes over the princess next door.' He sighed. 'OK, then, I'll have tea with my favourite patient. Who has a little colour in the cheeks today and a little light reading matter. Good God, what's this?'

After Helen's third day in hospital, the room had begun to look more like an office. The place was full of flowers, not arranged with any great care or skill, but extravagantly admired; there was a pile of books on the bedside locker and three files spread from the bed to the floor where they had fallen and she had not bothered to retrieve them.

'That's never work, woman, is it?' he gestured, horrified. 'A little something from your office, along with the blooms? Blackmail.'

'Doctor, that is one of my words, not yours. And

not accurately used in this context, if I may say so. Blackmail is the obtaining of a pecuniary advantage by threats. There are no threats, only flowers, and I am impecunious.'

'Oh you and your legal words. I meant the emotional sort of a bargain. I'd have anaesthetised your tongue if I'd known you were a lawyer. Always know a lawyer's health by the state of his mouth. When it's shut, he's dead.'

'Sit down for heaven's sake, you make me even more restless *and* you owe me fifty pence. Have a glass of wine since you can't have whisky. You can rinse your mouth out after. Tell me about the world outside.' They had become very comfortable together, dark Helen West and grizzled old Dr Hazel whose flecked eyes regarded her with affection. A tough customer physically, Miss West. Her recovery had been swift, and the thought of her itching to go filled him with an unidentified sadness. But then no patient of right mind ever wanted to stay inside a hospital, even if they were allowed to drink and smoke. In mute conspiracy, each lit a cigarette, his a Players full strength, hers milder.

'The world outside? Oh glory be to God, what do you want to know about that for? They've just lit the lights in Regent Street, the shops are awash with Christmas carols already. It's murder out there. The rest you'll find from your newspaper and why on earth did your bloody office send you files? Don't they know you're sick?'

She laughed. 'And since when, in your career, did a surgeon ever take any notice of that? Even when you were my age as opposed to the rude old man you are now? Physician, heal thyself; get to work.'

'The buggers wouldn't think twice. Bring out your needle, Hazel, my lad: we'll give you a chair if you faint and a mask to keep germs off the patient.'

'So. I get files in here because no one else can read my handwriting. If I hadn't volunteered, they'd find out how stupid I am. Can I pick your brains?'

'You'll be lucky.'

'Right.' She motioned to the file half on, half off the bed. 'I'm not really working, you know, I'm playing at it. Reading a report where there could be a question of homicide, but I haven't managed more than page one. Tell me, why should a woman of forty-six, non-drinker, non-smoker, healthy, until she dies in bed, simply die? No obvious physical cause at all.'

'She could have been very, very tired,' he suggested flippantly. 'Or she might have been contemplating Christmas. Known to kill many, the mere thought of it. Blood pressure? Heart attack?' He leant forward and leered comically. 'Poison?'

'No evidence of anything in a routine post-mortem. Blood test awaits. I've only half the report. Sleeping like an infant, she was, curled to one side.'

'Even less likely for asphyxia. I don't know why she died. And I don't care. Leave it to the coroner.'

Helen put aside the half-complete Police Report on the death of Mrs Margaret Carlton, relieved to do so, and the talk fell happily to more palatable reading matter. A glass of wine was poured while

Dr Hazel scoffed at other books now littering the room. The wine in her veins was preferable to the drip which had left in the removal no trace of a bruise or needle mark, sure sign of a clever anaesthetist. A little alcohol went a long way towards the recovery of the patient, but the verbal fencing was better. The merits of a favourite novelist were under attack. Hazel enjoyed an argument.

'How can you say this is a heap of rubbish, or is your eyesight bad?'

'Oh, get on with you; the woman is indecipherable . . .'

Exactly the kind of conversation which Bailey, that most literary of police officers, should have been able to join with ease, but his coming upon them ended the camaraderie, as Helen could have predicted without quite knowing why, his quiet arrival in that hospital room signalling Hazel's abrupt departure. Quite different from the nurses who simpered in Bailey's presence, there was something in Hazel which obviously disliked the aura of policeman inherent in his mild appearance, shied from it like a nervous pony about to throw the rider. A familiar syndrome which nevertheless provoked in Helen a sharp irritation. He often had this effect on people; the talking cadaver at the feast, as if he reminded them suddenly of a cold outside, conscience, and all sorts of old ghosts. He held the door for Hazel. The doctor neglected to thank him.

The irritation was reciprocal. Tearing across London from the grubby east to the smarter west, Bailey might have expected her to be surrounded with other visitors – Helen attracted nice and nasty without turning any way – but he had not expected to find the patient looking weak but well, wine in one hand and cigarette in the other, deep in conversation with some scruffy male party who was obviously besotted. Last evening he had found Helen scarcely mobile, but playing draughts with the same Dr Hazel: there was something vaguely insulting about it, as if his own protective, companionable role had been usurped. Then he sniffed. The air was full of flowers, tobacco; the sanctity of hospital lost, and the knowledge of that restored his mood. The hackles of insecurity rose and sank back while he registered the beginnings of a mess in the room, secretly rejoicing in this sign of recovery. His own two winter roses were thoroughly dead in a vase by the bed; she had a strange liking for half dead petals and was always reluctant to throw out flowers. Helen might be a peculiar kind of civil servant, but she was clearly impossible to institutionalise.

'Files,' he said caustically, lifting them from the floor. 'What's this, darling?'

'You may look,' she said with mock primness. 'That one comes from somewhere near you, not your manor exactly but near your flat. A chemist.'

'Mrs Carlton,' he read, before putting it down, sitting close to the bed in the chair still warm from Dr Hazel. 'Bugger Mrs Carlton. How are you? When are you coming home?'

'I've got four massive stitches,' said Helen conspiratorially as he bent to kiss her, 'on my Easter egg.'

Bailey drove straight back east into the dim car park of the police station where he worked most of the time. He was not seeking the panacea of work: nor was such available since his tasks were now the delegation of tasks, the current investigations run by remote control. He relied on the self-motivation of most of his men; no immediate panics, despite the unexplained deaths, the missing lorry loads, the Asian bride burnt in some feud they would never understand, the armed robbery of the wages van, and all the other weekly hazards of East Central London. Bailey had become a manager by default, controlled three teams of detectives, although control was not always the appropriate word. Respect was what they showed, co-operation forth-coming as often as not while, rather to his own surprise, they could be prevailed upon to confide both professionally and privately, allowing him to circumvent some of the worst disasters before they actually occurred. Such as refusing to authorise a search warrant requested without a shred of evidence, or deflecting the young sergeant about to punch a rival. Sometimes Bailey thought that his present post, his role as the near but still distant wise old man of the division, was a role designed to do no more than save the Commissioner embarrassment. For some time he had felt he was suffering from a new version of an old malaise, a growing disinterest in life, and he wondered if this managerial appointment was the cause or result of despair. For months now, ever since he and Helen had returned from outside London, ever since he had seen and heard a boy burn to death, he had felt he was slipping. Did not want to know any more the ingredients of these tragedies, see bodies or hear screaming. All in all, even while resenting many of his current tasks, he preferred welfare and discipline. He had lost touch with his streets; here, there was just enough to keep his mind ticking over, and the patience he displayed did not have to touch his heart. The role called for silence, contemplation, passive intelligence, and while Bailey would not have admitted to boredom he hoped that was all that ailed him.

Fog blanketed the ugly building that was East Ham station, Victorian brick-built, solid, but without the fortress appearance of more modern equivalents, oddly and quite invariably ill lit inside and out. Spotlights relieved the gloom of the car park, but once inside the back door, gloom prevailed on painted walls and everyone, uniformed or not, looked as sallow as the mustard of the decor. Bailey had a separate, although tiny, office with a door leading through into the CID room where several detectives sat by day, teasing a harassed secretary.

Some wag had stuck a Christmas decoration on Bailey's door, a loud Santa Claus with frogging on the shoulders and a tie in Bailey's favourite claret colour round the neck. He liked that: it indicated a measure of the popularity he never courted since that way lay madness. There were times when he would have liked to be hail fellow well met, able to drink with the team, share their outlook and be fêted as one of them, but, being himself, was rarely the subject of jokes, perceived as dry, stern, innovative without ever being revolutionary, the cynicism hidden and the intelligence far too acute for most people's liking. Bailey's own officers wanted to please, almost blushed at his praise, but they did not slap him on the shoulder.

Empty offices always reminded Bailey of empty schools, deserted markets; places which bore no resemblance whatever at night to what they were by day, so lonely he would have the feeling each time of having arrived at the wrong place. As he sat at the desk and dealt briskly with his in-tray, transferring most of it to OUT, the odd sensation of the quietness, punctuated by cars in the yard, murmurings from the front desk, became odder as he heard sounds from the room next door, strange little snorting noises, masked into anonymity by the constant murmuring of the antiquated heating which gave all occupants of this unsympathetic space the sensation of water on the brain. Bailey's long hands, as well equipped for the mending of his clocks as they were for the writing of clipped phrases in elegantly official prose, paused, lay flat on the desk as he raised his head, immobile with curiosity, invisible antennae ready for action although instinct told him there was no threat in these sounds. Burglars do not come into police stations for the purposes of burglary, but what crossed his mind was the unlikely prospect of one of his men working late, or, as likely, staying away from home. The last possibility was more illicit; some male with female officer, taking advantage of an empty room. In which case, best not to interfere: such delicate matters were not his concern. But just as he debated whether or not to move, or at least to clear his throat in signal, the noise became definable. Snoring: unrhythmical snores, falling and dying, ragged sounds not orchestrated or controlled. As soon as Bailey identified the snores, he knew who it was next door. Duncan, back from the pub. If he had driven here in his car, Bailey would skin him. Duncan Perry, Detective Constable, the muscle of the squad, the door breaker, *el machismo* incarnate.

As Bailey opened the door between his room and the next Duncan stirred, not woken, but reaching the natural end of what must have been an uncomfortable sleep. His bulky body, that of an athlete going to seed, was slumped into a chair, one leg extended, the other curled, maintaining his seat by a miracle, while his torso was precariously supported on the desk, head on one arm, the other arm dangling free and dragging him slowly towards the floor. As he woke, the elbow slipped, and Bailey saw him slide out of sight, his face transfixed with surprise. Reaching the floor, he let out a grunt of astonishment. Bailey, looking at the controlled mess of the room, reckoned a little more litter would make no difference, and also reckoned that although Duncan had fallen with quite a thump, he was beyond pain.

'Get up, man,' he said sharply. 'What the hell are you doing here this time of night? Ten o'clock, Duncan. Bedtime by the look of you. Is your car in the yard?'

'No, sir.' Duncan had struggled upright. 'I walked, sir. I'm not quite that stupid.' He was running his hand through his hair as if trying to discover if his head was attached. The words were humble, without a touch of defiance, and, rather to his own alarm, Bailey could see that the man's eyes were filling with tears. 'Didn't even have that much, sir, honest. I went and got some shopping.' He pointed at two supermarket bags in the corner, toilet rolls and tins spilling from the mouths. 'Very tired, sir. Bloody tired.' Bailey looked closer. Maybe Duncan was telling the truth and the manner of his sleeping, as well as the choice of venue, owed more to exhaustion than to alcohol although the latter certainly played a part. There was not a day in Duncan's life when alcohol did not play a part, but he was always disposed to be truthful. Work, truth, silly bravery, obsession and booze, the keys to a character that only appeared simple on the surface. Bailey liked Duncan, but not all of the time. Sometimes, even as men went, he was revolting. Lack of sympathy with Duncans was part of Bailey's condition, carefully hidden from mankind.

'You were supposed to be off duty at six. What the hell have you been doing between then and now?'

Duncan dragged himself straight, yanked up his trousers, and looked at the coat he was still wearing as if he did not recognise it.

'Had a couple of drinks, sir. Late-night shopping.' He pointed towards the carrier bags again. 'Then hung around a bit.'

Bailey sighed inaudibly. He might not join in the gossip, but it was his business to hear enough to have a shrewd notion of what hanging around meant in Duncan's case. Uniformed officers had slipped him the word once or twice about D.C. Perry's distinctive car being parked in the slip road behind Herringbone Parade early in the morning or evening, watching for his wife, and even without that, Duncan's distress had bleated itself into a dozen ears, month after month. Kimberley Perry was different. Bailey remembered her clearly from an annual party when he had talked to her for a full fifteen minutes, delighted to find an independent woman among the spouses, while Duncan showed her off like a prize bloom at a flower show. She had been brave enough not to run off with someone else. That alone made her uncommon. Christ, Bailey thought to himself. I'm getting cynical.

'I suppose,' he said gently, 'you were checking up on Kimberley. Seeing she was OK? And the boy, Tom, isn't it? Must be a big lad now.'

Duncan looked like a dumb ox, nodding his head in affirmation. 'Any chance you'll make up, you two?' Bailey ventured even more delicately, as if his remarks concerned nothing more than the weather. 'I mean, there comes a time, doesn't there, when you either have to make up or give up. Been a whole year, Duncan, long time.'

'She won't even talk about it,' Duncan muttered through clenched teeth. 'Never a word. I collect the kid, take him back, she smiles, shuts the door, 'won't let me do anything for her. Cold as ice, the bitch.'

'She's not a bitch,' Bailey interrupted quietly. Duncan turned on him one belligerent eye, sank back against the desk.

'No, sir, she's not a bitch. I almost wish she was.'

'Nor a fool. She can think for herself. Seems to have made up her mind, doesn't she? Got someone else, has she?' He was deliberately harsh.

'Yes. No. I don't know. I love her,' said Duncan with sudden intensity. 'I think she might be having it off with her boss. She can't do this to me, I bloody love her.'

This time Bailey's sigh was not disguised. How often these words were used as cudgels. I love her, therefore she must love me: therefore I must have her and no one else must . . . That obdurate hope, born and dying in stupidity, of love extracting its own reward. He felt a wave of impatience with Duncan. In front of him there stood a man intelligent enough to know that he could not force a prisoner to talk, make a horse drink or a car start, still thinking he could make a woman love him. There was nothing for Bailey to say.

'Well, you mustn't make a nuisance of yourself, or there'll be trouble. Won't do you know. Come on, I'll run you home. You're on my way,' he added. Duncan hated favours as much as advice. One did only what one could, accepting that people could not be changed.

'Thank you, sir.' Bailey turned away to his own room before the man bent to retrieve his shopping.

He had no wish to see what his lone, wilfully miserable officers ate for their suppers; wanted to help without being involved. Wandering outside to wait, he thought bitterly how this had become habit. Stopping people from talking, turning his eyes from suffering which might be stupid, but was still real. Seeing only what he needed to see.

'I'll have to talk to someone, just must. Oh God, I can't go on. Is he going mad, or am I?' Kimberley Perry stifled the feeling of panic, stopped herself running to the phone, running from one room to the other. Nothing to be achieved by that apart from waking fractious Tombo, who had sulked into sleep. There was no one to tell: Kim's stance on the subject of her own marriage alienated her family, pride made them the least likely of chosen confidants, and her thoughts turned to Pip. No, far too personal to tell Pip, as well as unfair, no extra burdens for such a new, if brave widower. Which meant that she could really do nothing at all if Pip were not to know, because even changing the locks on what was, after all, his flat, would be a signal of alarm. She knew what he would do, kind Pip: call me, he would say, whenever you're worried; I'll be round in two seconds. Pip was everybody's helper. For Christ's sake, it was not as if she had done anything wrong in coming back reasonably late, not as if she'd been out dancing till dawn with a rose between her teeth – only out for a drink, for God's sake. But it was the very fact of her being somewhere out of sight that Duncan seemed to dislike so much. Wanted to punish, so he must have crept into the flat with the keys they had agreed he keep against any emergencies on the understanding he never used them otherwise. Crept in here like an alley cat as he brought Tom home from an outing, sniffed around, marking her territory. Taken souvenirs, crept away. Bastard.

'Oh shit. Fucking hell.' Her voice, deep and strident, better suited for joking but no stranger to swearing, sounded harsh and defeated to her own ears, the fury in her tinged with guilt. She need never have suffered this if she hadn't been such a silly cow. Flitting round the flat, feeling sorry for herself, wanting a reminder of being a girl and not a motherly drudge. Searching for that special nightie, a thing of gossamer and satin, bought in headier days, honeymoon stuff, so frivolous it befitted a trousseau. Wanting it now to make herself feel lighter, prettier, even to an audience of no one. A reminder that she was getting out of this hole, going up some day soon and although she tried to pretend the nightie might not have been there in the bottom drawer where she had left it, she knew there was no mistake and it was gone. Along with two pairs of sheer stockings, and, left in place, a single small bottle of the type of perfume Duncan had unfailingly produced on Christmas and birthday. Looking into the drawer, Kim was afraid to look anywhere else, at least until daylight. The evidence of his obsession made her sick.

Who to tell, then, when all this became too much? There were few reserves of fortitude left to manage this new departure of Duncan's, the watchful jealousy worse since she had let him stay, just that once. The night after she found Margaret. Who to tell? There was no reporting policeman Duncan to his fellows and having him jeered down the street. Then an idea illuminated the darkness of the panic, a face swam hopefully into vision and her brow cleared slightly. Bailey, that man Bailey, Duncan's boss. The one she had talked to at the last Christmas party, the only one who listened to what she wanted to do and seemed to know by instinct how tough a time she had with a bleeding drunk spouse like Duncan. A man who had said, let me know if I can help, I doubt if I can, but talking is better than silence. And a man who might, just might be able to exert some control.

'No. Stuff it.' No one helped. No one ever had and no one ever would. You're on your own, gal, silly bitch. Broken all the rules. You, a chemist, don't make me laugh. She scrubbed at her face in the mirror. I'll handle this, sod you all, you wankers. I don't want nothing so leave me alone. Twenty-fucking-nine with eyebags and a maniac husband. Oh Christ. Kim thrust her bosom forward through her pyjamas to intimidate her reflection, the way she would with an awkward customer. She would cope. She would have to.

She knew her silhouette was visible from the window and did not care. The building site was empty, a newly established crane swinging silent. No one whistled and she missed the sound.

CHAPTER THREE

'Any signs of life in here? Yes? No. Oh well.'

How easy to feel extremely silly. In the atmosphere of soporific indifference which pervaded Helen's office, there had been no point in staggering beyond the portals wearing at the time a flashing bow-tie provided by one of her godchildren; pretending not to be tired while repeating a few thoughts. How awful to be here. No; I think I like it here some of the time. Possibly not today. The ten days' absence felt more like a decade, and in a minute someone would come in that door, look a little sheepish and say, Nice to see you and now you're better would you like to go to court this afternoon? She wanted to be able to say, look, buster, I could have swung the lead on the strength of one small operation and stayed off till after Christmas according to Civil Service rules; as it is, conscience got the upper hand so here I am, but don't push your luck. Seen this tie? Wish it was me with the spare battery. If it weren't for having only half a file on Mrs Carlton, I would have stayed home. Where the hell is everybody?

Helen recognised that talking to oneself had all

the ingredients of eccentricity, just as expecting some sort of welcome from her colleagues bore witness to an optimism which was futile at eleven a.m., most other times too. She dropped on a chair one polythene-wrapped hanger bearing newly collected dry cleaning, breathed in the dust with appreciation.

The emptiness was not surprising. There were never enough staff in any inner city office of the Crown Prosecution Service, such a romantic, well-chosen name, she had always thought. Made them sound remarkably like the firm which cleaned the towels, King's Laundry, or any other syndicate which happened to sweep up rubbish. At your service, sir, Prosecutions Incorporated, imprisonments recommended, also cheap eats and good excuses. Helen's untidiness hid her efficiency, and, though the office would have liked to make the same claim it found itself famous instead for failing expectations and losing papers. Justice on a shoestring, poor pay and lousy prospects. Being indifferent to ambition and careless about money, Helen had been in her post far longer than most, and was relied upon by beleaguered colleagues to do the work which no one else had ever done before, the big cases no one else knew how to tackle, the tedious dribs and drabs which had no real place anywhere and precious little interest either. She also supplied shoulders on which to cry (her own excuse for wearing shoulder pads), and, sometimes, the silly jokes.

The battery for the flashing bow-tie was uncomfortable against her skin and the effort of the tube journey more tiring than she expected. Rubbish, she was tired of being tired. One of the reasons for this pretend complete recovery was to avoid solicitude, far worse than any illness. Only as an adolescent had she craved to be pale and interesting like the consumptive heroine of a novel, but now when feeling fragile, she applied the maquillage of perfect health. Bailey had been so kind, so instinctively sensitive, that the attention provoked little but guilt. She was also sick of the idea of resting herself into boredom and drinking nothing but barley water. The door opened. Into the room staggered the case clerk, Mika, under a weight of files.

'Oh. 'Lo, Miss West. Where you been? Got some stuff for you. Redwood thought you might be back. Going to court this afternoon are you? Been poorly? Oh, look.' She pointed to the bow-tie, smiling but bewildered, as if the tie had nothing to do with Helen herself. Mika did not understand jokes. 'What's that?'

'It monitors my heart beat, Mika. How are you?'

'You joking, miss? Oh yes you are. Oh yes, yes, yes. Joke. Shall I tell him you're in? Oh here, Darren wants to see you. And Lefty. Shall I tell . . .'

'Give us a minute, Mika. Don't tell Red Squirrel until after lunch, right? I want to do a bit of reading before he catches me.'

'Right. Gotcha.' Mika grinned, to accompany an elaborate stage whisper, and pushed off to the clerk's room with the good news and her own bustle.

'Well, well, cover blown,' said Helen aloud, not waiting for the queue to form, but knowing, without self-congratulation, that it would. Case clerks, typists not suffering from flu, disgruntled doorman *et al* would all sidle in, one way or another. They did because they knew how much they could widen her eyes with their gossip or their problems. She could do nothing but listen, of course, but that was maybe better than nothing. The same way she listened to witnesses, defendants in waiting who tended to trust her more than their own representatives, and anyone else with a voice. Helen was a time-waster, Redwood said: appalling subject for a time and motion study. What's more she encourages the others.

Silence fell, the silence of the office inside court hours, an interlude for contemplative study. Helen did not want to contemplate, would have preferred to talk, but reading was mandatory and she had flogged in here purely to read. What had puzzled her so much about the Carlton file, blurred over in hospital, was the fact that it was incomplete. Tantalisingly so. A fine case of a Chief Inspector doing his beleaguered best with a bad grace. There was neither the need nor the official requirement to report an unnatural death to the Crown Prosecutor for the area, but if one did so, long before he read of it in the paper over breakfast and called for a report, then at least no officer of the law could say his back was not clear and he had not done his duty. But the indifference of this particular report was evident, an exercise in writing a few paragraphs to a person in whose existence he did not entirely believe and whom he certainly disliked. A little like the mad letters they got quite often, copied to the Queen.

'Sir. (The fact that the addressee may have been a woman did not enter into the rough calculations of politeness.)

'I beg to report the following incident . . .'

Who begs, thought Helen. I beg, you beg. To be heard, understood or have enough for dinner, he has no need to beg.

'Mrs Margaret Carlton (deceased) was found dead in bed on Nov third 1990. Her husband had been away for the forty-eight hours before the discovery of her death, he being a pharmacist, attending a drugs symposium/conference at a central London hotel. Since he had been unable to raise Mrs Carlton by telephone, he had alerted first his assistant, who lives next-door to the flat the couple occupied; she in turn alerted the local police the next morning, at his request. Police Constable Jones forced entry into the flat with Mrs Perry and they found Mrs Carlton dead in bed, but looking quite normally asleep. Since there were no signs, other than those caused by PC Jones himself, of forced entry – here Helen paused and smiled: Jones had obviously entered with all the gentle force of a battering ram – nor were there any signs of struggle or burglary, it was assumed that Mrs Carlton had died in her sleep of natural causes and her doctor was called. He confirmed that she was who she was, a woman of forty-six with no health problems apparent from his own records. She had been married to Philip Carlton, proprietor of the chemist's shop below the flat, for five years prior to her death, and by all local accounts, the marriage had been very happy. Mr Carlton was a bachelor who had spent many years nursing his own mother. The deceased owned the freehold of the shop and assisted in it. Routine post-mortem carried out, mindful of the fact that the deceased was living above a stock of drugs, but nothing untoward was found. Her husband says that on the probable night of her death they had consumed a meal cooked by himself: he then left for the conference. The departure is confirmed by his assistant. The deceased was not missed until the following evening, when Mr Carlton tried to phone her and got no reply. (Continues page two . . .)

There was no page two. The rest of the file consisted of a statement from the doctor and PC Jones, plus one from another doctor at the local hospital who had done the post-mortem, plus two bald descriptions from two ambulancemen, and a statement from someone who watched Mr P. Carlton identify the body of his wife. Helen could see the reason for the report, or thought she could. Chief Inspector whatever he was had some reason to believe there was something wrong here somewhere, didn't like chemists for the good reason that chemists had dealings with drugs, so a certain bad smell must always follow the unexpected demise of anyone near. Or whatever it was, this chemist was not to be taken lightly, according to information received, but all the same, the report, its bitty if formal preparation with all the crossings out, the case itself, starring PC Jones, had never been given the status of any kind of homicide. So where was the rest, if there was any rest. And why, apart from hospital nightmares, did it bother her so much? Slop, rubbish, voluminous, time-wasting things, were the stuff of daily life here; who picked whose pocket. Anyone who thought they joined to deal all the time with real crime etc., soon found out to the difference. But it was that damned shop, or a shop so like this shop, which fixed an uncomfortable, immovable image in her mind.

To say that Helen liked shops was an understatement. Shops and markets without discrimination. The liking was more of an addiction and one which Bailey failed to understand. Shop, she said to herself. Not necessarily the same shop, but she was sure she had remembered the ugly lettering on the outside, 'Carlton's Caring Chemist', with a market outside. Some weeks before hospital, which now seemed another life, driving back from Bailey's flat on a Saturday morning, a journey she could manage with her eyes half-closed and often did, she had found the market, stopped mid-stall with a pair of green tights in hand, arrested by the pain, walked into that shop, and up to the counter, muttering, 'Nurofen, please, anything that works.' Only then did she notice the dizzy interior of the place. Socks hung above the counter, frilly undies, every patent medicine under the sun, one poster showing flossed teeth in a wide smile, another showing the state of a smoker's lungs. The effect of this brightly illuminated variety, plus all the posters, warnings and directions, as well as the condescension of the proprietor – 'Got a headache, have we?' – had the same effect on Helen as psychedelic décor inflicted on a hangover. So much so she had only mumbled her thanks, taken her purchase and fled to the car. Swallowing pills and pulling faces at the taste, she forgot the image, the funny smell which was talcum powder, vitamins, bleach, dispensary scents, all mixed up with the sugary, bitter taste in the mouth. Then, in hospital nightmares, the same scents carried in by nurses and impregnated in the sheets, reminded her again.

So. A chemist's wife may die, sadly alone, like any other wife (Helen was alternately happy and sad not to be a wife), without the faintest suggestion of crime since tragedy and crime do not always go hand in hand, and if there was no sufficient suggestion of crime, then Helen had no business to linger over this or any file, because she was not paid for idle curiosity, only for the prosecution of those who were criminal by accident or design in some incident already established.

All the same, she dived into the in-tray, searching for the addendum or any additions to this scrappy and preliminary report which somehow held the imagination. Ahh. Page two emerged from the internal memos, notes on Christmas leave, law reports, other reports and letters which she allowed to fall to the floor, one way of forcing herself to examine them. An in-tray was a magnet for the meaningless, but full of hazards.

'Mrs Perry, the pharmacist's assistant, was questioned about the death, she being apparently well acquainted with the deceased and the person who found the body. She could contribute no information to explain the cause. However, Mr Carlton volunteered the fact that his wife was in the occasional habit of sniffing chloroform to induce sleep and/or well-being. Small bottle of same found in bathroom, but the dose found in the body was not enough to kill, being only half that necessary (see Pathologist's report). There were no other drugs on the premises at all, no chemicals, apart from the usual domestic range, bleach, dry-cleaning fluid, etcetera. Same have been kept. There were no stimulants. I seek your guidance on how much further this matter should be investigated . . . The family would like the body released for burial . . .'

Well, I can see his point, Helen thought. No murder suspect, no misadventure but the simple and unacceptable fact of death. Chloroform, self-administered, well, well. Twelve milligrammes, she read, not lethal. How did anyone know, since no modern doctor used the stuff any more? The arrogance of all this infuriated her. Why sniff chloroform when you live upstairs from a stockpile of pills you could drink in your tea? She rummaged in the top right-hand drawer of her desk, looking for the familiar store of apples kept to impose limits on her cigarette consumption, forgot there would be none, and found instead a packet of cough sweets which she ate, absently. She jotted on the blotter, phone . . . retest blood – for what? Chloroform in bathroom, body in bed. How? I hate facts, she complained to herself. I hate facts and smells.

Smells, obnoxious scents. She lived by visual images, second to words heard and things smelled, all of these senses acute and long-remembered. The cough sweet tasted of eucalyptus, but alongside that was another smell, reminiscent of a dentist, the mask coming down over the face, a sickly smell inhaled in mute protest. A little like the smell of the dry-cleaning she had placed over the spare chair on the other side of the desk, the polythene covering disturbed to release that waft of cutting scent, so suggestive of aggressive cleanliness. The smells in a pharmacy, as clear as a notice saying we have cleaned everything twice. She jotted on the pad again, 'Dry cleaning fluid: test . . .' How weird was the association of smells, worse, oh far worse than the association of words.

No, she did not believe. No one willingly dumped such cloying smells over their faces simply to sleep. Not if they had ever been to a dentist. Somewhere this report contained a lie.

Helen stirred, felt the still swollen abdomen, wished someone would come in to talk. She felt lazy, resented the prospect of effort; wanted back her hospital bed, tea and sympathy, but not this faint and dangerous scent of anaesthesia.

Tombo hated the smell for a start, nearly as much as he hated the whole occasion. Rotten fruit, not rotten but overripe, suppurating somewhere, ready to burst from boxes and dribble to the floor, fruit worse than the kind his mother packed for him every day and which he threw, extravagantly, towards the playground wall, like they all did. He joined in, afraid, as he always was, that some kid from Herringbone Parade would hit him. A party like this, full of these kids who tormented him whenever they saw him for reasons none of them could have defined, was the worst possible thing about living in Herringbone Parade. Life was better with Daddy – or maybe not. Daddy was better to think about and shout about, as in, You leave me alone, my daddy's a copper, between class, scuffling shouts repeated and rehearsed to perfection, losing their potency now. Boasting about Daddy was better than the actual experience of him every other Saturday when he didn't really know what to do and didn't really know where to go, apart from the pictures where he fell asleep and Tombo sat on, eating popcorn until he felt as sick as he was bored by the characters on the screen. Or playing inept football with Dad, even worse, since Dad was always so disappointed in him. Dad? Can we go and see *Omen Three*? Jimmy's dad took him to that and he said it was great. No, you can't. Here, catch. Got to make a man of you. Can't have you turning out a cissy, but no nightmare films either.

What a joke. As if anything was more of a nightmare than this party. Tombo had not been given the choice of refusing the party organised by Mrs Bum from the grocer's on her premises, but sponsored and bossed by Mrs Bosom from the clothes shop, names he had coined for the satisfaction of giggling himself silly. But while he was there, knew very well what a nightmare was. He felt the symptoms: a flush in the chest, a little sweat on the forehead, a feeling of hot and urgent panic, and only because he was strictly, if imperfectly, tutored about his manners, did he stay, suffering like a soul in torment.

They did this every year, Mrs Bum and Mrs Bosom, whatever they were really called, both in competition with one another, which ensured the continuation of this time-battered ritual. Mrs Bosom could not let Mrs Bum take the accolades for what had once been a philanthropic idea in harder times; nor could Mrs Bum stop donating her larger shop one afternoon a year for a ritual she privately loathed (although she always said otherwise, in case anyone should consider her mean and a person who did not like little kiddies, which she emphatically did not). So far, only the little kiddies could tell, and the compromise she had managed to make was to insist that this party, for all the children in Herringbone Parade, as well as all the children of the Parade's customers, be held at the very beginning of December, to inaugurate the whole festive season and at least not waste as much trading time as it might if she held it during Christmas week when everyone else had a party anyhow and their own efforts would not be noticed. She cleared the front of the shop as well as one of the large rooms at the back where they kept the new stock along with the old, now all piled against the wall, awaiting trimming and rejuvenation before sale. Her husband did not hump the sacks of sprouts because of his ulcer: Daniel did that. Daniel was useful, tolerantly despised. Never mind him being an addict; he was nice enough, not always reliable, but cheap at the price, without ever being comfortable. There were several cartons of melons he had carried indoors, a mistake, those melons, but the fairy lights were sound, tested here before Mrs Beale moved them to the window the week after next. Sod the little bastards, get them organised. Tombo heard her voice, but all he was really registering, by deliberately removing himself from all the other children around him, was the smell of the rotting melons, the dankness of the room, the unaccustomed sweat of his own terror.

'We're all going to play pass the parcel,' shrieked Mrs Bosom, who despite the alarming nature of her appearance, all shiny stuff and so big on top, entered fully into the spirit of this gathering. Mrs Bosom did not have children and still preserved the body beautiful, as well as a belief in childish fun. Currently, her voice was hoarse. 'And after that, boys and girls, hide and seek! With prizes!'

Tombo was quite beyond wanting a prize, the only carrot to be found in a grocer's shop: the disgrace of not getting one of the many prizes progressively less important, and besides, they had all been given a bar of chocolate already. They were ushered into a circle while a huge, light parcel was produced. Crackly music blared from the stereo in the corner. As the parcel passed into his hands, he threw it on with great violence as if his fingers were burning, then sat back, bathed in relief, his arms crossed over his chest, resisting the next contact or the touching of anyone else. Then the parcel lurched into his lap again as the sound of the carol faded. He looked down in furious disbelief, kicked it on savagely, survived for five terrible minutes. He fixed a smile while the chocolate he gripped changed shape in his sticky fingers and he did not know where to put it down.

But hide and seek was a fate worse than death, a sort of slow torture recalled from previous horrors, unavoidable despite pretending to go to the lavatory, finding whispering girls in the path up the stairs, retreating, holding himself, his need frozen in the greater desire simply to pass the time before he escaped, remembering to smile when he came back. Sent first to hide, he hid obviously enough to be found in seconds, then was grabbed and hauled back, only to understand that this was a trial and he had to do the same again. 'Make it harder, Tom, there's a good boy,' yelled one voice, but he could not imagine anything harder than hiding away to be found, pushed, shoved, squashed with the enemy in a dark smelly corner where someone would pinch. He hid behind the melon boxes, gagging on the smell, but his nerve was gone. They were counting up to one hundred, going slowly to give him time, all of them with their hands over their eyes, and the chanting '. . . twenty-seven, twenty-eight, twenty-nine, thirty!' ending in a shout at the end of each ten, sounded like the barking of a malevolent pack of dogs set to tear him to pieces. Vomit was in his throat: shame at his heels.

Tombo stumbled through the back room, not really looking at all. There were two back rooms to this, the largest of all the shops: one where they had partaken of the tea which lay so heavily on his stomach, the other no more than an ante-room to the little yard which led out to the service road behind, a cold, draughty annexe. Tombo heard the counting grow louder, speeding out of control before someone would turn out the light for them to come creeping after him, less like dogs now than rats hissing in the dark. The terror of humiliation became uncontrollable, lending him strength. He pushed against the back door, knowing the pushing was loud enough to be heard, not caring, kicking it shut behind him, running through the yard before stopping, suddenly brave enough to turn back and yell, 'Yer, yer yer!' very loudly, frightening himself further by the echo into the silence. His fist was raised, shaking defiance.

The greengrocer's was at the far end of the Parade, once a house, and the first of all the shops which seemed to stream out like a series of additions to an original idea. At the back, everything was featureless. Tombo knew exactly where he was since he had explored this service road, poked into the little yards and delivery bays, but never in the dark which made this unlit backwater endless. Half-day closing today, the party starting straight after school and himself not expected home before seven, Mummy probably taking advantage to be out.

Tombo breathed deeply, puffing out his chest as he looked round on the off chance for Daniel. Daniel often hung round here, no real fun, but big and company of sorts. At least you could sit with him. Tom looked hopefully at the building site. Empty. There was no sound in the wintery blackness apart from his breath on the cold air, a rasping noise which made clouds in front of his eyes. He remembered the coat left behind, hugged his arms to his chest, and then heard dim thumps coming from inside the shop. Like dogs and rats released, they would realise soon, follow him, hissing and barking, taunt him, put him inside one of the tall bins flanking the road. He began to trot bravely, going faster and faster past the back of the newsagent's, the off-licence, the butcher's, the takeaway, each with its own terrible smell, trying not to break into a run, pretending he was in control; not knowing what to do until he was level with the back of Carlton's Caring Chemist, no light shining out of his own upstairs home, and nowhere to go. Sometimes he had a key to let himself into the flat, a practice which made his mother so ashamed for all it signified, but not today. Any other day he could have waited inside the shop, but today they shut at five. Tombo stood, irresolute, becoming cold, then crept forward. Salvation. There was a light at the back of the shop where Mr Carlton's back room, his own, tiny dispensary, led on to a patch of ground below the stairs to the flats. Light shone from the window, so welcome he wanted to touch it. Better than nothing: he was cold.

Tombo had never quite brought himself to like Philip Carlton, whom he always addressed as plain Mister, nor could he rely on Mister to understand his predicament because Mister was clearly a person who liked parties, and because Mister always tried to be nice (call me Uncle Pip), but he did not believe he would be sent away. Formulating excuses and reasons, he crept to the window, which was, he had forgotten, the top half of the door. The light was the only sign of life. Thinking how sick he was of pushing unfamiliar doors either to get out or get in, he tried the door, which yielded suddenly to his touch, sending his light body into the chemist's back dispensary with all the grace of a jack-in-the-box.

'What the hell . . .'

Philip Carlton whirled round from the laboratory shelf which occupied half of the room, with the sink in the middle surrounded with what looked like medicine bottles, and a few very old and mouldy-looking books. It was the ante-room to the back room rather like the arrangement in Mrs Bum's but without stairs connecting with the upper landing. Philip's voice was thick with fury. He had seized a jemmy used for prising open cardboard crates and held it aloft in one hand, the arm lowering as he squinted, identifying his visitor.

'What on earth do you think you're doing in here, young Master Perry? I thought you might be one of those bad boys I know, come to steal drugs. You know bl . . .' he choked on a swear word, tried to stand up straighter, '. . . very well you're never supposed to come in here. Now what do you want?'

'Nothing, Mr Carlton, honest. I'm sort of locked out upstairs and I saw the light. I thought Mum would be back, but she isn't, you see not yet . . .' the fury in Philip's usually unctuous voice made Tombo gabble, come to a dead halt and stand there, hugging his chest. Then Mister smiled, very broadly, and Tombo felt another kind of doubt as he heard a complete change of tone, the voice becoming manically friendly, even a little dreamy.

'Oh, I see, I see, I see. Well that's fine then, absolutely fine. You'd better stay here until your lovely mummy gets back. Play with Uncle Pip, eh? Such a lot of fun we're having here, such a lot of fun.'

'What are you doing?'

'Me? You must mean me, ha, ha, no one else here, is there? Me? I'm making mixtures. For putting in bottles, keeping poisons safe and fit to use. Such fun, you see.'

He always repeats himself, Tombo thought, says the same things again and again and everything twice. Reassured, but unaccountably anxious, he couldn't help but notice there was something strange about Mister tonight: he was grinning so wide and his eyes were all sparkly, his movements expansive, so that when he waved an arm to usher Tom further forward into the room towards a chair, he knocked some books to the floor. Tombo was used to Mister being delicate and precise in all his movements, irritatingly, sometimes comically so:

the big waves and big voice were more often the surprising hallmark of little Mrs Carlton. Remembering she who was dead, this one-time friend of his, made Tombo even more uncomfortable. Death was not something he understood, except to know it was discussed in low voices.

'Seen these books, eh, Tombo?' Mister was pointing at the old volumes on the shelf which appeared to have been the object of his study before the interruption, although the whole bench was littered. The books contrasted oddly with the modern, laminated manuals his mother used for reference, but Tom was not curious.

'No,' he said.

'Well, you can look at the pictures, but not if you don't want nightmares, ha, ha. Mares in the night, don't you know. Why call 'em mares? Why not nightfillies?'

'What's in the books?' Tom asked out of politeness. He was beginning to get used to the glittering eyes and the strange smell in there. Nothing like the faintly dirty smell in Mrs Bum's. This was at least clean. As his father had noted with disgust, Tom had become a fastidious little boy.

'Shows you how they used to do operations, Master Perry, in the olden days. I got all those books when I was a lad your age, wanted to be a doctor, but not to be, not to be. Not enough money. A humble chemist, never an anaesthetist. My mean old dad, no ambition. Dead, of course, my dad.'

That word, dead; a signal to change the subject.

'What sort of doctor is a neethtist?' Tombo enquired, looking dutifully at the books, which were dull indeed, containing pictures certainly, but nothing in colour and only of things which looked like masks, strange contraptions, old nurses' uniforms.

'An an-aes-thet-ist is the one who puts you to sleep before you have an operation, silly.'

'Oh,' said Tombo, turning the pages. The atmosphere was oppressive: between the cleanness of the smells, the party tea rebelled inside him and he was developing a headache.

'What time is it, Mr Carlton, please?'

A watch was consulted with elaborate care. Mister seemed to have some difficulty in reading it although the light was extremely bright.

'Six-forty-five. Or quarter to seven, whatever you prefer.' He was laughing again, seemed incredibly happy.

'I'd better go and see if Mummy's back, then. She might . . .'

'Oh might she? Yes I suppose she might . . . Your mother . . . your mother is a wonderful girl, you know.' The voice was now thick with emotion. 'Tell her . . . Tell her, oh never mind.' He was suddenly back to his more familiar self. 'Anyway, come back if she isn't there. Can't have you wandering round on your own, can we?'

Tombo was beginning to think this might be preferable. With all the uninhibited instincts of his age, he was aware, where Mummy was not, of Mister's funny, grown-up, silly regard for her, the way his eyes followed her in the shop when she was not looking and Tombo was in there, waiting on his seat by the counter where he had felt safest with Mrs Carlton, even when she was at her worst. He did not analyse any of this but the defection of little Mrs Carlton through death made him angry with her: some form of safety went with her. Tom was also angry with Mummy who would, surely, if left alone, make friends with Daddy again. She had told him, categorically and often, that they were friends, really, Daddy and she, just not the kind of friends who should live under the same roof. 'You know how it is, pet; some people you like, but you can't be with them all the time. You've got friends like that in school.' Had he hell: the likening of his own situation to theirs brought resentment without a glimmer of understanding. Tombo was more used to yearning for friends: he could not imagine the luxury of turning them away; he could not even turn Daniel away, and if Mister here, with his great, wide, soppy smile and his glittering eyes . . . if this Mister thought he was going to step in where Daddy had stepped out, he had another think coming. Tombo slithered off his seat.

'Goodbye,' he said very formally. 'Thanks for letting me in.'

'Any time, old son.' Watching him for two steps, waving blearily.

Old son, new son, I am not your son, you, you stinker: you don't care about me at all. Tombo dawdled in the yard, hoping that the longer he took, the greater would be the chance of light in the

66

upstairs flat. He paused by the wall, half-hiding, aping the game of hide and seek he had so recently escaped, peering round the broken fence although he did not expect discovery. Then, from just beyond the wall, he saw the tail lights of a parked car flutter into life, slightly ahead and parallel with the back of the baker's, two doors down, but close. An engine choked softly and began to purr: he recognised the familiar sound in one great bound of joy, ran from his sheltering place, shrieking after the lights and the puff of exhaust, 'Daddy, Daddy, Daddy! Dad, it's me, stop . . . Dad . . . stop . . .' But it was too late. He ran after the car up to the junction at the end, where it slowed, turned, too dark for the driver to see behind, leaving Tombo, standing still, shaking his fist and crying.

He wiped his hand across his nose. Traces of chocolate clung like mud, mingling with the tears.

CHAPTER FOUR

'You are old, you are old . . . And your bones are growing cold . . .'

Old. Nearing seventy, facing the vacuum of an evening in a hospital room assigned for his use. Oh, Father William, you are old, and you hide your depression in a cold. The softest pair of hands, most catholic of knowledge, such talent in finding a vein, but nothing to do with all those hours before sleep. Dr Hazel was overly familiar with despair. His right hand stretched out for the brandy bottle beside his bed: then the left hand followed the right and slapped his own wrist. He squinted at the red mark he had made, faintly visible below the age marks on white skin. No.

As long as he stayed overnight in the room, he might be needed or entertained. Hospitals breathed by night: there were generators and footsteps, life and crises instead of the sterile death of empty rooms in an empty home. No one asked him to stay and look in on his patients, but he stayed. On the desk at home was paper, pen, the constant reproach of all he had meant to write and could not write. The same reproach lingered here, but not as pressing. No. Not the brandy. A lifetime's acquaintance with the unconscious patient left him prey to an inverted view of human kind: cynical depression was the curse of his existence. So much so, there was discomfort in the finding of an occasional kindred spirit who whetted that appetite for life he had been trying to kill, and awakened his talent to amuse and inform. He was not grateful to Helen West.

'Dear God,' he muttered, folding his hands in mockery of prayer. 'Will someone, somewhere, give me something useful to do? Rancid, I am, with stale knowledge and old clothes.'

The jacket had thirty years, cavalry twills twenty, outmoded like many of his drugs, only the fingers superbly useful. Retirement, the blackest gift of his seventieth birthday, yawned like a black hole and suicide beckoned less as a sin against the Holy Ghost than as the exchange of one hell for another. He picked up his pen and felt it freeze in his fingers. No one would want to know. He eyed the medicine cabinet in the corner, which, being his own, was never checked. A few drops of this and that, oblivion so easy. Again, no. He had his pride, although he despised it. His wife and son stared out from the photograph fading by the sink. Dead, buried along with his own dignity and reputation.

A little of the brandy, perhaps. Only a little.

Helen knew she was better. Familiar energy was returning to her limbs; she had ticked her way through two days in the office and one very awkward interview with the Chief Inspector in the Carlton enquiry, but recovery was reliably signalled by preparations for an evening out with friends and the beginnings of an argument with Bailey. Understated arguments were frequent preludes to such occasions. Bailey only liked parties after they were finished, had fond memories of some, and actually loved conversation, but getting him out there was not always easy. What irritated Helen was the fact that the sociable part of their not very sociable lives was invariably initiated by her, never by him. He had no conscience about refusing invitations, nor did he aspire to the kind of acquaintance she seemed to attract without effort. Taking Bailey out to dinner with others was an activity she compared with leading out a dancing bear on a chain; he grumbled and snarled slightly, grizzled, but followed and once there, found himself baited.

'I like that. You look good.' Helen's dress always pleased him; he took a rare interest in her clothes, would have encouraged even greater flamboyance than she ever allowed herself in the plain lines and strong colours of her choice. He was proud of her, liked others to see her, but he never said so, of course.

'So do you. You always do. Handsome. If a little formal.' There was no sarcasm in the words, only a familiar teasing. Bailey could not master casual clothing. There were suits and other uniforms for work; then there were frayed jeans and shirts for carpentry, gardening or mending drains, but nothing in between. Helen liked to see his long, lean frame adorned by a suit, and it did not matter what others chose.

'By the way,' she continued from no beginning, 'do you know a Chief Inspector Davies? On your division, not your station.'

'Yes, vaguely. He doesn't report to me. Nice man. Not made for higher things and doesn't want them. Collects teapots.'

'Oh, does he? Might have liked him better if I'd known that. He came into the office yesterday: we had a bit of an argument about that Carlton death, you know the chemist near you. He thought I was telling him how to do his job.'

Bailey frowned, a look of real annoyance replacing the resignation which had been present a minute before. He picked the car keys from the top of the fridge, where a large dish contained every spare item, bills included, which lingered, sometimes for weeks, in Helen's home, waiting for a place to rest. 'Well . . . were you telling him how to do his job?'

'Not as I saw it,' said Helen, feeling round in the dish for the house keys which also lived there, assuming a life of their own whenever she needed them. 'But he just wasn't interested. I was telling him I thought we needed another post-mortem, household stuff analysed to see if there was any more chloroform around, and a lot more background detail into the drug as well as the family before we could say that this damn chemist's wife really had died without any explanation. A good look at the shop. Stuff like that. Re-interview the woman assistant . . .' Her voice had assumed that airy quality which meant she recognised some form of criticism from him was on the way. Helen wanted to circumvent that: it boded ill for an evening already fraught with pitfalls, but she knew she was too late. Bailey did not understand blind loyalty – he belonged to no tribe, policemen or otherwise – but something in him rebelled against hearing a colleague being criticised. Strangers could do so, newspapers did so all the time, but not, please, his nearest and dearest.

'Listen, he's a Chief Inspector doing his best. They have the worst of all worlds, poor bastards, all the administrative nightmares, almost everything routine to investigate, hit and run, unexplained death, with none of the facilities given to the CID. You have to let him do the best he can and accept the result. If you interfere, you'll make it worse. He has a healthy attitude to lawyers, anyway.'

'Meaning we're really congenital idiots who know nothing about the real world? Sit in judgement like gods on the universe and never get our hands dirty? Yes, that is what you mean.'

'No, not what *I* mean, but what he might mean, especially if you dictate to him. Neither party does a perfect job, but the one shouldn't interfere with the other.'

'I thought I'd ask Dr Hazel, you know, my anaesthetist, for some help on the subject. What am I supposed to do, let it ride?'

'In some cases, yes, unless you have excellent reasons to say you shouldn't. Which you haven't here. There's no real suggestion of murder or manslaughter, any more than there is in death by glue sniffing. Helen West's insatiable curiosity is about to request the invasion of some poor citizen's privacy. Nothing to do with evidence, of course. And enlisting the aid of a deeply suspicious old man in the process.'

She did not leap to the good doctor's defence: that way lay serious argument, but she was uncomfortable. There was no evidence of foul play, rather the reverse, plenty to indicate nothing of the kind. Only the smells, the shameful scent of a wild goose chase and the wonder how anyone could bear the perfume of drugs without overdose first. She felt slightly ashamed as her hands closed over the keys.

'You wouldn't be able to have a placatory word with Chief Inspector Davies, would you? Put him on the amenable track, since you know him, smooth the hackles?'

'Helen,' he said warningly. 'You know I won't.'

'OK, OK, leave it for now, sorry I spoke.' She deflected serious irritation by pulling at his sleeve, 'Come on, we're late.'

Late for an evening of good food, multicoloured salad and veal escalope which he enjoyed, conversational jousting with him as the target, which he did not. It only needed one liberal bounty hunter who believed the whole order of police officers was rife with corruption to lead a pack of interrogators, primed with the questions they had always wanted to ask. There was a dentist, three lawyers, a magazine journalist, not an abnormal throng for a dinner

73

party. Helen, knowing he was far from defenceless and angry with him anyway, left him to the wolves at the other end of the table.

'No,' he was repeating wearily, 'no, I don't think London's policemen are particularly more wonderful than any other men: they do what other men do, think what other men think, are tempted in the same way by the same things.'

'Have you ever,' asked one intense woman, 'ever lost your temper, and you know, oh, I hope you don't mind being asked this, I mean, ever beaten someone, hit them? When you were arresting them, I mean,' she added hastily.

'I do mind being asked.' Bailey's voice was sharper, alerting Helen from her distance. 'But since you have, the answer's yes. Without much real excuse either. Not for some time, however. Hot temper goes hand in hand with youth, but also has an occasional association with courage. Difficult, in awkward situations, to have the one without the other.' He smiled at the woman like a piranha, making her duck back into her food, Bailey's most dreadful and terrifying smile, not deterring the man opposite. Oh, Christ, Helen thought; this was not one of the evenings worth leaving a fireside for, even to avoid cooking. She knew very well by the end of the second course that they would depart as soon as decency allowed, looked round at her own contemporaries. Better educated than Bailey, despite his law degree, painfully acquired through night school; better read for all his voracious reading; better mannered, certainly not. Bailey would

74

not dream of harassing a fellow guest. In his case, disapproval bred silence, so did uncertainty, and no serious conversation was ever so public, so rudely monopolising. It was not his fault that despite his erudition he so often resembled a bull in a china shop. She was proud of him, loved him, but occasionally, they embarrassed each other.

Finding the safety of the car after they left the house and in the certain knowledge of being talked about, Helen wondered if it would ever end, this social awkwardness. Probably not.

'Your place or mine?' he asked, the ordinary smile which creased the face into a thousand lines showing relief at the end of captivity.

'Any home at all, James, and don't spare the horses.'

Philip Carlton's late wife Margaret had never actually disgraced him in public, but, as he saw it, she had never actually raised his stock either. I mean, he told himself, in the privacy of his spotless kitchen, allowing himself a little of her favourite tipple although it was slightly sour from the keeping, she wasn't an asset. Pip scarcely noticed the taste, bought wine automatically the same way he consumed one glass each evening alongside carefully prepared food. One pork chop, two vegetables, one small baked potato, efforts the women in the grocer's and the butcher's found commendably sad and brave. Almost as swift to commend and sympathise was that Chief Inspector who had phoned in the first place to say that Margaret was dead. Sympathy had diminished with the discovery of the chloroform angle, ebbed and flowed since, but he seemed to accept Pip's apologetic explanations. Besides, the chemist's drugs were all in order, not a single poison unaccounted for, the records immaculate, and although the telephone voice was clipped, it was still reassuring. Pip remembered how he had kept them out of the back dispensary.

'Sorry to bother you, Mr Carlton. I said I'd come back to you about the . . . funeral arrangements.' He had been going to say, about your wife's body, but changed the words instead. Chief Inspector Davies loved his own wife solidly; he imagined most respectable men did the same, despite the evidence to the contrary often shoved in front of his nose. Besides, any one of the few questioned in Herringbone Parade (a sketchy questioning, he had to admit) found Philip Carlton wonderful. That, with the Inspector's naive belief in the integrity of professional men, put him firmly on Pip's side. Women, on the other hand, were always difficult.

'But anyway, as I said, we can't release the . . . deceased, not yet. And another officer might see you tomorrow. Detective Inspector Collins. I'm off the case.'

'Why?' said Pip.

'Well,' said Davies uncomfortably, 'I had to report to the Crown Prosecution Service. We do, you see. It's them, not me: they want a few more enquiries. That chloroform, bloody nuisance. Silly of her to play round like that.'

People dying in bed were a burden for a desk

already full of death and disaster mainly inflicted by motor cars. 'Nothing to worry about, the Coroner's doing his pieces, but there it is. Shouldn't take long. Only a matter of loose ends.'

'Can you bring back the things you took from the flat?'

There was a pause. 'No, not yet, sir, but please don't worry. He'll see you at twelve, OK?'

Pip was not worried, or not more than a jot. If they asked him more questions, he would only have to give them more answers since he had nothing to lose apart from the sympathy of another police officer. No one had yet asked for any elaboration, but he had never really supposed it was going to be as easy as that. What he and Margaret had done so often last thing at night might be considered odd, but hardly criminal. You would only have to look at a photograph of Margaret to see why. In any event, the entertainments of the evening had rendered him languid, full of confidence and bonhomie, and he was well on the way to believing that everything had been Margaret's fault anyhow. Bossy, officious, little Margaret with the lined monkey face and shattering voice, with her pathetic passion to be loved. Not quite as well off or as amenable as he had thought, this Margaret, owner of this freehold shop, all left by her dead husband. They had added this respectable wealth to the price of the house left by his mother when Pip entered into marriage for the first time. Margaret's fault too, if the glow had faded; she should not have been so bossy, so anxious to interfere with everything. He dwelt on this, working himself into righteous anger. It saved him from dwelling on the other. The shame, the hot, searing shame which pierced his groin as he sat in the kitchen, his hand moving automatically to guard his crotch. Small and perfectly formed, his mother had said, touching all the time and teasing. Alone and afraid, he could feel her fingers again, flicking and tickling his childish little stump, teasing him into life, that awful, disgraceful, involuntary life which Margaret had so craved.

He could feel the fingers. Pip suddenly screamed in agony. Sat back with his knees pressed close together, rocking to and fro until he was calmer, waited for the sweat to cool, still feeling hands along his spine and between his legs, creeping like insects. There was a knock on the door. His head shot up, the neat hair fell back into place and colour returned to his skin. Outside, Daniel was halfway down the steps. Daniel never waited.

'Oh. I was coming to see you. Heard you shout. Those boxes out the back . . .'

'No,' said Pip. 'Not now, tomorrow. It's late.'

'OK.' Daniel shrugged. A sly smile curved at his mouth, not a particularly pleasant smile. 'Don't want anyone going near your back room, do we?'

'Go home, Dan.' The voice was sharp.

Daniel went, his own pace never varying, carrying with him a cloud of discomfort. Ever watchful Daniel, that half-smile playing havoc. Pip was shaking. Memory stirred uncomfortably, a different memory from all that panic which had preceded the knock. Another memory of a figure outside in the dim light of pre-dawn, but Daniel was not a man with memory. Pip shook his head again, concentrated instead on the image of Kimberley Perry's rounded bottom as she bent down, her legs when she climbed the step ladder to the top shelf in the dispensary, her comforting bosom under the overall. Give her time, give her time, stay still for now. And then he would really know. For now, he would clean his house and his best suit instead. Ready for a funeral.

Whistling tunefully, Pip set about his domestic tasks, a little apprehensive about tomorrow and what he would say. He swiped at the stainless steel sink, already shining from washing-up liquid, plucked the ironing board from a cupboard and fetched his suit. Went to hunt for the dry-cleaning fluid he used for spot cleaning wool flannel. Gone, missing from under the sink he had just made new, gone with all the other rubbish hidden along with it, Jif, Sparkle, environmentally friendly washing powder, all taken by the police. Now that gave him a moment's pause for thought, not a nice moment, but a minute or two in which he sweated freely and was forced to sit down. Repeating a few mantra-like phrases to himself, such as, it does not matter, this will pass, they won't connect, nothing wrong anyway. I've got an explanation, and the one thing they'll never do is find evidence, no one old enough. Policemen are not chemists. Then the lassitude of the evening won again, bringing in the wake of the sweat a repetition of the earlier optimism which was his own hallmark, along with a feeling of recklessness. Perhaps he would go and see Kimberley. He rummaged in the drawers of the dresser: sweets for children, children like any kind of sweet, even the fusty chocolate bars which Margaret had provided to make him fat; a sort of memorial, never to be consumed. Armed with these, he made for the balcony, the thought of Kimberley sharpening his breath. He had to know: he had to find out: she was the only one who could show him, the only one he had ever desired . . . With his constant care for economy, he turned out the light before he opened the glazed back door. Stood by the rail, stung by the cold of the air, and heard, to his chagrin, his own name called from the road below.

'Never mind, Tombo, never mind. Honestly, it doesn't matter. Parties don't matter, only I wish you'd said how much you hated it last time and I'd have made an excuse for you not to go. What on earth made you think I'd be cross about something like that? You are a silly.' She ruffled his head. 'Anyway, you raced out of there, went to Uncle Philip while you were waiting for me to come back; you were lucky he let you in. No one's allowed in the back dispensary, not even me. Anyhow, then what did you do?'

'Sat on the step, in the dark. After . . .'

'After what?' She could sense he did not want to answer, but would answer if she was patient, stayed as she was, stroking his head which he always seemed to like. A worrying state to find him in, shivering without a coat, sick as soon as they came indoors. Put to bed with more ceremony than usual, attended by more than the customary guilt. 'After what?'

'After Daddy went,' he muttered, feeling the treachery reach to his stomach as well as to the eyes which still threatened tears. But he stopped when he saw that Mummy was calm and not even surprised.

'Just a minute, Tom, I'm getting a cigarette.' Out of the room to hide the shaking of the limbs, the feeling of shock. She lit the cigarette hurriedly and came back, disguising distress in the smoke and apologies. Tombo at his tender age was remarkably puritanical about smoking: so, at the best of times, was she.

'I didn't know Daddy was coming this evening,' she said conversationally. 'Though he does come quite often, I know. Just to check we're all right, you know. He doesn't have time to come in.' If only that were true, she thought: if only I had never let him have a key. If only he did not watch us, watch me, rather. He doesn't watch over Tombo enough. Nor does he steal Tombo's nightwear. Nor does he cross-examine him every time they meet, like he does me.

'What time was it roughly, tonight, when you saw Daddy, I mean, and did you get a word with him?' She slowed down the frantic puffing on the unfamiliar cigarette, pretending to try and blow smoke rings, pulling faces to make him laugh.

'Only ten minutes before you came back. I wasn't waiting long, honest. Bit cold though.' He was feeling comfortable now, warm and loved, sleep intruding into the corners of his busy brain.

'Bet it was, you poor old thing. You'll have to wear your anorak for school in the morning. I'll go back and get your coat from the grocer's, Mrs Beale. I know you call her Mrs Bum, but I can't call her that. Wouldn't I like to, though. Pretty good name, isn't it? Suits her.'

Tombo giggled, giddy with the relief of being part of a pair. Mummy was laughing: she rarely laughed but when she did, laughing with him, like now, he knew with great certainty how ready she was to fight for him, look after him, if only he asked. Asking was the trouble. Pride was a barrier the size of a reef. Nor was this invisible support, this fervent love, so tangible now, always beyond doubt in a school playground which stretched for a hundred miles each side, to say nothing of the pavements of Herringbone Parade.

Mrs Beale was puffing on the customer's side of the counter at Carlton's Caring Chemist, enjoying a sense of her own importance and only faintly apologetic. Ever so sorry to bother him, she was, but she guessed he'd be in (he was never out and nor should he be, widowed so recent, wouldn't be right), and her need was greater. Mrs Beale did not believe in the local doctor, a gentle man admittedly but never a gentleman because of being as black as the ace of spades and called Dr Gupta. Not good enough for her mother-in-law's ulcer, oh no. Pip Carlton was the man for that, any damn chemist with a stock of pills was the man for that and bloody Mother playing up like a baby because of all the disruptions of that party. Pig. She had an ulcer from eating like a sow and complaining every alternate breath, serve her right. Truth to tell, she had been trotting up the back road simply to be out of her way as much as because she thought she needed medicine. Herringbone Parade might have been full of neighbours by day, but was certainly not particularly neighbourly by night, not like the old days. Not like it was in the days of the dim-remembered war. There was a proper spirit about the place then, Mother said; never stopped talking about the bombs which wrecked the landscape in the Blitz. Now, nothing stirred after seven o'clock, when the service road assumed the silence of a grave, the odd, snorting car, nothing else. So it was nice, very nice to have a word with Pip, who was never out of patience, never said no, was ever so caring. Yes of course, Mrs Beale, but how are you? Can't give you anything you could only get with a prescription, mind, but I think I've got something which is just the job; can you come round the corner to the shop? Never keep anything like that in the flat, you know: Margaret wouldn't have it. Mrs Beale was touched by the way he always spoke of Margaret as if she were still alive, maybe because they hadn't had a funeral yet. Sad, that, but not very. She was well aware that Margaret would have sent her packing, protected Pip from the inconvenience he actually liked and told her to call a doctor.

'I'm ever so sorry,' she repeated for the seventh

time, although she hadn't meant it the first, 'but she does play up, you know. Wouldn't get a wink if I left her like that, would I?' 'No, you wouldn't,' said Pip with a twinkle in his eye. 'You could always, you know, distract her. How about one of these nice nighties here while you're at it?' She roared with laughter, always appreciative of his little bit of flirting. 'Oh get on, can you see me in one of them? I'd have a heart attack just looking in the mirror.' 'Sold one to your friend in the dress shop, you know. How was the party, by the way?' She ignored the question, but not the roguish glance, the raised eyebrows at the mention of the lady whom Tombo called Mrs Bosom, the chance of poking a little fun at that glamorous rival too good to resist. Not that Pip ever said anything nasty, but the look was enough. 'Did you now?' Mrs Beale murmured. 'Did you indeed? Just tell me what colour and I'll never mention it again.' His turn to laugh, handing her the medicine, putting both hands round hers as he pressed the bottle into her palm. Pip always touched first, before he was touched. 'More than my life's worth, Mrs B, you know that, more than my life's worth.' They beamed at each other in mutual approval.

'Come back for a cuppa,' Mrs Beale said. 'Not late, is it? Don't like to think of you on your own. Mum would love to see you. Talk about old times.'

Pip looked gratified, hiding the wariness. Ah, the love of the neighbours, the various kinds of love Margaret had denied him, but old Mrs Beale had known him as a boy, half a mile and a million years away. She had known the family, the aunts and his mother, the only person in the Parade who did, and Pip was not ready for reminiscence. 'Oh, you are kind, but not tonight. Work, I'm afraid.'

'Well, another time then. You look after yourself.'

Ten doors down, Mrs Beale senior sat by the fire, waiting. She wondered why, with her compendious knowledge, the police had never been to see her, sat as she had sat for weeks, in a state of silent offence.

Solitude was onerous. There were times when Hazel bore it as lightly as he carried his shambling fifteen stone; other occasions when these night hours were so oppressive he felt them suffocating his heart, remembered by logical association the anaesthetics he had used as a childish man. A believer in science and the power of healing, dear God, those were the days. Holding down a patient and making them breathe their escape from pain, even while they resisted. No, this was his imagination: he had never actually done so. That was what was done in the olden days, the earliest, mid-nineteenth century anaesthetics, when more patients were killed by the new discoveries than had been killed before, even when they screamed their way through hideous surgery, removed from the populous hospital wards so that other patients might not hear the yells. Well, as he reflected when looking at his collection of books, at least they gave the poor bastards a choice of death, these knock-out fumes applied at first by the surgeon himself or whoever happened to be around, magic formulae in unsteady, ignorant hands, administered with such liberality that the patient need not wait to die by the knife. There was no such animal as an anaesthetist then: there was simply a student or a nurse with the mask, looking like an executioner, often inadvertently fulfilling that same function. Sean Hazel knew all this and knew he would not have such nightmares if it was not his habit to read such history. There was in his brain the dream book, the papers he had never written, the story of these lives, as told by his own father, read in these dry volumes, known by himself, as one of the few doctors old enough to have used the same stuffs. The new breed did not want to know and did not need to know, what history was like. Or how they owed respect to their elders for their very existence, even if those elders, like Hazel himself, were burdened with useless knowledge.

He was talking to himself again, getting ready for bed in the cabin-like room, gesturing to his books, the old Victorian manuals, to prove to himself his own point. 'You'd manage best in the jungle, boy, surely. You'd know how to improvise.' The thought was satisfying, pointless self-flattery, he knew, but still reassuring. He looked towards the brandy bottle: only two fingers gone, good lad. He had tried them all, alcohol last; none of them worked. Oblivion was the hardest thing of all, fatigue the best he could ever achieve to blur the pictures in his mind or rid his nostrils of the smells.

He had used chloroform on his son.

There had been nothing else.

Helen had gone to work with Bailey's admonitions ringing in her ears, not a lecture, only the same few words, very softly spoken. 'Don't interfere: let others do the work they are paid for . . .' She had not told him how the self-same advice had already been given by her own superiors, and since she was never immune to advice or to criticism, she was beginning to think she should listen. Arrogance was so foreign a sensation she did not really know what it was: conviction was another matter entirely, but as she strode up the corridor, armed with the second-best suit from the dry cleaner's, conscious of feeling well, wanting a quiet life with Redwood, Mika and everyone else, she was feeling blithely co-operative, ready to apologise to the world for causing it trouble, anything to keep the peace.

Until Mika came into the room with a memo, on her face the reproving glance given to the person who is late by the person who has arrived early. 'Chief Inspector Davies has been phoning. I wrote it down. He'll phone back, but he had to go out.'

'Oh, shit.' The in-tray was full again, the Carlton papers still on the corner of the desk. 'Chloroform', said the memo, the one word carefully dictated to ensure the spelling, never Mika's strong point, was correct. 'Chloroform in dry cleaning fluid.'

'He was going on about something else,' Mika said. 'An . . . afro, afrodissy . . . something to do with sex. Rude.'

'Aphrodisiac?' said Helen.

'That's it, that's it. You'd better ring him. He's ever so cross.'

'Shit,' said Helen again, and dropped the dry cleaning in her arms to the floor. It was the mere thought of the smell. Anti-aphrodisiac, and the world was not only bad, but mad.

CHAPTER FIVE

'The truth, the whole truth and nothing but the truth, so help me God.'

Helen looked up from the document in front of her, met the eyes facing her own. The new officer, Detective Inspector Collins, was anxious to please without being deferential. So far, she liked what she saw. He caught Helen's expression, allowed a half smile.

'I didn't make him say that, Miss West; he insisted.'

'Well, that's quite enough to put me off.'

She had begun at the end, reached what she privately considered the greatest indecency in Philip Carlton's statement. Pleas to Jehovah, promises made on my mother's life, all that hypocritical hogwash in promises of truth, raised alarm bells as well as the slight tendency to be sick.

'I don't understand why he couldn't have said any of this before. It was the obvious thing to say.'

'Didn't want to shock, he said. Anyway, neither Mr Davies nor anyone else asked him. No one would have asked him, or looked at all the stuff under the sink if you hadn't, well, insisted.'

Inspector Collins coughed in polite deference, a repeated cough. Helen considered offering one of the cough sweets in the desk drawer, decided he would be even less at ease if he had to sit there with a lozenge in his mouth. 'No one knew there was more chloroform until we got the dry cleaning fluid tested. Anyway, he explains that. Says he really did use it to clean clothes, much better than a normal solvent, he says. But really, none of this makes much difference, does it? Still an accident.'

'Accident. Only it turns out the poor, daft chemist's wife has been taught how to sniff this stuff by her bloody husband. She wasn't a pharmacist. She was only a shopkeeper's daughter. The bastard.'

'An accident,' said Inspector Collins firmly. 'Nasty accident, but not a crime. So far. Nobody made her sniff dry cleaning fluid. She was on her own.'

'I'd like to think about this,' said Helen firmly. 'For a day or two.'

'Is there anything else you want me to do? I could do some house to house, but it's not as if we're investigating a murder.'

'You'll check his alibi, of course?'

'I was going to do that again. He was definitely in his hotel, but we can check the details again. I should have said.'

Verbal rap on the knuckles, a reminder he knew his trade.

'And you've checked his shop?'

'Of course. Davies did that thoroughly: I don't think I need to repeat everything, yet. That chemist keeps immaculate records of all his prescribed drugs, very thorough, not that they have much choice, you know. He isn't exactly dangerous. They have to account for everything they prescribe. He has chloroform, for preparations, but that's legal. For him anyway.'

'Fine. Well I think that's all for the time being.' She smiled again reassuringly. Don't tell the man how to do his job, this one knows perfectly well and the sound of nagging was creeping into her voice. Anxiety put words in one's mouth. Helen's renowned patience was a sham half the time, a question of pretending to be the mild professional instead of someone who, once alone, strode up and down her own messy room, the pacing an attempt to subdue the energy of frustration and the futility of ignorance.

She looked at the statement again.

'. . . I once told her chloroform could be an aphrodisiac. We tried it, for fun. You pour some on to a clean duster, sniff it for about sixty seconds. Not me, of course, I told her about it from one of my older pharmaceutical books: I only kept some chloroform in the flat for spot cleaning a suit. Then I discovered she syphoned off some of her own. Used it to help her with sex and give herself a high. She knew I disapproved, but I couldn't really stop her . . .'

Chloroform? An aphrodisiac? How little one knew in this world. Helen had thought it put people to sleep.

'While ignorance is bliss,' Sean Hazel wrote, 'knowledge is dangerous. Especially pristine knowledge, untarnished by experiment. Or rather by experience which is the multi-plural of experiments. Experience also tells one not to trust, to use a small repertoire of drugs rather than a larger range, because the manner of use is as important as the quality of the substance itself, and the brain can only remember so much . . .'

Or very little, as the case may be. He wanted to write, in the form of a pamphlet, a history of futility. Something to show how doctors were prone to behave like dangerous sheep, getting others to chew what they had just been sold, but the written word, which he had hoped would be the solace of old age, turned any message from his pen into porridge. The analogy was distasteful: he had hated porridge as a child and he was very tired. 'Our little life is rounded by a sleep,' he said to himself, 'Only soon, I hope.' He could not wield a pen; cigarettes, whisky and wild women were also out, apart from the cigarettes and whisky. So what else? Nothing. And then, a voice on a telephone, needing knowledge which no one else ever even requested, let alone needed. A delicious voice, at that.

'It's Helen West. I'll say hallo properly in a minute, but listen. Chloroform, Doc. Tell me about chloroform. Everything you know.'

After a few hours, the day had turned foul. A grey, wet wind hinted at sleet, cut through clothes, lifted umbrellas, attacked faces. Inside offices, noses streamed; pub windows were thick with steam and the bare bent trees dripped dirty London rain. Even these ugly winter trees were in short supply on Bailey's route between Whitechapel and Bethnal Green through the concrete and redbrick jungle where the remnants of old squares, invisible to traffic, formed the only saving graces of the area in summer. In early December, there were no green compensations. Out of interest, he cut through Herringbone Parade, the address stuck in his mind from Helen's talk, less free on the subject than she might have been. He parked behind, leaving the car to be covered in dust, looked over hoardings in to the pit of a building site beyond. Further on was an elegant terrace, a pre-war remnant housing a mosque and a hundred families; the earth between was red. Bailey shivered. The London of his boyhood had been punctuated by wartime: nothing so different now even after two generations: he often wondered what lay beneath. Something had happened in the Carlton enquiry which had stimulated Helen's eclectic interest, but since he had warned her against interference, she had been silent on the subject. They were often thus, reserve descending on them like summer rain. Only a two-day silence, not one she would maintain, since Helen, unlike himself, was quite unable to hold still, always told him in the end. Perhaps she always tried to teach him by example a greater openness, or perhaps she was aware of the feeling of drabness and boredom which was now almost a fear in him. He did not like the idea of that. Turning the car into the lights of the Parade, all blazing in the premature dark of the afternoon, he realised that Helen paying silence for silence was actually quite justified. She had said nothing of new developments, which hurt a little, but on the other hand he had not mentioned his knowledge of the Parade and his knowledge of Mr and Mrs Duncan Perry. He would tell her, though: she would help. Had to do something to deal with Duncan, but not now. He could advise the wife, console the husband, but for this and all purposes, he felt quite unfit. Bailey felt fit for nothing.

Herringbone Parade was not a place anyone would choose to live and die in, he decided; more the sort of place in which a person fetched up, beached by fortune and left to make the best of it. But for all its older inhabitants, who had indeed been hostages to fortune, shipped here from older buildings, people who remembered his parents' war, it was a brave place for all that, lights blazing, a few Christmas decorations showing in misted windows, people huddling from one doorway to the next. Passing the Pharmacy, he saw two customers bundling out of the door, conversation frozen by the cold. Bailey laughed at himself. In other days, he would have come here for the market. Now he had come for the idle curiosity he professed to despise. To examine the geography for other purposes still quite unrelated to Helen's legal conundrums. He slowed down past the shop, blocked for a moment by a van offloading from a stall, then turned the car easily left into the service road. He manoeuvred past bags of rubbish and watched with distaste as his headlights caught a mongrel dog jumping away from a rubbish bag, dragging a chicken carcass. Winter cold brought out the predatory instincts even in a pet, but chicken bones were bad for a dog, Bailey remembered, too brittle for the throat: the silly brute might choke. He was slightly ashamed of his indifference. The animal slunk away, ready to watch him leave before returning for the best of human detritus. Dog eat dog. Let them.

As Bailey cruised the back of the street, Helen emerged from behind a shelf in Carlton's Caring Chemist. While her eyes had examined a dusty display of suntan creams in the shop window, her mind beset with the domestic detail of why they were there, she had sensed, in that flash of recognition reserved only for the acutely familiar, Bailey's car and Bailey's brief presence. Separated by a few feet and two sheets of glass, so far and yet so near to the sixth sense which made her duck as if to read the full particulars of factor sixteen creme, suitable for babies. Something akin to shame, but definitely unshameful, made her blush. She regretted this necessary secrecy, this subterfuge to hide a nature which was curious but cautious and still afraid of criticism. She suffered as well from that guilty fear which afflicts any reasonably conscientious person who has lied in order to leave work indecently early.

'Can I help? Gawd, what a mess.' There was, as

she rose, a large, red-skirted behind, level with her face, with shapely legs gradually disappearing from view in a dim impression of red and black striped tights, an adventurous ensemble which owed more to experiment than taste, all dignified by a statu-esque shape, large black belt on a small waist and the sensation of a very nubile body striving to get out. Half bent, Helen stood level with the kind of bosom she had craved at eighteen, and still admired; looked up at a face of intelligent, preoccupied friendliness. Big eyes, blue mascara, wide mouth, all the features of an artless Brigitte Bardot with none of the sophistication.

'No, I was just . . .'

'That's fine, then. Take your time. I hate people rushing me in shops, don't you? We got everything here. Watch out for the toothpaste stand won't you? Only it ladders your stockings.' The behind, as if drawn on its own momentum, moved out of sight with brisk undulation as Helen straightened. She felt small and inept.

There was nothing peculiar in what she was doing, Helen told herself, with the bag of files uncomfortable against one shoulder. She was simply looking because it was imperative to look, and she rarely disobeyed imperatives. Helen West knew what she was, and, as usual, never rebelled at the limitations. Her role was to act as a conduit: the shifter of knowledge, rarely vouchsafed the first-hand view, but at least allowed the second before the crown court stars got up and did their bit. Rather like being the dresser in a theatre as opposed to the lead player. Or an offstage producer, the peruser of post-mortem photographs rather than the pathologist or the sonorous barrister. A researcher, a broker of evidence, a gofor, a back-room person. No accolades anywhere, for what she did, and she never minded how limited was the view she was allowed, provided she could do what she did, well. What she could not stand was no view at all or any opinion either. She was damned if she would be denied a squint at the *locus in quo*. In any standard murder case, she would at least see the face of the body on the slab; be able to express a brief and unbusinesslike pity; or see a video of the house where the corpse was found, put colours into the scene, note the furnishings, the wear or tear which gave an impertinent clue to the pressures of that life and death, the very clothing a feature of the story. Part of her task would be, in photographic terms, to weed out the most obscene photographs from those showed to a jury, but here with dead Mrs Carlton carried away in a white wagon like any other routine death, without the benefit of a single flash bulb, Helen had nothing. No clue to follow except the smells, no perspective to what she had read in soulless, typewritten sheets. It was not prurience which dragged her here, but the need to feel the framework and the literal desire to be informed.

She had been patrolling the shelves, smelling the smell and blinking in the neon light, breathing deep and doing as she would always do at relative leisure in a shop, which was browsing. No one could deny that a pharmacy was bound to contain some item of necessity. Shampoo, corn plasters, Tampax, instant diets, new lipsticks, a lifetime supply of toilet rolls, dusters. Ye gods, dusters. It was a shop where you had to scan each shelf, from the very top to the depths. Stooped again, transfixed by the daffodil yellow of six artificial chamois cloths, her own slender rump in a full khaki skirt, and from above her own dark head, another voice, saying the same thing.

'Can I help? Was there anything in particular you wanted? We do like to help.'

Helen hated being hounded in shops; she resented the voice. They were identical heights when they stood, Helen West and the caring chemist, accidentally so close together as she rose, and Helen stepped back sharply. Her heel encountered a packet of cotton wool, an unpleasant yielding under her foot.

'Was there anything in particular?' he queried. She gazed at him, mesmerised, her face forming an apologetic smile while her eyes and ears were full of the scent of him. Lavender water, some subtle smell of baby powder mingling with other scents clinging to a white coat pressed to perfection. Helen thought of a spruce waiter when she looked at this man, so small, so neat, so deferential. His well-manicured hands were crossed below his waist: he stood as if a half bow were natural: his shoes were polished, his collar points faultless, his tie held with a pin. Not a hair on his head was out of line with the furrows of his comb. A sallow skin, and the palest eyes she had ever seen. Bleached blue as if the colour had drained from them, ostensibly smiling, but lifeless. A man well versed in pretence, powerfully vulnerable.

'Oh! These things.' She placed a small collection of wares into the hands which rose like a begging bowl to receive them.

'Anything else?'

Helen sensed a mutual frisson of dislike and the knowledge of being hustled to the counter.

'Not from round here, are you?' he was enquiring conversationally as his little fingers tapped the till.

'No,' she answered shortly. Somehow she had no desire to reveal any more, looked round hopefully for the red legs of the girl.

'Have a nice day,' he intoned, handing over the white polythene bag, the pale eyes unmoving, and suddenly, Helen was weak with conviction. I'm right! The internal voice was shouting so loud she felt he must hear. I'm right, I know I'm right. There would be nothing natural about a death in this man's house. He would never lose a wife by accident: he would never allow such loss of control. And the smell of him. So clean, a sniff of sanitised threat.

'Thanks.'

'See you,' he answered.

Not if I see you first. Helen trod the route back from the door, aware of him turning away towards the high voice of the girl speaking from the room behind the counter. A sweet sound of normality so ill suited to the strange artificiality of her well-groomed employer, Helen found the cheerfulness unnerving. I should not have come here, she told herself, while knowing she should. What was worse was the knowledge that she could never confess her reactions.

'Don't forget you said I could go early today, Pip. Sure that's all right?'

'Oh, sure, sure.'

She hesitated. 'Pip, what did the police want with you yesterday? You were gone for hours. Was it about Margaret?'

He cleared his throat. 'Yes, as it happens. Look, there's something I want to tell you. Do you mind?'

Kim did not know what she was supposed to say to that since she did not know what it was, but chats with the indiscreet Margaret did not make her relish the prospect of marital secrets now. She had been dreading this moment, but knew it was inevitable. All through the busy surgery hours that morning, she had been aware of Pip watching her, as if testing her sympathy in advance, his distraction so complete he could not even count pills into the pill-counting machine or handle the prescriptions in order. They were sitting in the dispensary now, Pip's back room beyond hidden by boxes as it often was by day, each with the cups of tea which were the punctuation marks in every single day. All sorts of tea; camomile tea, ordinary tea, peppermint tea; he insisted on experimenting. The shop outside was quiet. Rain stopped play, and apparently, pain.

'I'm afraid they discovered Margaret's little secret. The police, I mean. I hoped they wouldn't you see, but they did. Thank God you saw me leave the night before she must have died, you know. Otherwise I'd be in the frame. They'd think I gave it to her.'

'Gave her what? Sorry, Pip, love, I'm not following.'

He shifted on his stool, appeared to gulp at his tea when she mentioned the word love, shot her a look so full of sadness she could feel herself melt. Kim's harder edges dissolved when Pip looked so soulful, like a puppy with enormous eyes. He was so kind, no wonder Margaret had loved him. He was actually not bad looking either, although Kim was young enough to consider him a little old.

'Chloroform. I'm only telling you because you may well find out anyhow and I don't want to hide it from you, although I certainly don't want the rest of the street knowing. Listen, when I met Margaret, she was a junkie. Yes, I know it's a surprise and it never showed, but didn't you ever wonder how she got so thin? She'd been weaned off, then weaned on to tranquillisers and you know what they're like. So, from the hard stuff to the valium she'd done them all and she was starting in on the alcohol. Then I once made the mistake of explaining to her . . . she was always asking questions, you remember, always wanting to get involved . . . anyway, I told her how a person could get a high from sniffing ether, or even chloroform. I didn't have any ether, no need for me to stock it you know, but I do make my own chloroform water. For keeping morphine, if I have to stock it, which isn't often and never for long, of course. I showed her for fun . . .'

'For fun?' Kim echoed. Bloody hell, she thought, strange notion of fun. Wouldn't have thought she had it in her, never can tell. She could feel her jaw dropping, slightly.

'Yes, for fun. It can't do you any harm, and it kept her distracted from anything else she might have wanted to take. I put some on a clean duster, just a little. You hold it above your face, never on your face, breathe deeply, and hey presto, you feel fine. Happy. She liked it so much I hid it, said if she ever wanted to use it, she could only use it with me there.'

'What kind of duster?' Kim asked stupidly, for lack of anything else to say to prevent the shock showing on her face. She remembered Margaret Carlton's unnatural thinness, her silliness and her ebullience, but there had never been a hint of unpredictability. Margaret had always been the same, laughing, irritating, perhaps a little hyperactive. A great person for silly detail. Pip looked surprised at the irrelevancy.

'One of the dusters we sell. The yellow ones. We had dozens. Always the same sort. I told them that, too.' He looked more cautious, pathetically worried about her response, turning back to his tea to hide his face, trying to speak casually. 'Did Margaret never mention any of this to you? She did talk to you, liked you so much . . .'

Kim was even more embarrassed, and muttered, 'She never told me she'd been an addict. I didn't know. But she did tell me she thought you needed . . . don't know what she meant, none of my business, but something. To improve your love lives.'

His loud and nervous laugh rang through the small room, so shrill she jumped.

'Our what? We didn't have a love life, she couldn't bear it, really could not bear it. I did hope, when she got better, but . . .'

'Couldn't you have locked the chloroform away?'

'Oh yes. But better the devil you know and it isn't addictive. Listen, Kim, I knew what my duty was with Maggie. I had to look after her as best I could. And it wasn't good enough. I go away, just once, God alone knows, I rarely get the chance, and when I come back, she's dead. And now they tell me she died of poison. She had twelve milligrammes of chloroform in her blood. Oh God, oh God, you can't imagine what it's been like . . .'

He rested his head in his fists on the counter used for bottling prescriptions, his shoulders heaving. Kim had seen him cry like this when he came back from the mortuary, the helpless sobbing of a young child, reminding her of Tombo in his furies of grief. And all this time, he had laughed and carried on as normal, bearing these dreadful burdens, poor, poor, Philip. Kim was easily moved by another person's tears, especially male tears, a weapon Duncan had never used, although with her they would have been the bluntest and most effective of all. Begging sickened her: tears worked.

Amid a genuine pity, came secret relief. She had

had an absurd suspicion that violent, obsessive Duncan had somehow been involved in the untimely death of Margaret. Kim had never thought through how this could have been: maybe he scared her to death with his nocturnal lurking; maybe he crawled into the wrong flat and took the wrong underwear. No, no; he wouldn't do that; he would notice the size. But all the same, the dark thought had grown, and now she knew for certain he was innocent of something at least. There was also relief in the knowledge that there was nothing perverted about Pip, as his wife had once vaguely suggested. Among all those accounts of diarrhoea, dentistry, minor operations and such, what malicious ideas Margaret had sown, each conversation promising more than the last: the merest hint of something strange about her husband beginning to emerge. Kim felt a surge of dislike for the dead wife, moved to Pip's side and put her arms round his bent back, resting her head against his shoulders. 'There, there, oh, please don't be upset. I understand, honestly I do, oh, poor Pip, I wish I could have helped . . .'

He flinched at her touch, like a child shrinking away from the adult who patted or tickled, but then he held her hand briefly, fished in the pocket of his white overall for a handkerchief. Kim wondered how it was he both liked and hated to be touched.

'You did help. You always help. And it was awful for you, being there when they found her. I'm sorry, what a baby to cry like this, not very manly, is it?'

She hugged him again, harder, then let go

abruptly. Standing on the far side of the shop counter, watching intently, was Daniel, his face split in that half smile which could just as easily have indicated contempt as curiosity. Kim realised in a split second why Daniel raised her hackles. He saw so much and was far from a fool. She patted Pip on the head, making him jump, flinch and turn. She watched, puzzled, then spoke without embarrassment, but still stiffly.

'Daniel's here, Mr Carlton.' Daniel beamed at her. Kim had always been gruffly kind, brisk, but with time for everyone, never asking questions. Even let him talk. He shuffled, deliberately slow.

'Delivery van outside, plus all that stuff from before, do you want it all moved now?' he asked, the face all innocence. Pip blew his nose noisily.

'Yes, if you've time. Yes, yes. You get off, Kim. You wanted to go early, go on, good girl.'

She went, the embarrassment of Daniel's cool regard lost in her haste to get upstairs, clean up a bit, put on her face and go shopping for Christmas. All that she had heard overtook her own unease. She was alive with the knowledge she had just acquired, full of pity, flattered to be the confidant. It made her feel wiser and stronger. She tidied the living-room, noticed the dust on the surfaces as she stuffed away magazines and Tom's toys. Stopped for a moment, puzzled before moving on, shaking her head. She had been there when Margaret Carlton was found. Calling Margaret's name to no response, entering the door of that pristine bedroom, full of stale air, unmoved by breath, she had known without further test that Margaret was dead, had not lingered to inspect that lined little face never yet seen without lipstick, but had raced instead for the other room. Minutes later, safe in early morning sunlight which made it all so harmless, she had ventured a brief, further look, but could not recall, not now, not then, anything resembling a yellow duster.

Enough: she was sorry and she was late. In view of other people's problems, tragedies rather than woes like her own, she felt surprisingly good. Anger and anxiety fizzled out of her. The thought of confiding or complaining, being weak all over again, drifted downhill like the breeze-blown rubbish in the street outside. Whatever there was, she would cope.

Kim put on her yellow coat, a bargain from the market and very short. Leg warmers, bright as the lipstick. Teetered past the shop on her way to the bus. She missed the hungry eyes following her through bright, misted windows, watching like a hawk.

Daniel found enough to do around the caring chemist's for at least half an hour a day. On a good morning, Kim made him tea and sometimes he acquired things to eat. He did a further half-hour down the road for Mrs Beale, but although she thanked him and gave him apples, she never paid, didn't believe in it, she said. Nor did Mrs Kennel in the dress shop, although Ahmed in the off-licence lent him videos and gave him the occasional free can of lager. They provided well for him, the whole Parade, with supplies or generosity, but only Mr Carlton and Kimberley Perry actually gave him money. Margaret, the all-time fixer, had fixed that. Money, she said, he needs money. Which was strange since there was no need. Whatever he said, whatever he did, he was bound to this dispensary as surely as if he had been tied, would have done whatever he was asked, but how mean of Pip to forget to pay. He had come to rely on it. Neither could Pip ever see how Daniel needed smiles, for instance, as well as cash occasionally for the sweat of his labours. Even recognition of their mutual manhood would not have come amiss. Pip would not talk about drugs the way Daniel liked to talk about drugs. Dan was fascinated: he learned from his own condition. He knew a lot about Pip and quite liked the idea of how little Pip knew of how much he watched.

'No, not in the back dispensary,' Pip said sharply.

'Why not? You've forgotten these.' He pointed to a pile of boxes, 'And there's no room for them out here.'

'The back room's not for storage,' Pip responded angrily, 'and I didn't forget.'

'Oh, yes, your favourite place. You like it in there. No records in there. It's like one of those priest holes. Do you know, I saw you in there the other night. And the night your missus popped her clogs. Oh, no, the night before. No, I'm wrong. You were looking out of the window. In the morning, early. Very early. I like getting up in the dark.'

Daniel meant nothing sinister by this: it was merely a thought which popped into his mind to dwell for a second, without any real association between one winter's night when someone had died and the next. Daniel was used to death: most of his peers were dead and the timing of any death soon became a blur. Margaret was someone he regretted without mourning, since he was incapable of mourning. He knew Pip ignored him the way he did not ignore other customers and for the moment he wanted to be seen. All these words were no more than a longwinded attempt to jog Pip's memory on the subject of money. Only a pound coin here and there, but every little helped.

'What's so precious about the back room anyway?' he grumbled. 'Not as if you have to make up any of your own stuff, not this day and age anyhow. You can get it all in packets. Kept you away from the missus, I s'pose, but not a problem now, is it? No need to stay out of Kim's way. Quite fun to bump into. Slowly.'

He stooped over a pile of boxes, laughing a little, straightening the sides, about to continue. Then he felt a blow to the back of his skull, a dull, heavy, stiffening blow, delivered by an iron fist. A bloodless shock, a hand pressing his neck into the dusty floor; words hissed into his ear.

'Shut up, shut up, shut up. Shut it, you piece of scum, you bastard . . .'

Tombo scuffled home from school with a large hole in his nylon satchel. There was also a large hole in his trousers and he was not sure which he should explain first, that or the graze on his forehead. He was numb with misery. Today had been one of those days when his own credibility in the playground had failed, not there, but on the way home, when they had seen his vulnerability. He should not have boasted about Dad's car coming to school, had them waiting as he waited, jeering, then fighting. Daddy was supposed to meet him, Mum had said, and he had promised. Failing which, she had said, come home with someone else if you can, try not to go alone, and if I'm not back go and wait with Uncle Pip in the shop. He had not believed there would be a 'failing which', but he was alone, skulking down the back service road like a thief. Dad was a bastard, a bum, a stinker, a sodding, sodding . . .

There was absolutely nothing he wanted to do, nothing at all, and no one he wanted to see. So profound was his misery that the odd cut and bruise did not matter and even the dark service road presented no threats. He was walking down the back of the Parade rather than the front purely in order to avoid any contact with Mrs Bosom or Mrs Bum, who might just enquire why he had run away from their party. Mum had explained, but he knew they would ask him direct. There were few enough children actually living in Herringbone Parade for him to stick out like a sore thumb, only enough of them to field one dreadful party, and he felt as if the graze on his forehead was the colour of scarlet. But slowly, the quiet worked some sort of calm. Even traffic was distant here, and the wind and rain had died away to a solid cold. Tombo, delaying the time he would have to go and wait in the chemist if Mum was not back, took three steps forward and two steps back, looking round at last for anything to absorb his rage.

The ground at the back of Herringbone Parade was good for nothing but storing the tall rubbish bins which frightened him a little because they were big enough to hide a man inside and he always imagined being placed in there, head first with his feet tied together. One way they might have dealt with him at the party. The bins were full, only half the garbage bags had been taken away carelessly that morning, leaving stray bits to dance in the wind. They often did that, the rubbish men: got fed up halfway through if it was cold and left their task for the next day so the service road was never swept clean. These were things he noticed, the high spots of the week. Nearing his own home again, Tombo found rubbish dropped in the street: they were often careless like that. A torn sack gnawed by a dog leaving a trail of bones. Something of interest at last, near his own back door; a bent-up wire coat hanger, maybe two, formed into a ring with wire crossing over the top, making it look rather like a skeleton hat. The contraption projected from a knotted bag which had once sealed it, and the careful covering somehow added to its value. Tom thought at first the thing was the framework for some sort of helmet, looked around and put it on his head. The wire sat comfortably: he regarded it

as a find, slightly ashamed of himself to be so
delighted, as well as curious to see what on earth
he looked like. Really, he knew he was too old for
make-believe, all those silly pretend games, but he
liked the hat all the same and knew he would keep
it. Things collected had a way of becoming more
precious than anything given, because then you
were burdened with the effort of saying thank you.
He made a little feint towards a bin, growling; then
looked around for somewhere to see himself trans-
formed into a fierce space invader. Or a soldier, if
he stuck in branches and made himself camouflage.
The glazed window of his own back door was probably nearest and he trotted towards it, ready to
examine his own blurred reflection in privacy, hide
the hat in the torn satchel and only then go round
to the front for a boring hour by the counter if she
wasn't ready. Already he was reconciled to tellings
off, excuses, tedium.

But not yet. His foot on the step contacted something hot and his heart flew into his mouth. Tombo
almost stepped on the figure huddled there, leapt
backwards in a jolt of fear and prepared to run, until
he heard the figure moaning. But retreating more
slowly to a safe distance, even in the dark, he was
suddenly reassured by something familiar, a scent,
a familiar slouch which told him not to be afraid,
for himself at least.

'What do you want?' he hissed at the figure from
the safe distance of six feet. The form on the steps
groaned, moving slightly, the groaning turning into

a singsong sound of despairing pain, 'Oh God, oh God, oh God.'

'Daniel!' Tombo said louder, moving closer. 'What's the matter? Don't be silly, what's the matter? Stop playing about, you scared me.'

'My head,' Daniel slurred. 'My head. Someone kicked my head. Hurts. Can't properly see. Hurts.'

'Who kicked your head? Where? Out here, just now?' Tombo had approached, touched Daniel's shoulder, looking over his own, conscious of danger. Daniel did not answer, resumed the keening moaning, his hands across his chest, rocking himself to and fro. As Tom touched, he shrugged him away. Tom withdrew his hand as if he had touched a live wire.

'Wait,' he said. 'Wait just here. I'll get help. Wait.' Daniel merely grunted: Tom thought he saw him shake his head. He ran to the end of the service road, round the corner, panting up to the door of Mum's shop, pushing between the shelves on his way to the counter where two people stood waiting. Shocked to find Mum not there, immediately visible, he stumbled behind the counter, forgetting his excuse-me's, and thrust his head into the dispensary, holding the doorframe with both hands. 'Mr Carlton, Mr Carlton, you gotta come quick. 'S Daniel, not well, very poorly.'

Pip turned briefly, then turned back. 'No children in here, Tom, you know that.'

'I know, I know, but you gotta come. Quick. You could go through the back. Daniel, I said. You know, Daniel.'

Pip smiled over his head, out to the two women waiting at the counter. He shrugged his shoulders in a what-can-you-do-with-them? gesture. They smiled back. 'Yes, I know Daniel,' he said gently, condescension lacing every syllable. 'And there's nothing wrong with him, nothing at all. He was in here a minute ago. One of his turns, Tom, old boy, nothing to worry about.'

'There is, there is . . . you gotta come and see.'

'No, Tom, can't you see I'm busy?'

Tom turned to the waiting women with a look of appeal. They smiled back. 'I should come out of there if I was you,' one of them said, irritated by being kept waiting. 'You heard what Mr Pip said.'

Tom had heard, clearly. And seen the ingratiating smile on Uncle Pip's face, which he returned with a look of hatred, a look which bounced back off the granite of that smile. He turned to go, pushing past the women again, so that one of them tutted in disapproval. Halfway to the door, slower this time, he heard Pip's voice hail him back.

'Tom, here, if you want to be useful, take Dan his prescription. Shouldn't let you have it, but I don't think you'll eat it. That's all he wants. Addict, you know; very sad,' he added in an undertone to the women. The hand was extended beyond the dispensary door, holding aloft a white carrier bag. Tom had seen this before, carried it once or twice. Daniel, he knew, collected this every day, but the bag he took was heavier than he remembered. He gripped the slippy plastic and ran.

Perhaps, he thought later, Mister was right and

that was all Daniel had wanted. Back round the corner, into the dark, stunning dark after all the lights of the Parade. Daniel still there, himself full of breathless explanations. 'He won't come, Danny, he won't, got your prescription.' Daniel laughing, unbelievably laughing, a funny, sobbing sound. 'What should I do, Daniel, come upstairs with me, we'll just wait for Mum . . .' and then, both of them blinded by the flashing lights of Dad's car, slewing to a halt where they stood. Daddy, with whom he had been so angry, getting out, saying 'I'm sorry, son, I'm sorry, couldn't get to school . . .' and Tombo, standing his ground for a second or two, unable to prove his point by waiting, running towards him, awash with words. He stumbled over his lines, rushed them, pointing backwards and forwards, round the corner in a storm of explanation, then back to his friend. Father detached son and they both approached. Daniel watched them, boy with father in hand, a unit which excluded him completely and one of them a copper to boot, spoke his first articulate words. A poetry in lonely hatred.

'Piss off, why don't you? Just piss off. I'm fine.'

Then he had just got to his feet and stumbled away. Tombo remembered him, all in the black, in the dark, the only visible bit of him the white plastic bag. He knew he should have stopped him somehow; dragged him back to be with them, but there was Daddy, big Daddy, forgiven in a second for the whole hours of weeping distress he had caused by being late.

Bailey was home first. Helen's place, by prearrangement, himself armed with shopping since he liked to cook as much as she loathed it. Left to Helen, they would never eat. At least the East End was rich in markets, including Herringbone Parade, and Bailey found that cooking, mending clocks, keeping busy, was the best panacea for his current existence. Less taxing than people, who could all go hang, apart from Helen. Bailey's loyalties had always been few, but intense.

He could tell she was well by the way she came downstairs, crashing through the front door, across the corridor, down the steps to her basement, everything flying. Bailey could visualise her long, thick hair escaping, as it did by this point every evening, from the slide which held it on top of her head, her brilliant blue coat, bought as an antidote to boredom, left flapping open. And he knew, with absolute sureness, that she had been on some expedition before coming home. The pub, probably.

Not that he minded. Each had a life to be followed but he was sometimes aware of his own vulnerability, his social isolation as compared with hers. She was aware of it too, included him as much as possible in everything she did, as generous with friends as with money and time, but he was still an outsider. When Bailey thought of this, he was perplexed, although never for long. They had care of each other and no one else did; he as vital to her sanity as air to her breathing. To have this place in Helen's heart, that enormous love she reserved for him, was enough, but he was well aware she had room for others, too. Being jaundiced with humanity was only his affliction, his particular cancer. He hid it, since she did not seem to suffer and he had no wish to infect.

'What was it this time?' he asked mildly. 'Somebody leaving, somebody getting engaged, or just Monday evening?' She grinned, not about to say immediately. He brushed her cold, pink cheek with his own warm face, waited for her arms around him, Helen's affection, which so delighted him but which he could not initiate.

'I've got egg on my hands,' he said, wanting to return the hugging.

'And me on my face. Doesn't matter.' She shrugged off the coat.

'I've only been shopping.' There was something a little evasive about this, but Bailey did not mind. 'Oh, and I spoke to Dr Hazel today. I promised I'd keep in touch, I liked him, you see, and he liked me and he's lonely. And he's helping me with the Carlton case.'

'How?'

'Chloroform. He knows all about it. So does Mr Caring Carlton, I'll tell you. Only Dr Hazel is going to write me an essay on chloroform. Did you know it was an aphrodisiac?' She was prowling round the kitchen, sniffing, alert to the smells, excited.

'No, I didn't know. Why don't you bring some home?'

'Actually, no. And anyway,' she added demurely, 'I don't think we need it.'

'Oh, I don't know. I'm getting on, you know. Ten years older than you.'

'And wiser, most of the time. And a better cook. You often make me feel redundant, you know. You do every bloody thing better than me. I'm a cretin compared with you.' There was no anxiety in the tone, no teasing either, only a genuine humility. He looked to check on that, turned back to the food, smiling to himself. She had her ways of reassuring him after all.

CHAPTER SIX

Despite a pathological reluctance to listen, Redwood found himself almost fascinated.

'Yes, yes, yes,' he repeated, nodding energetically towards the tableau of faces six feet beyond. He had agreed to listen, but, as branch Crown Prosecutor, regarded Helen West as one of life's dirty tricks. Helen had been placed under his command in the more peaceful areas of village Essex, from whence she had departed to his enormous relief, only for him to find that the promotion stakes of the Crown Prosecution Service dictated he follow. Bit of city life, Redwood, do you good. You're bound for higher things and we have to see how you survive in the jungle. A far cry, this grubby office, from the civilisation of Branston, dull though it had been. Redwood struggled in these waters, and he knew, again with a clenching of the jaw in his pouchy face, that his survival owed much to this rebellious professional, who was never insolent, never crossed him, always deferred to him, but was never, ever entirely under his control. Never a particularly passionate man, he harboured a strong dislike for Helen that was mixed with resentment, and made worse by the fact that he needed her desperately for all the thing he could not do. Such as keeping the office in harmony. A closet subversive was what she was; too clever by half and far too popular.

No one but Helen would haul into his office some ragtail of a wizened medical man with some time-wasting story. In semi-rural Essex, Redwood had been in the zealous habit of ordering the prosecution of everything which moved, but now the sheer volume of work in the inner city had wrought huge changes in his practice. If there was any excuse to turn away a case, he took it, in a desperate attempt to control the huge numbers of files which rolled through the office day in, day out, like volcanic lava, hot, inexorable and suffocating. Without the sort of evidence which would survive a legal firing squad he dumped that case in the waste bin. Reports not submitted in double-spaced typing were rejected and any case requiring the valuable and unavailable resource of man hours was likely to go the same way. So, despite the story-telling he was hearing, he regarded today's exercise as no more than an hour's entertainment. Something to tell his wife when he got home. He was beginning to consult his watch, listening to the medic, noting the pleasant Irish of his voice, distrusting him more than somewhat. Medical men, anaesthetists, surgeons, whatever, should not look like that.

Dr Hazel was in fine form. Work, a project of any kind, had lent wings to his mind and freed his tongue for an audience.

'Twelve milligrammes,' he was saying jovially.

'Not necessarily lethal, your pathologist said, and he was right. Just about the equivalent of light anaesthesia in a patient, but quite enough to polish off someone vulnerable. The difference is that the far higher doses on record, twice as much or near enough, were administered with oxygen. You can take far more that way. Chloroform used to be the darling of anaesthetists, but there were a few hazards. For one, the poor devil of a patient would fight it, never liked the smell, sick and heavy, like the fumes themselves. A very heavy vapour. Fight too hard with a weak heart, off you went. The other curse was taking too much, slowed down your respiration so much you were likely to give up the breathing business altogether. Then, once they got the dosages right, they discovered a dreadful effect on the liver, especially children's livers. Degenerated afterwards, so they died when they should have been cured. The whole thing improved when the heavy-handed gave oxygen with the vapour. The problem, you see, with any anaesthetic you inhale, is getting enough to put you under while getting sufficient oxygen to keep you alive at the same time. They managed that with a metal mask. Used masks, for chloroform and ether . . .'

'The *surgeons* used metal masks?' Redwood asked, clearly horrified at the vision of an operating theatre full of highwaymen.

'No, no,' said Dr Hazel kindly, 'but do you ever remember a mask on your face when you went to the dentist? No, perhaps not, you're not old enough.' For this flattery, Redwood was grateful.

'No,' Hazel went on, 'they would put a mask, more like a frame over the patient's face. A sort of wire structure, with a tube inside to give oxygen in the more sophisticated versions, but anyway, really no more than a metal circle with struts, on which you put gauze. On the gauze, you dripped the chloroform, or ether – both evaporate quickly – and the patient simply breathes in the fumes without the liquid touching the skin. It burns, you see, chloroform, leaves a white mark. All in all, ether was better. Pleasanter for the patient, so fewer heart attacks, didn't slow down the respiration either.'

'Why didn't they use that all the time then?' Redwood was beginning to be irritated. Time was short, his stomach was rumbling and medical details made him queasy.

'Fashion, for one. Combustion, for another. Ether is highly combustible. You could never have used it in the same room as a bunsen burner and a lot of primitive operating theatres would have had those. As well as a surgeon who smoked a cheroot during surgery.'

'How disgusting,' commented Redwood, a fervent anti-smoker at all times. Helen, who was longing for a cigarette, remained poker-faced, and Hazel, in similar state, merely continued. 'Besides, ether had a frivolous reputation. Ether frolics, not unknown, sniffing the stuff to make you high, a social pastime by the same sorts of people who might now snort cocaine. Chloroform too, clumsier, though. Made a fellow sexy. They once used chloroform as a truth drug too, you know. Gave it to a suspect in police custody, to make him talk. Couldn't see you people getting away with that now.' He chuckled, to Redwood's mind, obscenely. Redwood shuffled in his seat. His irritation was becoming obvious. 'We're not the police, you know,' he began, but the only effect was to make Hazel talk more.

'The stuff has a use in crime, too, of course. A woman was supposed to have murdered her doctor husband with chloroform and a few teams were up before the beak for using it in robbery. Not likely, I'd have thought. Takes too long to work, and the amount you could clap over someone's mouth would only work for a minute or two. Which is the point here, don't you see? Miss West and I agree on that.'

'Yes,' murmured Redwood, lost. What an unholy alliance, Helen West and some scruffy eccentric, making something out of nothing while he needed her to go to court or sit inside with a mammoth fraud case which had been lingering here in the corner far too long. Get on with it. If stupid chemist's wives wanted to ape dilettante Victorians, and sniff disused anaesthetics, killing themselves in the process, it might all be very interesting, but not the business of the Crown Prosecution Service. Of which, he was, he reminded himself, the local leader, with no time to spare. He was only interested in proof, and not as in whisky or drugs either.

'You see – ' Hazel was leaning forward confidentially on the side of Redwood's desk ' – you can only inhale chloroform, you can't drink it, or at least, never of your own free will, and anyway, there was none in her stomach. As far as I can see, you cannot, by yourself, get enough in your blood to anaesthetise you, let alone kill you, do you see? Somebody has to help you, do you see? To get that inside you, you need an anaesthetist. That's why we buggers were invented, you see? For the simple reason that you have to go on inhaling after you've gone to sleep. The point of this case is not whether twelve milligrammes is lethal or not. The point is you can't self-administer when you're unconscious.'

'Oh,' said Redwood, light dawning. 'Yes, I do see.'

'All right, Duncan?'

Bailey's question did not demand any real reply. Any kind of grunt would do to answer this expression of concern. Bailey had thought Duncan looked better over the last few days. Perhaps he and the wife had patched things up, or perhaps DS Perry had seen the futility of haunting the back of Herringbone Parade in the hope of finding her in need, finding her out, or simply seeing her, this wife of his. He knew this would be no use to the wife, but he was no stranger to the self-defeating nature of Duncan's kind of love. Nor was he unfamiliar with Duncan's kind of need. Less directly, and many years before Helen, he had discreetly haunted his own ex-wife, who had rejected him with more mad violence than Kimberley Perry could ever have summoned. Kimberley was at least sane, and unlike

Bailey's one-time spouse, had a living child, not a dead one. Bailey understood far more about obsession than his bland expression could ever indicate and somehow Duncan recognised he would not be speaking into a void.

'No, sir, I'm not all right. Not really.'

Bailey got up and shut the door between his office and the next. The voices on telephones, the clack of a typewriter, another detective telling a joke, faded significantly. As soon as the door closed, the joke ended and there was a burst of raucous laughter. Duncan flinched.

'I crunched the car,' he said. 'Outside Kim's flat.'

'Were you drunk?' Bailey asked in neutral tones. Duncan snorted.

'No, but I was later on. I got a taxi home, don't worry. Sodding car was towed off. She came out and screamed at me, see? Because I was late picking up the kid and he came home from school by himself. After that, I'd picked him up from home, took him for a hamburger, and when she came in, been shopping or something, she didn't know where he was, only that he'd been round the corner into the chemist earlier and then disappeared. So she screamed, really tore me off a strip. Said I should sod off altogether, not come round the place any more, stop stealing her things and hanging about. Stealing her things? She got hysterical, I tell you. So I said, what the fuck did she think she was doing anyway, out at work all the time, and letting the boy play round with a junkie? He does, you know, he told me.' The memory of all this screaming was making Duncan agitated.

'Hold on, how old is the boy?' Bailey was always uncomfortable when the professional lives of Helen and himself were enmeshed, but for the moment, he was grateful that her conversation about Carlton's Chemist made him vaguely familiar with the lives of all who sailed with her. Otherwise Duncan would have been difficult to follow. People in distress, he had noticed, assumed you knew far more about them than you actually did.

'He's just ten,' Duncan said, as if Bailey should have known. 'And most mornings, this bloody junkie takes him to school. Oh, he's a tame junkie, not black either, stable, comes into the pharmacist every day for his prescription. But I ask you, still a junkie. Who does she think she is, to tell me off? Even I could do better than that . . .'

'But you were late for the boy, and you did take him off without telling her where you were going, or leaving a message. She must have been worried sick, you idiot. No wonder she shouted.' His voice disguised any hint of lecture or disapproval. Duncan looked at his hands.

'All right. But I got so mad when that poncey little chemist, her bloody boss, comes out from somewhere and tells me to piss off. He tells me, stuck up little fart, seems to think he's God's gift. I know Kim's always said there's nothing going on there, and I know his wife's just died, but I don't believe her nothing going on, what with him shaking his fist, putting his arm round her and taking her back indoors, my wife. *My bloody wife!*' The recitation ended in a shout. There was a sudden silence from next door.

'That's right,' said Bailey evenly. 'Let them all know, go on.' He looked at his watch. 'Come on, we'll go out for the rest of this. Leave your coat.'

Rather than running the gauntlet through the CID office where the laughter was now quiet, they both went out through the front office, raising the heavy flap on the counter to go through, Bailey nodding en route towards the custody officer behind the desk. In the small lobby which fronted the grey outside world, three people were waiting, one black, one white, one female, all dejected. Missing cars, missing friends, perhaps; they had not arrived to celebrate good news. 'Got a quorum there,' Duncan remarked. 'You know, one black, one white, one woman.' Bailey smiled at the signs of normality. The custody officer watched them go, as he listened to a man explaining why he was without a driving licence. Easy life for some, coming and going as they pleased. Form-filling with one laborious hand, he picked up the phone with the other, listened, breathing heavily. 'No, not here, mate. We can't send anyone from here, we don't cover Herringbone Parade. Yes, I know it's only down the road but we don't cover it here. I don't care if you've got Sophia Loren. Phone up Bethnal Green, good lad, OK?' Looking at the departing back of DC Perry, he scowled. Pull the other one sunshine, looking so miserable. He'd heard it all. One of these days, Bethnal Green would do them a favour. Catch Perry mooning around drunk, and good riddance.

'What exactly was it you wanted to achieve, Helen? I mean, Miss West?'

Oh, ho ho, no signs of a democratic set-up here. We are all Mr, Mrs, Miss. She never let show her constant amusement at Redwood's frightful pomposity.

'Well, at this stage, not a lot, beyond the fact that this death is most unlikely to be accidental. Which means it could be criminal. The purpose of introducing you to Dr Hazel was to show I'm not alone in my view. If this should ever come to trial, he could act as an expert witness, but, for the moment, I only want your blessing to pay him to do further tests.'

'For what?'

'To show how long it takes to inhale twelve milligrammes of chloroform vapour. To see if a person could do that by themselves. If so, no case.'

'Doesn't look like much of a case whichever way you turn it,' he grumbled.

'Granted. But we have to know, don't we? And Dr Hazel won't charge much. He came here this morning for free.' Helen cast a glance at the budget sheets hidden beneath other papers on Redwood's desk, sorry for him, relieved, not for the first time, that she had avoided promotion.

'Right,' he said, looking at her with resigned exasperation. 'Keep it cheap. Oh, and . . .' Helen was halfway to the door. 'Check the chap's credentials, will you?'

She nodded, avoiding his eyes, unwilling to confess a suspicion that these credentials might not be entirely immaculate. She had nothing to base this suspicion on other than the knowledge that she liked Hazel and knew full well how rarely she liked anyone with a blameless past. To Redwood, for one gratifying moment, she was merely five foot four slender inches of deferential servant. Until she smiled.

'Don't waste time on it, Helen,' he snapped. 'Plenty of real cases here.'

A dance, Helen thought. The law is a long, slow, dance. You learn the minuet in stages and you never hurry. No room for a sense of emergency anywhere: never frighten the decision-makers.

The whole day had gone on too long.

'You made him do it, Mummy. You did, you did. So why should he say he's sorry? You made Dad go right back into that wall, you did, by shouting at him.'

'Tom, I told you to stay indoors. And Dad lost his temper. He wasn't just reversing his car, he was trying to reverse it into Uncle Pip's car, which was naughty, to say the least. He deserved to go into the wall.'

'He didn't mean it. Why would he do that?'

Tom could guess why Dad should, and sympathised. On the way home from school with Mum, he was arguing for the sake of arguing, still angry from the night before, without tears, simply cold recrimination. She put a hand on his shoulder as they walked down the Parade, but he shrugged it away, deliberately hurtful. She pretended not to notice. At least there was conversation, unlike this morning when silence had governed breakfast. Kim felt very old.

'Daddy was cross with Uncle Pip for interfering,' she said mildly. 'And I was very, very cross with him for not meeting you from school, then taking you off like that. Can't I go out, once in a while . . . Oh, never mind. Anyway, I'm sorry: I shouldn't have screamed. Neither should he, so we'll both say sorry. All right?'

'All right.' He kicked a paving stone, felt his satchel thump on his back, the metal helmet inside digging into his spine. He wanted to show her the wire helmet, unsure whether she deserved such privilege. The sulk was receding, started only because he was sick of being asked to see Mum's point of view and he knew he deserved a better reward. For being good, fielding off all Dad's questions, saying Mum was fine and no, she didn't go out with the chemist, or anyone else, and then all Mum did was scream at Dad. And have Uncle Pip put his arm round her, so now Dad would think he, Tom, was a liar. You never resolved anything with grown-ups. They never listened.

Mrs Beale stood at the door of her shop as they passed and Tom cringed, too late. 'Evening, Kim. Oh, there's Tom. How's my little man, then? Don't like parties too much, do we?'

'No, I'm afraid not.' Kim stopped to answer for him, laughed. Asked, 'How's things going then? How's your mother?' Got Tom off the hook of questions. She was careful to be nice to the neighbours, natural in any event since she was full of defensive kindness, but Tom never guessed how much she passed the time of day for his sake. To cure their isolation, make them accepted. A vain hope while Mrs Beale gazed at Kim's voluptuous figure with envy. Thinking almost aloud how a girl like that, as edible as ice-cream, couldn't possibly be up to any good.

'Heard anything more about Mr Carlton's wife, then?' asked Mrs Beale, retrieving from the shop front an apple softened by the Christmas lights, thrusting it at the boy. He thanked her with a mumble and put it in his satchel. Tom hated apples. 'No, nothing,' Kim said. 'I mean, there's nothing wrong or anything, but they don't seem able to work out what kind of heart attack. More than a month now, dreadful, isn't it? Poor Mr Carlton, can't even have a funeral.'

'Well, you look after him, sweetheart.' Mrs Beale, hungry for scandal, delivered a grotesque wink, which Kim ignored. They moved on.

'Oh, isn't she awful?' Kim muttered to Tom, and the agreement united them. He felt too old to take her hand, someone might see, so he clutched the sleeve of her coat instead.

'What does she mean, look after him?' he hissed, running to keep pace.

'Just that, darling, look after him. Like he looks after us.'

At this point of accord, Tom did not risk going any further. Resentment had a habit of draining away long before he had said what he wanted to say, asked what he wanted to know. Or dared venture to Mum how he hated Uncle Pip, for everything, really. Such as putting his arms round his mother and even more particularly for that awful moment in the shop when he refused to come out for Daniel. Daniel was something else. He had been on Tom's mind all day.

'Did Dan come in the shop today?'

'I didn't see him, but Pip says he came in for his prescription this morning, so he must be OK.' She had heard a little of the saga of Tom's errand of mercy, but not how abruptly he had been forestalled.

'So Uncle Pip was right, wasn't he? Nothing to worry about.'

Nothing at all, but Kim was afflicted by the vaguest discomfort, marring yesterday's bullishness, and the odd kind of catharsis there had been in screaming at her husband. Although she entrusted Tombo to Daniel from time to time and only out of necessity, she did not even really know where Daniel lived. Around and about; one of the clutch of bedsits above the pub, a stone's throw, an address seen often on his record, but never quite visualised.

'You never go indoors with Dan, do you, Tom?'

'Nope. He never asks me. He lives down this end. Doesn't take me there.'

'Well, if he asks you in, don't go, will you?'

He looked up in surprise. 'Daniel's a bit dirty, Mummy. He's all right, but I wouldn't want to go.'

Don't want to go. Pip had not wanted to go the evening before. Kim thought of that as they climbed the steps up to the flat, she irritated as ever by the lack of light, still unsure after a day's thought whether Pip's not wanting to leave after another cup of tea gave her a feeling of warmth, or whether the memory of that proprietorial hand round her shoulder made her cold. Let's face it, Kim, she told herself later, when Tom had yawned peacefully to bed halfway through a video and well beyond another battle over homework, let's face the fact that you could do very well with Mr Carlton. You'll soon be a qualified pharmacist, only another month until you can register, but no hope in hell of ever getting a shop of your own. Play your cards right and good old Pip would help you. All you'd have to do is love him a bit. Carry on where the wife left off, be looked after, Tom too. Do a bit of looking after herself, and go to bed with him, of course. There she stopped and sighed, pulled her dressing gown around herself defensively, huddled back into the depths of the second-hand sofa and remembered how futile it was to dwell for a minute on what Pip could provide. No use whatever her thinking she could even begin to string along some man she did not fancy, and the merest touch of Pip was enough to show her that however much she admired him for all that industry and enthusiasm, sex, God forbid, was another matter. She'd rather

Duncan. And come to think of it, she'd not liked Pip shouting at Duncan, telling him to shove off. She could say what she liked – she could scream like a fishwife; Duncan was still her husband – but if anyone else interfered, even on her behalf, she resented the insult. 'No, my girl,' she grumbled to the electric fire, a thing of such ineffective ugliness she despised it along with all her lousy furniture, 'there aren't any easy ways. Wouldn't mind a bloody good cuddle, but not Pip. Ugh.' The thought chilled her. She got up to go to bed, late. Bed had been her destination more than an hour ago; the lights were out apart from the artificial glow of the fire, invisible outside, but all decisions to move had postponed themselves. The parade, visible from the living-room window, was lit but silent apart from one passing car a minute: behind her, on to the service road downstairs from the kitchen door, a stillness she could feel through the walls, punctuated by that scrabbling sound, only now beginning to register on a mind blurred by fatigue. A scratching at the window, then at the door, nothing visible shadowed through the glass or the net curtain. Kim stood between kitchen and living-room, paralysed, listening, gazing at the handle of the kitchen door fixedly, almost willing it to move, imagining it did. If Tom stared long enough at a clock, he could see the hands move. Now her own eyes took in no more than a fraction of play on the door handle, a soft, scraping sound outside, insistent, audible with straining effort, undetectable to a careless ear, a background to her thoughts, she now remembered, for five minutes or more. She was suddenly cold; then hot in a damp sweat of fear which cooled into a trembling. Each of her hands gripped the opposite forearm, fingers digging deep into her own skin to still herself, injecting pain enough to control the desire to shout.

'Duncan! Is that you? Well, fuck off.' The silence was ominous; into it crept the continued sound of the creeping scrape, no footsteps. The handle of the door was still.

'Duncan, don't be silly. I'm giving you ten seconds to go. One, two . . . or I'll call your boss . . . three, four . . .'

She spoke loudly enough for him to hear, softly enough not to waken the boy, spitting the numbers out of her mouth clearly and very slowly, as much as anything to calm herself, stop herself screaming her message. Then she walked towards the light switch, flicked it, opened the back door with a violent fling.

There was nothing, a big blank space of nothing. Silence, no car, no light other than her own streaming into the darkness. The pitted site beyond, a crane punctuating the horizon.

'Duncan?' she called again. Then, more doubtfully, 'Daniel?'

Still silence, but drifting around the concrete balcony, scraping against the rough surface, a white polythene bag, glowing in the light, fluttering in the breeze which had wafted it upwards from the rubbish in the dirty road, moving around like a live thing, frisking in the tunnel the balcony formed.

No one hung washing here: the dirt defeated everything. Kim slumped against the doorway, dizzy with relief. A bag, a bloody bag, rustling. Moving the door handle, no, there had not really been any movement. Only a bag in a breeze. She closed the door, wanting to believe what she had cause to believe, put her hands over her ears, in case she might hear footsteps.

Bailey parked his car at one end of the grim service road, feeling a little sheepish and wondering what he would say if some police car, not from his own station, should ask what he was doing loitering in these parts. Looking for what, sir? A bit of nice Asian tart, sir? You're on the wrong side for the posh Chinese restaurant, sir. No, no, of course not, but what would he say? I'm out looking for a rogue copper, don't make me laugh. He did not doubt he would cope with such questions and also that he would be able to avoid them. The number of patrol cars was pathetically small, and the service road less threatening than it seemed. Unlike Tombo, large bins, nooks and crannies held few fears for Bailey. He seemed to have developed a sixth sense, like a heat-seeking missile, for the dangerous presence of human warmth; a sense which would send him, with apparent aimlessness to the other side of the street, avoiding the corner glowing with malevolence. Bailey had several scars, kneecaps, elbows, the back of the skull, the ribs and the psyche, knew very well how to fight and what it was like to lose control. Which was precisely why he preferred to avoid the conflict. The same knowledge influenced his dealings with Duncan, younger than himself by more than fifteen summers; at the age when he could not have been taught anything either, would always have known best. There had been no point then, in some wiser, older sergeant saying, wouldn't do that if I were you, or I should give up while the going's good, boy; or, when a woman's left, she's gone, old son, find another. He knew he would not have listened then any more than Duncan would listen now. They had spoken at length, the two of them, Duncan attentive to the warnings, the advice to woo and accept his wife if he wanted her back, taking it in like a balm on the skin, not really listening at all, the same obsessive jealousy as much in evidence at the end as it had been at the beginning, determined to go back. Two pints and more hypocrisy, Bailey well aware that he was saying, do as you should, but not as I did. Duncan was not murderous, Bailey decided; but as an officer capable of conspicuous bravery and equally conspicuous drinking, a man with a mission, little reflective sense and no other humanising influences than a one-time wife, he was possibly dangerous and certainly a nuisance. Duncan's problem was, in part, having nowhere else to go and nothing else to do but haunt his woman and embarrass everyone. Duncan came from the same streets as most of those he arrested; they did not read books. He needed the blunt approach of being found in the act and stopped like a criminal.

Which was why Bailey was walking down this road in his brothel-creeping shoes, soundless and almost invisible. The wind whipped rubbish in his face, the detritus of neglect and a neighbourhood of which few were proud. There was another cause for concern in his active mind, another cause for feeling ever so faintly hypocritical. All that stuff he said to Helen about never interfering, let be what will be, let people find out for themselves and don't sweat if you can't help. Load of rot, in view of what he was doing. He might have said, I am paid by the Commissioner to keep my men working, but he doubted the Commissioner expected this. Out at midnight, catching an obsessive husband who happened to be a policeman, in the hope of confronting him with his own stupidity, making him ashamed to be no better than a slightly ridiculous prowler.

Bailey ducked behind one of the enormous bins, an instinct, nothing more, squinting towards the door and the stairs where he had never been, the exact location deduced from inspecting the front of Herringbone Parade. Kimberley Perry's flat, almost like all the other ugly flats. Next door to the chemist's flat, so close an agile man could cross from one cumbersome concrete balcony to the next. A car parked, without lights, next to the chemist, not Duncan's damaged car: a man walking away round the corner, an energetic walk, no skulking to it, no conscience either. Duncan, he thought, without being sure. Anyone really, but a windcheater like Duncan's, Duncan's brisk walk which Bailey had seen him maintain, drunk or sober. More silence. The figure rounded the corner, disappeared. Then Bailey heard the moaning.

'No, no, no. Too much . . . he did. Help me, uncle . . .'

The sound of it was borne to him on the wind, a hopeless sound of one human being not in agony but *in extremis*. He followed the pathetic half weeping from where he stood, into an alcove which formed an entrance to the yard behind a fruit and vegetable shop. Bailey could tell roughly which shop by the smell of vegetable, something reminiscent of a market stall after hours, or a school kitchen, a dead leaf smell, sweet rather than rotten. Mixed, as he bent over him, with the smell of this figure sitting with his head on his crossed arms, over one raised knee, the other leg lying as if he had already abandoned part of himself. The head, when Bailey placed one hand under the chin to raise it gently, was that of an old man, the indeterminate age only betrayed by the thick, lank hair. There was no protest against such summary handling: the breath snorting from the mouth was full of decay. Bailey squatted by his side.

'What's the matter, lad? Not well?'

'Oh God, oh God, oh God. Him, he hit me. Hit me. Gave me the wrong stuff, too much. Oh God. Don't know why. Him and his back room. Saw him come back.'

Bailey did not know what he was talking about in this gasping mumble of words, asked because it seemed what the man wanted.

'Who hit you? Who came back?' He could see eyes, glittering.

'Him. I saw him. Doesn't matter now. Help me.'

There were rules in a dozen police manuals about dealing with vagrants, drug addicts, filthy specimens in poor conditions. No artificial respiration without a tube, call for ambulance and only handle with rubber gloves, carefully. They scratch, they bite, they infect with Aids, hepatitis, they must never go inside a car which is not equipped. Bailey knew the rules: he had taught them. He embraced the man, warmed him for a minute, shocked to find thin cotton clothes with only a raggy sweater for warmth, spoke carefully into his ear.

'Wait here for a minute.' One claw-like hand clutched his coat. He detached it gently, ran down to the end of the service road where his car was surreptitiously parked and drove back level with the man. He picked him up, and fed him gently into the back seat of the car, a manoeuvre that took minutes since the body was heavy. Saliva fell from the open mouth on to Bailey's coat: as he put one hand over the head to protect the man's skull from the lintel of the car, he felt on the back a swelling beneath the sticky hair. Bailey could have knocked on a door, run for a phone, taken a number of other options which would avoid the future embarrassment of explaining his own errand in this godforsaken service road, but none of them crossed his mind. For someone needing a hospital, this was simply the quickest way. But in shutting the door, and driving away by the swiftest route to the nearest casualty, Bailey sensed he was already too late. There was a rattle in the throat of the man behind, and he fell over in the back seat, covered by Bailey's coat, his face pallid, profoundly unconscious, the car's warmth scented with death.

CHAPTER SEVEN

'Tra la la, fiddly di dee, what a mess. The breath of life is the stuff of life, so it is. Without which one becomes a stiff who doesn't give a stuff. One forgets how much fun this was, a lifetime of drugs. Don't breathe now, there's a good boy. What a jolly time we're having here, Hazel, my dear. Tinkering, and being paid. Avoiding temptation, of course. Never did like the smell of this stuff, but ether, well ether was different.'

Sean Hazel turned away from the bench where he worked and took a deep breath, then fished in his pockets for a cigarette on the right side and the small hip flask of brandy on the left. Withdrawing both hands simultaneously, he regarded the contents with puzzlement, unsure which to broach first, weighing the pleasure of one against the other. He put both down, easily distracted, picked up instead a copy of *Playboy* from the opposite bench, a magazine absorbed with relentless enthusiasm by the lab technician who did not care who knew what he read. Flicking over the pages, Hazel was puzzled and alarmed by the dimensions of the women in the photos. 'Glory be to God,' he muttered to himself.

'They'd eat you alive.' And he wondered vaguely about the lab technician's preferences. Behind him, there was the steady sound of disembodied breathing, eerie in the emptiness.

He sat far away from the bench on which he had rigged an automatic ventilator, a device which mimicked human breathing, pulled paper and pen towards him, then wrote in his indecipherable hand, dictating to himself as he went, 'This is what I did last night. First I folded an ordinary, large, yellow duster in various ways and poured chloroform on it, just to see how much it would hold. About fifty milligrammes at best, if the duster was soaking not dripping, but difficult to handle. Holding the duster over my own face, I breathed it as long as I could, but within a few minutes, while I was feeling dizzy and sick, the whole of the chloroform had evaporated. A heavyish concentration like this is rather unpleasant, and if the drug was being used for frivolous purposes, pleasure in other words, I doubt anyone would use that much. It might, however, have been sufficient to knock out a small woman, though not enough to keep her knocked out for more than a minute or two. Chloroform is many times heavier than air; much of it is wasted by falling around the face . . . Oh God,' he interrupted himself, 'even I find this complicated to explain. Now what the hell did I do next? Ah yes.' He walked three steps to the left, two to the right, counting.

'I took a sample of my own blood and had that lab technician test it today. Barely a hint of chloroform, a mere milligramme. And I certainly didn't feel randy, but I suppose that depends on the company.' He chuckled to himself. 'So you don't get anything like twelve milligrammes aboard even by the most determined sniffing, and since it evaporates so quick, you'd never get that much from one duster full, not ever.' He began to pace round the room, continuing his lecture. 'In fact, it occurs to me that it would take about twenty minutes' solid inhaling to get that much aboard, you just couldn't be faster. But looking at the books, old boy, and all the recorded levels, the average person would be out for the count, temporarily, that is, after five minutes inhaling a concentration like this, and five minutes was roughly how long the old anaesthetist would take to put them in the land of nod, holding them down too. Now, Miss West, and Mr Red Pig, how the hell did this woman take in the rest? Self-administered whilst already unconscious? Novel, but not possible. She could only take in twelve milligrammes if someone held the same duster over her face while she was unconscious, then poured on to it another fifty milligrammes, and then another . . . Whoever did this held the chloroform vehicle above the face and away from the skin, no burns, no contact with the mouth, you see . . .' He turned back to the lung machine, breathing with the sound of a regular heartbeat. He wished the sound of breathing had been as reliable in every patient he had put to sleep, but this was simply a machine, pushing air in and out. 'No heart, my dear,' he said, patting it. 'No anxieties, no lungs affected by a lifetime's fagends, etcetera, etcetera. But in a little while, I shall measure, if I'm sober enough, the levels of chloroform round this mouth which has been breathing in this stuff for a quarter of an hour . . . Then I'll think of a way to put into words what that bugger did . . .'

He looked at his watch, turned off the ventilator. The whole thing would be done again tomorrow. Over the mouth of the machine he had placed the mask, a souvenir from former times, the conventional anaesthetic mask. Covered in gauze, to be soaked with chloroform or ether, different thicknesses of gauze for each. He remembered; he remembered well. The Schimmelbusch mask was the one he liked most. An oval of thick wire with crossed struts and a rim to catch liquid. The one that looked like a helmet. Hazel sighed. He had last used this in the war with bombs falling around him. Buried bombs, memories and now disinterred ideas.

'Helen? Sorry to wake you, but . . .'

'What time is it?' Bailey always knew the time, as if a clock was placed at the back of his eyes.

'Only two in the morning. Not very civilised, but . . .'

'Are you all right? You're not hurt, are you?'

There were times when he loved her particularly, for making the obvious enquiry and failing to be annoyed. For sounding asleep, like a person talking from the far end of a tunnel, but responding without impatience.

'No, I'm fine. It could wait until morning.'

'No, it could not, or you wouldn't have rung now, would you? What is it?'

'Oh, nothing.' Self-deprecation, an automatic downgrading of emotion was a feeling they both shared, and one she understood perfectly.

'Nothing . . . but I went to that street, you know, Herringbone whatever. Where your chemist lives. To look for the sergeant who's mentioned in your report, just to see if I might forestall his arrest for loitering round after his wife, make a fool of him before a dozen others tried it. But I found a man instead. Dying, I think, drug overdose.'

'So you picked him up, I suppose?' Helen asked, knowing this was exactly what Bailey would have done. 'Blew your cover?'

'Yes, of course. Took him to Casualty, too late, I think. Can't have been very old, looked older. Left him there, comatose. Bit of a mess.'

She knew then the purpose of the call. In the face of meaningless, wasteful death, Bailey became angry, bewildered, moved for a while at least, in a fog of grief and fury.

'Want to come over? Or shall I come to you?'

'My car's warm. And I'm dressed.'

'Get a clean shirt then, see you in ten minutes. Drive carefully.'

The instruction was lightly given. Bailey drove with a racer's flair, but careless speed was a symptom of rage. She knew him, she thought, fairly well, when he was not a stranger. Began to guess how it took the cold breath of tragedy, the casual brutality of his own native streets, to bring Bailey back out of the doldrums and into life.

Kim enjoyed working alone in the shop. Pip chose lunchtimes to leave her in sole control, since it was only then that the morning trade from the doctors' surgeries dried. Between ten and twelve, there would be a steady stream of people, clutching their sheets of prescription paper which they handed over to the pharmacist together with a small fee in return for lotions, potions and pills. Pip stuck the prescription forms on a stake, like a short order cook in a kitchen, and they dealt with them in sequence. Kim could do everything but dispense direct to the public until her admission to the Pharmaceutical Society, which was imminent. Patients and customers did not understand when she said, 'Come back later, I can get it ready for you, but Mr Carlton has to check it, sorry.' 'Why?' they said. 'Well that's the way it is, I'm afraid,' for another month, and as far as she was concerned herself, the time would not be too soon. This morning she felt as if she had taken the soporific cough medicine which had such an exaggerated effect on her, but recognising that she was simply tired did nothing to help her cope with the effects, which were, irritation, an acute awareness of Pip's bossiness, and something she could only describe as a longing to escape, simply to something different. That mesmeric building site and all the rubbish in the streets, she told herself; rubbish creating ghosts which only died with the early-morning rumble of the cement mixer over the road, all these sights and sounds which made her feel imprisoned, while logic would tell her this was not imprisonment at all. Kim was not given to introspection: there was no time. This extra awareness of everything was unusual. Tom had been sweet this morning, making up for his previous sourness in that way of his, showing her some treasure picked up from the street. A wire helmet, someone's idea of fancy dress which she had not appreciated. And then Daniel, scheduled to appear for the school run, had failed to materialise.

All of this together created the disaffection, rising slowly after Pip went off to see some drug firm representative and left her alone. Facing her at the counter, a small old lady was shaking her prescription and trying to proffer gifts in a bag.

'For Mr Pip,' she kept saying. 'He'll want these, he will, he will.'

'Want what?' Kim asked, irritated by the customer's insistence and her own inability to help. 'What will he want?'

'These,' said the woman, her voice sinking as if about to impart a disgraceful secret, but still clutching the brown paper bag. 'This stuff. He said I had to bring it back if we had too much, and now, poor sod, he doesn't need it.' She leant forward, confidentially, beckoned Kimberley towards her with one crooked finger. 'And I found some other stuff too. From when Dad died.'

'What?' said Kim, desperately seeking clues, but already guessing. Pip had so many devoted, but harassed ladies, often old, not necessarily wise. He delivered to them in person, their medicines and their support stockings; they shared secrets and jokes to which she could never be party, jealous with his influence and his popularity, never letting her near so many of his own favourites, she suddenly realised with shock. Nor near those who crept in like this specimen, armed with something rattling in a bag. Leftover potions, the sort of poisons and medicines all members of the public were encouraged to take back to their pharmacist if any of them should prove surplus to requirement. Especially those few, termagant carers of the terminally ill, who were armed, for a short time at least, with the worst of the poisons. Heroin, perhaps, morphine sometimes, milder derivatives more often. Old-fashioned remedies in new-fashioned capsules, delivered as a last-ditch or very short-term remedy for those in acute pain or near the end, those who would not or could not get in the ambulance. The last brigade who thought of the hospital as their grandfathers thought of the poor house. There were a few round here. Survivors of a war, remembering desolation still, persons to whom the welfare state meant nothing more than access to a doctor who should never be bothered because doctors were too important to be bothered. Or the Asians, to whom care of their own in whatever state was a matter of intense pride along with a fear of hospital. They did not leave each other, these people, and though Kim did not understand them she had come to admire them for their dogged, obdurate, sometimes stupid courage. They waited, they obeyed, they gave heroin obediently to their dying, took any advice which meant he or she would not leave home, accepted the death. And then, like this scarf-swathed woman, who trusted Pip as she would have trusted God, continued to obey local customs and brought back the remnants of the medicine. Looking at the face, resigned, shrewd, trusting, all in one, Kim felt humble. Despite her qualification in pharmacy, she felt stupid and ignorant.

'Ah, I see,' she ventured, more kindly. 'I think I remember. You looked after your uncle, cancer, wasn't it. You wouldn't let them take him in . . . I'm sorry, I didn't know.'

'Can't be helped,' said the woman brusquely. 'But I don't want this stuff in the house. The cat might get it. And I want some medicine for myself. Night Nurse, it's called. Got a prescription from the doctor.'

'Do you want capsules, or the linctus?'

'Linctus, I said. The other doesn't work.'

It was on the tip of Kim's tongue to say, you don't actually need a prescription for any kind of cough linctus and the capsules are made of exactly the same thing, but, sensing that anything prescribed by the doctor would be preferable to something bought over the counter, she simply wrapped the bottle carefully and presented the parcel like a prize. In turn the woman handed over her own.

'Morphine, he said it was. Fat lot of good it did too.'

On her way out of the shop, the woman dislodged an arrangement of toothpaste with her bag on wheels. She carried on regardless, letting the tubes cascade to the floor behind her and Kim moved forward to tidy the mess, stopping as she realised she was still holding the paper bag. The possession of it made her feel guilty, as if she had just intruded on some secret, and when the door sounded to let in another customer, she started, stuffed the packets back and retreated behind the counter without looking to see who was coming in. With the bag still in her hand and cheeks slightly flushed, she faced the customer with an air of confidence. Smiled in relief.

'Dr Gupta. Nice to see you. Did you want Pip for something, only he's not here.'

He turned on her his bird-like, nut-brown face, then looked back towards the street, and jerked his head to where the woman could be seen standing on the pavement, uncertain where to go next. 'Poor soul,' he said. 'No one to look after now. Should have been a nurse. Now, what did I want?'

Kim laughed at him. Dr Gupta was sanguine, incessantly busy, frequently vague, and rarely came to see the pharmacy which served his patients and his practice. When he did, it was always for a purpose, such as giving a word of warning about one of the patients who was not above playing doctor and pharmacist off against one another in order to obtain the medicine he or she privately thought appropriate. 'Ah yes,' he said, 'I remember. Daniel. I'm a bit puzzled about Daniel.'

'Why? Isn't he well?' Dr Gupta looked surprised

and consulted his watch as if the dial could give him important information.

'You could say unwell. Dead, actually. Didn't you know? But then there's no reason for you to know. Hospital phoned me this morning. Someone brought him in. Methadone overdose, they think. Or he might have taken tranquillisers along with his methadone, lethal sort of mixture. Obviously fell over, which didn't help. Large haematoma on the back of his head, but not fatal. Only the methadone. What bothered me was where he got the extra that pushed him over. I know it wouldn't be here, but it did occur to me that Pip might know if he was going somewhere else.'

'Oh.' She was shocked, felt close to tears. Daniel had flitted in and out of their lives like a wraith, but he was still Daniel and the abruptness of his departure was difficult to comprehend. Kim slipped into the dispensary and pulled out Daniel's record. A daily collection of oral methadone, without fail. Nothing untoward. She came back to the counter slowly.

'He can't have got it from here. We order his stuff exactly as we need it. You know how strict they are. Dan only had his regular amount this week, same as usual. We never have a surplus microgram of anything on the premises. Pip says it's too risky even it it wasn't illegal. That's the one thing he stresses. Keep the barest minimum of poisons.'

Even as she spoke, one eye on the paper bag beneath the counter, Kim knew she was not telling the truth. Somewhere on these premises, Pip could easily have a cache of poisons, little bits of heroin, physeptone otherwise known as methadone, morphine. Returns, they were called; all those little bits brought back after the funeral, like today's offering; tranquillisers no longer needed, a selection of drugs given to the chemist for safekeeping. Pip always handled all of that: she had been excluded, but what he did with the surplus, Kim never knew. They abided by the strictest of rules with everything ordered, but on the disposal of returns, there was no real control.

'What's more,' she said, putting conviction into her voice, 'we've been looked over by the police recently. Since Mrs Carlton died, you know.' She remembered that, too. The officers had teased her, never ventured into the sanctum of Pip's back dispensary. He had steered them away and she had helped.

Dr Gupta sighed. 'Oh dear, oh dear. I didn't think he could have got anything from here, that's not what I was asking. Pip's far too efficient. Did he go anywhere else, that's what I want to know? Could he have bought it from a friend, for Christ's sake? Makes no difference now, anyhow. Get Pip to ring me, will you? Not that I like to bother him. Poor fellow. Poor Margaret. He must miss her.'

She had been thinking ill of Pip this morning, but just then she felt the more familiar loyalty, remembered what he had told her. 'Oh, he keeps as cheerful as he can. But didn't he have a lot to put up with? I mean, I never knew she was an addict . . .'

Dr Gupta cocked his head at an angle in another, puzzled look at his watch. 'Addict? You must be thinking of someone else. Margaret Carlton? Treated her for ten years. Hypochondriac maybe, always hoping there was some magic drug to improve her life, fascinated by pharmacists on that account and willing to try anything, but addict never. The idea. Anyway, you won't need any more methadone for Daniel. Sorry about that.'

He was a little man, on little plump legs. As he raced for the door with characteristic speed, he dislodged the toothpaste stand she had just re-erected. She watched him go. Sat down to think, leaving the stock, with the promises of perfect dental whiteness, littering the floor. Teeth did not seem to matter. Daniel's teeth, cleaned intermittently, had been yellow, but Daniel's eyes inquisitively bright. Always seeking, always curious, knew his own dosage to the last detail. Not a careless man for all his other afflictions, only occasionally sly. Kim wanted to weep for him but found herself dry-eyed.

Bailey found the unfamiliar police station slightly intimidating. Not because he was walking down a yellow corridor of the kind which was quite familiar to him, or knocking on a door and entering a room which was almost a carbon copy of his own, or finding himself afflicted by awkwardness; all of that was par for the course. What unnerved him was that tic in his left eye which told him he was breaking one of his own rules, perhaps pulling rank a little, something a good leader of men did not do. Never interfere in another man's case without wishing on yourself a very cold shoulder, and do not let curiosity rule the head. Instinct is a dirty word. He knocked and entered Inspector Collins' office, feeling every inch the interloper he was. Honesty was the only way out.

'Sorry, Jack. Got a minute?' Detective Inspector Collins looked up from his telephone, replaced the receiver in its cradle and stood up. There was no need for that. Between his own rank and that of his visitor, the difference was less apparent and far less abused than lower down the line. No one saluted any more and good riddance.

'Listen, this case you have. Margaret Carlton. I've got two interests to put on the table. One, my sergeant, Perry, is married to the woman who works in Carlton's shop. I went to pick him up from there last night and found a chap in the street, which you might hear about, so I thought I'd tell you first. I want to know about this man and I gather he was a customer of your Mr Carlton. Secondly, you're dealing with Miss West in the CPS, with whom I live, most of the time. Which means I have no right to know anything about the whole bloody business, even what I do know, but I want to know. You can tell me to fuck off if you like. Or I might be able to help. If you like.'

The delivery was brusque, the patter swift. The timing, by accident, was perfect. Collins felt he was swimming in treacle. His face, almost as severe, but younger than Bailey's own, broke into a smile.

'Sit down, Geoffrey, will you? I was just about to report to your lady friend. About an alibi.'

For one absurd minute, Bailey thought the man was talking about himself.

'Whose alibi? No one's accused of anything.'

'Carlton's alibi for the night his wife probably died. I've decided I don't like this sedulous little bastard. Too keen to please. Can't stand people with blameless lives. Forty years looking after his mother, then looking after a wife. No wonder he was staying in a hotel the night she copped it. Being wined and dined by some company making contraceptives. But if he'd wanted, he could have got home overnight with no one to see. Plenty of time. In theory.'

'In theory. Why do people who make contraceptives give dinners to chemists?'

'Why do you think? So next time I buy a rubber, which I don't have the luck to need, I'll know some shopkeeper has been given a perk to sell it to me. Funny line of business, pharmaceuticals. The clean end of dirty.'

Bailey grunted, grinned.

'As if we can talk,' he said, 'about dirty and clean. Tell me, this pharmacist, did he . . . ?'

'What? Murder his wife? Naa. No chance. Something funny, though. I've been trying to find someone who knows anything about chloroform, but they're all dead. I don't understand any of this. Does your lady friend think he did it?'

'Seems so. From a long way off. And I think she's also found some bloke who knows about chloroform. You're right. Doctors in that category have to be pegging on a bit.'

'Shame. She did seem, your lady . . . Miss West . . . She's not a Ms, is she? I always get worried when they call themselves Ms. Sounds like a wasp. Anyway, she did seem to have got a bee in the bonnet.'

Bailey felt more than a little guilty. Talking about Helen felt like treachery, but needs must: he was loyal, but pragmatic.

'Well, yes, she has a bit. The bee in the bonnet I mean, but she has this uncanny knack of being right.'

'Bangs on about work a bit, does she, if you'll excuse the expression?' Collins was frankly curious about what it might be like to live at such close quarters with one of the legal breed, even an attractive one like that. Solicitors were funny animals, best lodged in a zoo, on display for purely educational purposes.

'Well, she likes work, you know. Very conscientious. And anyway, you know, women . . . All the same.' Again he felt more than a hint of treachery. Never mind: Helen would understand; she was a pragmatist too. Collins laughed.

'Yes. Women. Ever asked yourself why we say bee in a bonnet, never bee in a trilby? Or a titfer? Or a helmet? Because only women wear bonnets. Obvious isn't it? And go on like that. Anyway, thinking of proof, fancy a pint? I'll tell you all I know. You're welcome. Shouldn't take long. I could write it on the back of a postage stamp. And none of it secret. Women.'

Bailey thought of his own office and the longing for a pint grew steadily. The CID room in his station was taboo, struck with a fever peculiar to the time of year and quite equal in fervour to that of a newly formed murder squad. Fourteen detectives, including three women, were discussing, with all the intensity and argument of a parliamentary debate, the final details of the Christmas party to be held next day. Bailey was not supposed to know. He liked Collins.

'Fine. I tell you what, since it's so close, why don't we take in the pub on Herringbone Parade? Close enough, could be useful.'

'Bloody awful place, but OK, if you insist. The beer's not bad. Only the people.'

There were no signs of conventional Christmas weather as they left, lowered themselves into Collins's car in a back yard identical to the gloomy area behind Bailey's almost identical station, and drove the half-mile to Herringbone Parade. Collins left his Ford Granada parked on a yellow line, saying, 'Oh stuff it', as he hauled himself out of the driver's seat and led the way at a fast trot towards the Lion and Unicorn, last remnant of old architecture on one corner. He was obviously having a bad day, Bailey thought, whereas he himself was beginning to have a fairly good one. As days went, and up until now, this one had ranged from tedious to downright dull. Part of him envied Collins, a man still allowed to ask questions, still relatively free of the endless meetings which came with managerial rank.

'See what I mean?' Collins asked when they were safely ensconced. 'About the people?'

Bailey privately thought Collins was wrong about the pub, which was, frankly, nice, with its etched glass and brass rails around the bar, worn chairs badly covered in plastic disguised as leather, a flowered carpet faded by dirt and use into something his own eyes found entirely acceptable. The reason for the dirt was easily apparent. Outside, it was market day, and although a subdued market day, where the awnings on the stalls flapped in the wind and the cold bit through clothing, the road was dirty. And this was a pre-war pub, an unbombed island surviving rebuilding, made for a time when pubs weren't supposed to be clean. Hats and scarves carried indoors with the inevitable refrain, 'Brass monkey weather, this. Fucking cold . . .', but none as dirty as the navvies playing cards in the corner. Now they, Bailey thought, were really dirty, coated in mud from head to foot, yet indifferent to the fact as if what they wore on the front of their donkey jackets was no more than one extra layer of insulation. Mud and dust flaked round their feet where the working boots could not be distinguished from the trouser cuffs. He looked at them, drinking casually, beer with spirit chasers, three rounds each and back to the mud. Only an hour to work that off. Steady drinker though he was, Bailey knew he could not compete. He and Collins were both conspicuous because of their suits. He saw the latter adjusting his tie, caught his eye and grinned.

'Well we are on the edge of the City,' he said. 'We might be mistaken for gents. Or management consultants.'

'No way,' said Collins. 'Well you might. Not me. I look like a brick shithouse dressed in a suit. Feel a bit of a wally, too. No way,' he repeated. He took a long gargle from the pint, his throat working until the glass was half empty, then put it down, obviously relieved.

'Anyway,' he went on, 'the bloody City with one square mile of a thousand banks might be next bloody door, but Jesus, it's a hundred miles from here. The City gets rebuilt; this just gets patchwork. Bet these geezers don't come down here to do their shopping. Anyway, we haven't got the right kind of suits. Mine cost fifty quid. Probably fell off the back of a lorry. Fair bit of that sort of gear passes through this pub, as it happens. Got mine in a sale.'

'You must have canvassed this place before, by the sound of things?'

'Oh yes, course. Bit of local gossip never comes amiss. Like Coronation Street, down here. Only don't go repeating none of it to your DS Perry, might give him ideas. Had a word, we did, with a few of the shops round here. They got their ideas about Mr Carlton and Perry's missus. Quite a disappointment she is, as well. Not fulfilling local expectation if you see what I mean. Lady in the grocer's shop tells me she expected someone to catch them in bed long ago, even before his old woman snuffed it, but she never plays, Mrs Perry, I mean. Doesn't even seem to know that old man Carlton had the hots for her as soon as she stepped in the door. Too busy to notice, but she was the only one didn't. They like her round here. As much as they like anyone who hasn't lived here for ever.'

Bailey grunted. Collins took that as a benign hint, plucked from nowhere and told the story from the beginning.

'Anyway, like I said. Christ, that went quick . . .' The straight-sided pint glass was empty. Bailey did the honours and bought himself a whisky, to go with the half. He had never really liked beer beyond the first round and the habits of the navvies were catching.

'Ta. It's a bugger, this case, you know. Because it isn't even a case, and whatever there was got screwed up in the first place. Tried to explain to your brief, but there it is. Police get called to break down a door because some wife's gone AWOL, find her dead, but laid out so nice you'd think the undertaker'd already got there. So he radios in and gets the body shifted. Accidental death. Why not? No photos, no forensic, no nothing. No one's broke in, no injury, no struggles, right? Pathologist just out of school, doesn't give a fuck, does the necessary and gets a surprise. Some old-fashioned drug he's heard of but don't know nothing about. Funny, he thinks, but not enough to kill her, I don't know why she was snorting it, do I? Which is what Davies thinks too, bit worried for his precious little chemist. Why? Because he's the best there is round

160

here. Delivers to little old ladies, he does, not that anyone pays him for it, but he seems a good bloke. Time for all of them, can't get anyone here to say a bad word, know what I mean? Wife a bossyboots, not unpopular, but not great either. Tries to stop our Mr Carlton from delivering to the old ladies, ordering in stock which don't make a profit, all that kind of stuff. Swept the floor when the builders came in looking for blister cream and rubber gloves, bit of a pain really, but not so bad anyone hated her, kind in her own way. Thinks her husband the best thing since sliced bread, absolutely worships the ground he treads on. There you go.' He took another, extraordinarily long draught at the beer in the glass. Bailey sat silent. He knew very well when not to interrupt a flow. Either beer or information, especially from a colleague having a bad day.

'So, as I said, we're fucking well scuppered. Because we never got the body, see? Because nobody looked in the first place and after that it's all over bar the shouting if they don't. We can't prove anything from the scene and by the time anyone's gone back for a second look, Carlton or whoever has had plenty of time to hoover the place, remove hairs, semen, anything like that. Not that there was any sign of sex on her, not a trace. Only he forgot to take the chloroform from under his kitchen sink, which was why he had to tell us about it. And his alibi's not watertight. Which is all we have.'

'What if someone can prove the chloroform

couldn't be self-administered? I mean, if it could be shown someone must have given it to her?'

'So what? It means we really would be looking for a murderer, but who? She could have let in the local drug addict, that chap you found, and yes, I did know about it. She could have been knocking off one of the builders. Kimberley Perry could have slipped in and killed her, for that matter.'

'You don't think so?'

'No, as it happens, although she could have got in. There were spare keys to the Carltons' flat in the pharmacy, and she had keys for the shop because she had to open up for herself and a relief chemist while he was gallivanting away, but she says she didn't know about the flat keys. Anyway, I've given up thinking.'

The straight glass was empty apart from a tracing of froth. Collins eased himself from the rickety table and over to a gap in the bar with the skill born of long practice, returning with two identical orders. The beer did not appear to have touched him. That's what we've both learned, Bailey thought; how to drink. Pity DS Perry had missed out on such invaluable knowledge.

'What do I say to your Miss West, then?' Collins asked with mild belligerence. 'How do I calm her down? Sorry, mustn't make chauvinistic remarks. Maybe she doesn't need calming down. Men and women created equal and all that. I've been sent on a course so I know. Told me not to denigrate the fair sex or call them rude names. Wait a minute, that's not the same Helen West who got beaten up by some psychopath? Coupla years since? Your case, wasn't it?'

'Yes,' said Bailey uncomfortably.

'Stone me,' said Collins. 'The poor cow.'

They parted on good terms, Collins sympathetic, if slightly incredulous when Bailey said he would linger where he was and shop on the market.

'Apples and oranges, potatoes, that kind of thing,' he said.

'And a few pills from the chemist?' Collins asked, his whole face a question mark.

'Maybe. If you don't mind.'

'Nope. Not this time. Tread on my toes any time you like as long as you tell me before it hurts.'

'Thanks,' said Bailey.

Tom Perry, on strict instructions from his mother which applied, and were often ignored, on any of the rare days she could not arrange for him to be met, boarded the bus slightly ahead of the crowd leaving school, sat downstairs near the door and clutched the handrail until Herringbone Parade hove into sight. Then he ran down the road like a lamp-lighter, jumping over the rubbish which heralded the end of the market, closing down amid shouts and wind and darkness. His eyes darted left and right, looking for Daniel. Daniel, greeted with indifference, but somehow necessary to life, was always out here on market days, hoping for a tip, but it was difficult to see. Always so dark; you went out in darkness to be the first at school, you came back in the dark and you never, ever became used to being in the dark.

By contrast, the shop made him twitch, an effect he noticed in others all the time. They came in here, blinking like moles, all except Mummy, who never minded the light, only complained about headaches and drank more tea to forestall the next, never noticing anything. He sat on the high stool by the counter, wishing she would give him the key and let him go home out of sight, eating a sweet, bored as usual. Sometimes he tested her, like now, holding a book upside-down to see if she would notice while a short queue formed at the counter. Tom rummaged in his torn satchel for entertainment, looking for another of the sweets swopped for apples, noticing that the metal helmet, which he carried everywhere, had worn an extra hole in the fabric. He took the thing out, laid it on his knee, and continued to forage elbow deep in the mess in the bottom of his bag. Mummy did the same with hers. Pip came out to the counter, speaking across Tom's head.

'Here you are, Mrs Jones: three times a day, if you please . . .' His eyes fell on the helmet.

'Where'd you get that thing, Tom, old boy?' The tone was jovial, the expression fixed in a smile.

'Outside. At the back, I think. Maybe it was somewhere else. Don't know.' He wanted to say, what's it to you where I got it, but any words, even tame words like these, provided the chance to put a sneer in his voice and imply the insolence he felt.

164

'What a strange contraption. Thought you might have made it at school. Can I look?'

Tom's hands tightened on the metal hat he was going to give to Daddy.

'No,' he said, and pulled a face.

Pip smiled and shrugged. 'Suit yourself, old boy, suit yourself.' He leant forward, and pinched Tom's cheek playfully. Tom continued to smile, even when Pip's red fingerprints remained livid on his skin. He fingered the metal, slowly, to stop himself yelping. Pip still stood there; it seemed imperative to behave as normal.

'OK, then, at least tell me where you got it. Interesting.'

Tom thought wildly. His mother was in earshot and he remembered the slapping from the last time he'd collected rubbish.

'Daniel gave it me.'

'Are you sure?'

'Course I'm sure.' He was beginning to shout and the louder he spoke the more he believed himself. Daniel never cared what anyone thought: let Daniel take the blame. He was immune.

The eyes which held his own finally faltered, and turned away with a look of obscure satisfaction. 'That's right,' said Pip. 'I might have seen Daniel with something like that. Scavenger.'

Tombo did not know what a scavenger was, but it sounded rude, made him defensive enough to want to confess the truth.

'Have you seen Daniel today?' Tom asked. 'Only I thought he would be in, haven't seen him . . .'

There was a long pause. Tom was surprised to see Mister looking faintly uncomfortable.

'Ask your mother,' Uncle Pip said.

CHAPTER EIGHT

'How's your mother?' Helen asked the man at the door.

'Oh not so bad these days, Miss West. Better. She likes Christmas, see. Cheers her up.'

There was something about buildings which made them unwell, welcoming or not. The disease of Helen's office building was obvious. Stuck down a small side street, there was permanent twilight on account of the enormous block which stood opposite and stole what little light there was. The difference in the seasons was difficult to determine from inside, apart from the temperature fluctuating between two different kinds of heat, the dry and the cloying, hotter than average in winter. There were days when she could hardly bring herself to push open the door, shrugging off her coat as she did so. Full of petty economies elsewhere, this part of the Crown Prosecution Service was content to fry the staff alive with its central heating, rendering them zombie-like by mid-afternoon, while the most unfair thing about Redwood's superior room was the fact that he was the only one actually able to open his window. The psychology behind this had the accidental effect of keeping them all out of doors rather than in, which Redwood encouraged. Real work was done in court where success or failure was manifest. Preparation and consideration always came second since they tended not to show.

Helen saw the tinsel hung in the corridors, a coy reminder of goodwill. Mika had been busy and Helen's heart sank lower with the first unavoidable signal of Christmas. Even in robust health, Helen hated Christmas. Christmas made men and women mad. Redwood would be infected and tonight was the first of the parties. Bailey's party. Or at least, Bailey's CID party, where they entertained the whole district. Where she would stick out like a sore thumb, the way she had last year and the year before. Unable, quite, to charm herself into some sort of acceptance or dull the nerves by getting drunk.

Her carpet was like patchwork, and the office had once been a showroom. For some reason quite beyond the ken of any man, the original, cheerful blue and all pure wool carpet left by the previous incumbents had been torn up for replacement by inferior, all synthetic yellow. They had protested, stood on the carpet, yelled on the carpet, and in Helen's case, even lain down on the carpet, but acrilan now dwelt where wool had been and the door frames tingled with static electricity. Why the hell do I do this? she was saying to herself: why do I work in this crap heap when I could earn twice as much somewhere else? With a secretary and fresh flowers daily and luncheon vouchers and a free car . . . Because you would be doing nothing but guarding other people's money, and you would be bored. That is, in general, what other, richer lawyers do.

Right. No moaning then. No whinging about how awful it was to be thus employed but how nice, how wonderful it would be if it were not quite such a struggle. According to Helen's calculations she spent half her life doing her job, with at least the other half devoted to the sheer mechanics of getting the simplest thing done. All that diplomacy, all that energy, like steam from a kettle, all spent creeping into the photocopying room, saying, would you mind terribly, come on, Dot, please . . . Or getting a letter typed, bended knees to a typist, blandishments and promises given like a tart. Prostitution was a useful analogy too when it came to getting major decisions made. Smile while you still got teeth. Convince the boss it was his idea, suggest, never dictate, wheedle, whinge, undermine with charm, talk as if talking were just invented, duck and dive, cajole, persuade, like a hockey player dribbling the ball up the long field to goal. That was the exhausting part, the time for losing judgement. Half a day, every day, coping with a hierarchy in order to do the simplest thing. In a place as hot as Hades.

The end results, of course, were not rewards. Such as this morning. She looked at the watch Bailey had given her. She had been thinking of Bailey, not always calmly, ever since she had met him, in an office like this. At least he was an honest ally, some of the time, even though his present job had threatened to turn him into a bureaucrat. Before he found dying persons in unfashionable streets. Enough. None of that was going to help her survive Bailey's party. She went into reception, where the man on the door was mopping his brow from the effort of greeting Dr Hazel.

'You'll know your way here by now, Sean. How've you been?'

'Better each time you phone. Do we have to go and see that little man again? Wee piglet?'

'Not yet. In theory, he takes all the decisions around here. We call him master.' She was mimicking his brogue. In the lift, rising towards the welcome ventilation of Redwood's room, Hazel grinned at her and frowned at his own reflection in the doors.

'What's that baggage you're carrying?' Helen demanded. Dr Hazel was armed with a small, bashed-about suitcase.

'Change of clothes,' he said. 'In case you ask me to stay.'

Redwood heard the sound of laughter going past his door, paused on his way towards his desk and sat down abruptly to polish his glasses. His once spacious office now contained three chipped desks, facing his own. Each one was covered with documents and the sight of them, as well as the sound of laughter, remained no more than a hollow suggestion of loneliness. Somewhere in all of this was the vain hope that the floor would sink into the basement and lose all this paper without trace. Bring him back to the camaraderie he had once enjoyed, and perhaps the blessed heat of the lower floors. His window was warped by winter, permanently open, and the back of his neck was frozen against the hackles he used to find rising occasionally round the hairline, all his instincts dulled by complaints and budget sheets, and Christmas too. He envied Helen West; he envied all the others. If she entered here, looking warm and flushed from the pleasures of meeting the public, he thought he would understand the meaning of the word murderous.

'Murder,' said Dr Hazel, 'is what it was.'

He had ended his peroration. They sat, Collins and Helen, facing him across a table in the messy basement room used for meetings and rudimentary library, both of them spellbound, Collins frankly shocked. His flushed skin told the tale of a celebration the night before, but he maintained the bearing of a soldier. Hazel looked like a tramp, but for that moment and the half-hour before, he had commanded their attention like a maestro, and thought he would never forget it. On the table lay a report, complete with diagrams, computer models, references and lucid articulate prose. He knew, as he finished, that he would actually write the book he had always planned to write. The thought filled him with grave exultation.

'I'd like to see you in the witness box, Doc. You'd slay 'em,' said Collins.

'Ah, now,' said Hazel, putting up his hands in a

warning gesture, a look of alarm crossing his face, 'no one said anything about that. I doubt if . . .'

'Say it again,' Helen interrupted quickly. 'About this thing.' She pointed to the metal frame which sat atop the report.

'The mask? Imagine you're the patient. You are about to be anaesthetised with chloroform. Imagine an operating theatre, if you will, full of men in frock coats, all addressing each other as sir. You lie back, thus . . .' Hazel grasped the metal object, an oval-shaped frame of wire with two crossed struts, and tilted back his seat to a dangerous angle, holding the mask across his face. 'The mask is a patent by Schimmelbusch, long since dead, and has a groove round the rim to catch surplus liquid. Sits over the face, wide enough in circumference not to touch. Gauze is placed on top, and chloroform is gently dripped on the cloth. The vapour sinks through, the patient breathes. Give him oxygen simultaneously and he can take more and last longer, as I explained.'

'Why a mask at all?' Helen demanded.

'Keeps the gauze and the liquid from the skin. Doubtless for the benefit of the doctor. These gentlemen in frock coats who started this did not have rubber gloves. You could, of course, manage without the mask – I have – but a fastidious man would use it.'

'And a chemist would know about this?'

'If he were interested in history, yes. Otherwise it might be a piece of forgotten undergraduate knowledge. Not all pharmacists are interested in the power of life over death but you might be surprised at the number who enter their profession because they have an unhealthy fascination with drugs. Drugs are power, you see.' He replaced the mask on the table where it made a satisfying clunk and reminded Helen of an empty crash helmet.

'If only,' said Collins, 'we'd had some chance to look at the room. We might have found something, I don't know. Like dents in the pillow. Wire sculptures. All Davies found, at Miss West's insistence, was chloroform.'

'Chloroform,' the doctor observed, 'would eradicate fingerprints too.'

'But it's all guesswork,' Collins complained. 'Apart from this.' He tapped the report. 'Apart from this reconstruction of how long it would have taken. Twenty minutes, you said.'

'At least. Longer without the mask.'

'And most of that time, she's unconscious? Christ, it's so cold-blooded.' Collins stood upright, disgusted by the images. 'A man standing there over someone asleep, keeping a mask in place, quietly putting more on the cloth. It's worse than a slow strangulation.' He breathed heavily as if avoiding contamination. 'Shall I go and get a warrant?'

'He wouldn't have seen her face,' Hazel reminded. 'And the only sound would have been breathing.'

Helen tidied the papers on the table into a pile. 'No warrant without permission from above,' she said, jerking her head towards the ceiling. 'And only if I can put my hand on my heart and swear there was absolutely no possibility of suicide. No chloroform under the bed?'

'No one looked,' said Collins bitterly. 'And besides, what difference would it make? If he was there?'

Upstairs, Redwood heard the footsteps coming towards his door and quickly shoved his newspaper out of sight. There was no idleness in his reading the local rag since consumption of all relevant headlines was mandatory. 'CROWN PROSECUTION SERVICE COCKS IT UP AGAIN.' 'WRONG MAN ARRESTED: RIGHT ONE RELEASED.' Yet more horror stories and a few writs in the offing with the words on the page reaching out to grab him by the throat. His sensitivities were as raw as the back of his neck. Entering his room, report in hand, refreshed by the icy blast from the window, Helen looked at his face and knew perfectly well what the answer would be.

'And?' asked Bailey later.

'And nothing. Sweet nothing, apart from no, not yet if ever. A warrant for whom? Bring me proof, he said. Bring me some connection between this man and this so-called murder. Knowledge, I said: knowledge is the connection. Rare knowledge. Christ, why is everyone so slow? Opportunity. Motive.'

'There is no motive.'

'Yes there is. In marriage, you never need a motive.' She flashed a glance at him, one mixed with frustration and mischief; then resumed brushing her thick hair with quick, irritated strokes. Bailey looked casually, noticed her nerves. Not for this case, he knew, only for the CID party, and he could not for the life of him imagine why. Her fears and braveries seemed to have no sense of priority, ranging as they did from a peculiar recklessness about life or health to this telling, acute irritation before a simple celebration.

'He must have liked Hazel's report.' Bailey squinted in the mirror, knotting a tie.

'Loved it, very impressed after he'd read it. Reluctantly. Said without that, there'd be no case at all, and without Hazel, I'd be told to put the whole thing in the fire. Hazel is just about my only bloody witness. Hazel and his immaculate reconstruction of events, with mask.'

'Helen, I've something to tell you . . .'

'Oh, ho. Is it a story? Will I like it? I feel absolutely frustrated by the deliberately obstructive regime of things. Let's have a drink.'

'Yes, to the drink. On second thoughts, the story can wait.'

'Everything's got to wait, but I'm not finished yet.'

Bailey was uncomfortable, but she chose not to question. He knew more than he said and would only say in his own time. He went into the bright spartan spaces of his huge living-room, the room which was really the whole of his flat, looked for the wine, found only whisky, gin and a pile of tangerines brought from the market.

'The whole investigation may take time, Helen.

You're so impatient, but once you've got Collins interested, you can leave it to him. No rush, is there? Even if the chemist killed his wife, it doesn't follow he's a danger to any other soul alive.' He thought of the man he had found in the back road to Herringbone Parade, then held his tongue, while Helen, not to be comforted, spoke his own words out loud.

'Bugger the stupidities and reservations of the law. I've been told I can't risk an assault on Mr Caring Carlton's civil liberties. So what if there's risk? Of course he's dangerous. Anyone who can mimic an anaesthetist is dangerous. Once you know what it's like, you don't relinquish the power over life and death.'

'Rubbish,' said Bailey. 'Sweetheart, you do talk rubbish.'

'Make us a tea now, there's a darling.'

'I'm just doing this, won't take a minute . . .'

'Well, now means now. Not later.'

He spoke very mildly, tapping the side of a plastic container of pills into the counting machine, his eyes fixed on the dial, muttering to himself, 'Four a day for fourteen days makes fifty-six. Tea, soon, please.'

The please was an afterthought, and Kimberley knew in that precise moment how none of the changes in him was the product of her imagination. Before Margaret's death, even before the last police visit, she might have answered back any peremptory order, teased his passion for tea, made light of his frustrations and bossiness, Uncle Pip, ruler of all he surveyed with the whole of this damn Parade in thrall and half the surrounding neighbourhood too. Make the tea, there's a love, sixteen times a day. In one month's time, she would be able to call herself a pharmacist, practise in her own right, and yet he ordered her to make tea, run errands. Kimberley remembered the back dispensary, its sacrosanct secrecy; remembered how Pip had always made the simplest things seem complex, adding mystique where common sense would do, all to make this career appear more difficult than it was. She did not think all of this at once: her mind was with Tom, bound to be awkward as always after an evening with Dad. She was yawning. Then Pip reversed the mood in one of his sudden moves, restored the balance.

'What am I talking about? Sound like some foreman, or school teacher. Stay where you are, I'll make tea. Sorry, Kim. I must have sounded short. Short! Ha! Like pastry. Just like I feel. Let's have some of that new herbal tea. Good for our nerves. It's all those Irish builders tramping in and out. They're behaving as if that site had a jinx. Wish they'd at least finish the foundations and go.'

It was on the tip of her tongue to say she did not want tea: she wanted sleep and an end of dreaming. Sleep without imagining things scuffling on her balcony. Sleep without this longing for Duncan, that brusque lover and husband who could still make her cry if only he waited to watch. Occasionally brutal Duncan, the treader of dreams, but oh, so certain in his certainty.

'It's OK, Pip, I'll make it.'

'Oh, no, no, no. Me. I mean I. Eye for an eye and tooth for tooth. I owe you plenty. Not just tea.' The last of this was muffled as he retreated into the alcove between the shop dispensary and his own little room. The alcove housed the kettle, and behind a door, the lavatory. 'Now look here,' he was saying, 'we seem to be able to do better than tea.' The hand in front of her face was flourishing a bottle of sherry. 'Nectar in a measuring glass,' he murmured, turning his back on her, rummaging on the shelves. Kimberley was so relieved not to have to drink tea simply because he had made it, the sherry seemed a good idea. One of these days, she would wake up and think of nothing. Maybe that was what Duncan sought on his binges. Waking up to the clear blue sky of nothing, with nothing to do, had to be a worthwhile state, however temporary. Kim had taught herself not to think: kept all observation to a minimum for the sake of her own peace of mind, and in one brief bout of recognition, she knew why Duncan drank.

'Yes, please, Pip. Sir. Lord and master. Just a large one.'

'And tea?'

'No. To tell the truth, I'm awash with tea.' He handed her one of the measuring cups, the sherry reaching up to the point of sixty millilitres. Rather a lot for a tired head. They sipped in a silence which was not quite companionable.

'Are we nearly finished, Pip? Only I've got to get back. Duncan's bringing Tom home, by seven o'clock, he said and it's nearly that now. Don't want him hanging about. He'll be off sharpish, though, Duncan I mean. Got a party, or something.' She remembered the Christmas parties she had enjoyed, thought of the lack of them this year and sighed, not listening.

'How about a Chinese takeaway, then? I'll come round later.' The invitation was slightly listless, as if he expected her to refuse, but she caught the same hint, that suggestion of an order which she was beginning to dislike.

'Sorry, Pip. I'm really tired. The wind last night: I kept hearing things and the blasted concrete mixer started before light. And I've got to tell Tom about Daniel.'

His silent offence only increased the feeling of helplessness. Carlton's Caring Chemist was becoming a place of isolation. Tombo rebellious, Daniel dead, Duncan obsessive and no one liking anyone else. Pip domineering and the wind howling.

'Another time, then,' he said mildly, back turned as he fetched more sherry. 'Do you want me to stay with you until they get back? In case Duncan's awkward?'

'No,' she said sharply. Every utterance she made seemed to be a refusal and she did not know how to soften any of them. 'Wow,' she muttered, rising from her stool and feeling giddy, steadying herself on the doorframe. 'Strong stuff, this.' Through her own efforts to stay upright, she could hear his smooth voice. 'Too much tea,' he was saying, 'and not enough food. I'll bring in some sandwiches for us tomorrow.' She was too tired now to recognise that same proprietorial tone, beyond resentment. Now which of them had been the bossy one of the two? Philip Carlton or his wife? The distinctions were becoming confused.

Kim plodded round the corner, slowly upstairs, searched for the key to her flat in the mess of her handbag. If Duncan was late, he need have no worries: she was too tired to shout, far too indifferent. The road was lighter than usual, a fact noticed by accident as she turned to prop the bag on her knee. Beyond the building site, she saw the huge crane which governed their view lit up with fairy lights across one magnificent, outflung arm, a red, blue, green salute, disembodied in the black sky, a sight so stunning in its savage but synthetic beauty that she could feel tears of sentiment and sheer surprise. She remembered tales of old paraders, memories of a sky lit by flames, night-time terrors, and suddenly felt their overwhelming fatigue. She left the door on the latch for Tom and stumbled inside.

Pip Carlton retreated to his back room, and closed the flimsy door behind him. The shaded light reminded him of a wartime he had never known and a secrecy which was second nature. Having drawn down a new blind on the back door window, which exaggerated the impression of a blackout and had the desired effect of making him invisible from the street, he began to feel safe. In contrast to the muddle outside, both in the real world and the ante-room to the shop, this place was now tidy: jars, boxes, pipettes, measuring jugs were all accessible: there was a large, locked cupboard which he patted vaguely. From outside, he heard the sound of a car, one door slamming and the hint of a childish voice, high with anxiety in its goodbyes. 'Go upstairs, you little runt,' Pip muttered, 'and tell me if she's asleep. If only you weren't coming home.'

There would be fantasies with these experiments. If not the real Kimberley in his arms, a dream instead. Pip reached for the yellow duster, soft and dry by the sink, sat in the armchair next to it. What cocktail tonight, what treat in store. He could not be heard in the shop, where the lights still blazed as they would until morning. He was dimly conscious that the car he had heard was revving to depart, the driver infecting the engine with his own impotent anger. Pip lay back, duster in hand, a smile of benign joy on his face. He smoothed the crotch of his trousers beneath the white overall, watched the bulge forming. Oh, Kimberley Perry, oh my darling.

Helen saw the crane, lit with lights of many colours, prominent from Blackfriars Bridge, and wanted, for one uncontrolled second, to clap her hands at the first thing which made her rejoice in Christmas. One brilliant arm in the sky, standing solid; a spectrum of light seen for a few seconds like a firework display against black clouds. She could not even say, Look, look, for fear of spoiling this childish pleasure, and wished they were going home from this party instead of being en route. Earth hath not anything more fair, a poem on Blackfriars Bridge: the poet had imagined this crane twinkling against the water. No poet ever dreamt of attending a policeman's ball.

Number Two Area's CID party was the daddy of them all. An effort frantic with munificence, blinding with glitter, stiff with shoulder pads. Gone was any sign of epaulettes and caps, the jeans or worn suits which Helen privately preferred: the men were in mufti, some following instructions to wear silly hats. A joke, Len, a joke: I knew you'd believe it. You don't think we'd have a party and turn up in hats, do you? We only said hats, to see if some silly wankers would fall for it. This is plain clothes, Len, remember. Nothing plain in sight, except Helen's rather elegant dress, calf-length, red, without any adornment whatever, and in it, she felt like a misplaced grandmother waiting and hoping to be sat in a corner with tea and smelling salts. Helen did not know the meaning of snobbery: she would not, in general, have noticed who was black, senior or junior, but the prospect of a good old knees-up in company with five hundred others made her quail even more than the risk of being thought a snob. Which was saying something, since she knew of no greater social fear than that. Stupid, said Bailey; ridiculous. You are the last person in the world anyone would ever call that: you are, sometimes, too egalitarian, too indiscriminate in your likings for your own good, whatever that is, and besides, it really does not matter what people think. It does, she was thinking now: it matters because they are your colleagues, your peers, and I have helped to isolate you from them: it matters terribly what they think.

Not only they, but also their wives. Always find a nice woman at a party; female solidarity, the comfort of life. Helen was deeply suspicious of any woman without good women friends, but standing by that was sometimes an uphill struggle on occasions like this. The wives and girlfriends gathered to powder and puff, adjusting earrings which half covered profiles, teasing fresh hairdos, pulling down their short straight skirts which skimmed their shiny knees; excited and stinking of perfume, a breed of butterflies allowed to flutter three or four times a year. And as she crossed the floor of this old-fashioned dance hall in a converted cinema, housing three hundred people for bingo three times a week, Helen could see why the sparkle on the women's clothing, in their hair, round their necks and on their ears, was so necessary. If you had nothing about your person to catch the light from the revolving globe in the middle of the ceiling, you were lost for ever. She had joked with the ladies in the loo, yielded her place by the mirror as they all scrabbled for lipstick, but when they heard her accent, their jokes diminished into shyer smiles. Although she realised this was her own fault, Helen regretted it all the same.

She struggled through an anonymous crush with

a dozen excuse-mes, gently pushing past the soft and solid suited bodies of all the men. Policemen one to one were fine – she knew how to deal with almost all – but weaving at sea in so great a volume of them, many the subject of awkward professional interviews, was a minefield of embarrassments. At first, she was the only woman at the bar. At this kind of party the men collected the drinks; the women hung back and awaited collection themselves. Helen was wrong again.

'Cor, look at that,' said a voice by her ear, the masculine appreciation sent straight over her head in the direction of the female huddle.

'Triffic. All right for them. Not enough to go round, is there? She'd have to be a right prune not to get lucky tonight. Ger in there, Dave. Oh, hallo, Miss West . . .' She grinned at a familiar face, aware that his guttural appreciation of the others was being swallowed in the knowledge of what she might think. Bailey was standing alone, the way he so often seemed most alone in a crowd, removed from these men by so many attitudes, rank and temperament, but pleased, like some paterfamilias, to see them relaxed. Helen took the proffered drink, gin and tonic, dispensed from barrels below the bar, free booze all evening and plenty of those present showing the signs already. She yelled in his ear above the din, 'Hey! Is this a party or a cattle market?'

'Both,' he yelled back. 'There's food over there.' He was itching to move, do his duties, meet what wives he could. He would abandon her to whatever she could find, confident she would manage with her usual panache. 'You all right?' he yelled, bending to impart the most commonly said words in the whole evening.

'Fine,' she bellowed back. Smiling encouragement, wondering quite what to do next and thinking, You bastard. I'd like to get revenge on you at our party where policeman guests stand around propping up the walls like a load of spare parts, but I suppose this is a fitting revenge for all those genteel dinner gatherings you've endured with me.

The generosity of policemen always amazed her: a party, by God, was a party. There was enough food for the feeding of the five thousand. Peanuts, crisps, curled sandwiches, scotch eggs, enough chicken drumsticks to have caused the death of a whole flock of hens, pies, cheeses, bread, a gesture towards salad. The whole groaning table, where the lightest thing was paper plates and plastic forks, was a reminder of the presence among the guests of almost every publican within a ten-mile radius.

More familiar faces approached: more conversations stilted by deference and the mistaken belief that solicitors could not laugh, however easy their manner. Helen found one lone woman in the gloom, and chatted with greater ease, but most of her own sex, determined not to be wallflowers, occupied the middle of the floor, some dancing dutifully round their handbags. They were kind and welcoming, and she liked them, but no conversation could be uninhibited as soon as she opened her mouth. And if life were about building bridges between yourself and others, there were times when it was better not to try too hard. She was the stranger here.

'Wanna dance?' a lanky young man with quite a few beers on board stood by her elbow, dared by a friend. Never refuse, thought Helen, so they danced in an uncoordinated but enthusiastic gyration from one foot to another.

'Hats!' he was shouting. 'Bloody hats, I ask you. Told us to come in hats, so the rest could have a go. Didn't half feel a berk.'

Smiling and nodding was the only possible response.

'Wass your name, then?'

'Helen.'

'Dave,' he shouted, pointing at his chest. 'Come on your own, did you?'

'No. With Superintendent Bailey.'

'Oh,' he said again, lower, in time with a lull in the music and an obvious lull in his mood. 'Well, hallo, Mrs Bailey. Nice to meet you.' It was neither the time nor the place, but she could rarely resist it. So pedantic you are, Helen, sometimes, said her own inner voice, too slow to prevent the words. 'I'm not Mrs Bailey. I'm his girlfriend.'

'Shit,' said Dave, slowing to a standstill. 'Where's his wife then?'

It was so easy to tread on toes, and she knew this floor was full of sensitive feet even though Christmas had already made men mad and driven them into the kind of drinking which might precede a year of drought. The music was louder, the voices correspondingly shriller: there was an argument raging on one side about someone being rude to a girl and quite soon there would be some woman crying in the ladies' loo and the careful settling of a few animosities outside. She had seen it before, could smell the sweet hilarity of a drinking crowd in danger of going sour.

At least there was Bailey if anything came to a fight, as likely here as at any gathering of the predominantly young and fit, trained for conflict, never mind if they were paid to uphold the law. There was something about Bailey, she thought, as she perched on a stool beyond the edge of the dancing but in reach of the drinking, chatting to another stranger. She knew that Bailey would protect her, unlike the previous partners of her life, her divorced husband, the other men of her own ilk. He would fight if need be and she was aware that he would fight to excellent effect, if not always to Queensberry rules. Not like a lawyer who would worry about his image, his suit or the consequences, and the contrast was one which gave her enormous pleasure. Some compensation for the vigorous display of good will and the sheer hard work of parties like this.

These might be basic, their food and celebrations might be primitive, but, thought Helen, she would really rather be around them than any other men.

Helen stood on the top rung of her bar stool in time to see the now swaying mass in the middle of the dance floor part to admit a large man with his arms clasped round the waist of a woman. His head was pressed into her back, whether for support or affection was difficult to tell at first sight, but in any event the total effect was restraint of the woman, who obviously resented what was more an arrest by force than an embrace. She was plucking at the hands fastened round her middle, screeching in protest, looking round wildly for some protector, and she was patently someone else's property. So much was obvious to the others, hence the shouts. 'Here, Duncan, leave it out . . .' 'You daft bugger, Duncan, bloody let go.' 'Sod off, Duncan . . . Piss off out of it . . .' He seemed oblivious, swaying to his own beat, his hands not loosening but splaying over the slippery fabric of the woman's dress, dragging down the modest décolletage to dangerous levels. There was panic in her expression. The man Duncan, his face obscured, was wearing a metal helmet slightly too small for his head, some makeshift wire object scarcely worth calling a hat. The others had abandoned their hats after initial teasing: the metal of his was digging into the woman's shoulder.

Somebody hit him. The one hand visible to Helen clawed at the bosom of the dress, and tore off a bright button reflected in the revolving light which distorted each movement and each expression as he slid to the floor and the hordes crowded in. Helen was afraid, paralysed afraid; and then she saw Bailey, pushing people this way and that, straight to the centre of the crowd where heads were bent and obscenities uttered. A man's arms were raised, a profile twisted as a foot was raised for a savage kick, bitterness caught in the light with a smell of sweat and an expression of surprise as he was pushed aside. The music went on: she could sense Bailey's voice below the pulse of sound, somehow being obeyed. Seconds later he emerged from the mass, dragging a man by the elbow. The metal hat rolled on the floor: Helen leapt off her stool, Bailey shoved the body on to her seat with the torso of it slumped fully over the bar and they sat down again in a trio. In one quick action, sign of an automatic tidiness in anyone else, Helen retrieved the metal hat. Duncan stirred, swore, looked at Helen with a leer and then looked straight ahead to all the bottles above the bar. Bailey coughed and straightened his tie. The gesture was so automatic that Helen wondered, not then, but later, how many times in his lifetime he had done exactly the same.

'Helen, meet Sergeant Perry. One of my best, at the best of times. Which this is not. Say hallo to the lady, Sergeant.'

''Aloo, Mrs B. Let me get you a drink.'

'He doesn't need a drink,' Helen murmured, fascinated despite herself. The truly drunk *were* fascinating, whenever there was someone to guard you from them.

'Yes, he does need a drink,' said Bailey. 'One more will make him malleable. With a bit of luck, even unconscious.'

'Fine, if you say so,' said Helen, signalling to the man behind the bar, rallying, even beginning to enjoy the situation. 'Who's going to take him home?'

'I am,' said Bailey. 'Will you wait for me? Shan't
be long.'

'I'm coming with you.' Duncan was fixing Bailey
with a baleful eye.

'No.'

'Why?'

'He might be sick.'

'And I have his hat. Nice parties you have. Come
on.'

The car cruised onwards in silence. Stopped at
traffic lights, started, behaved. 'How do people gen-
erally get home from police Christmas parties?'
Helen asked. 'If they all turn out like that? I didn't
see anyone sober for the last hour.' Bailey coughed.
'There are ways,' he began. In the back seat,
Duncan snored.

'Always wondered,' Helen was saying, 'about
what you do on the nights you don't get guarded
by me. Ferry round unconscious people in cars. So
it seems.'

'Not every night. Hang on. He's awake.' From
behind the driver's seat, there was the sound of
weeping. Copious, noisy, suddenly sober weeping,
sounds of such desolation from so large a man,
Helen was moved to pity. Turning round to the
back seat, she put out her hand and found it grasped.
A limp, hopeless grasp which made her curl her
fingers round his while the smell of him hit her
nostrils.

'Don't leave me,' said Duncan, 'Please don't leave

me. Take me home. Please take me home to Kim.'
Drunk. Lonely and desperate, clutching at hands.

'This is home,' said Bailey, brutally. The car stopped and he hauled himself out of the door and round
to the back while Helen, less practised, jumped out
of the front.

'Can we leave him like this? I'll come in with
you . . . Poor bloke's in some kind of pain . . .'
Detective Sergeant Perry was leaning out of the
back seat, threatening to fall. Bailey dragged him
upright, shoving one sagging arm round his own
neck.

'No,' he said with one backward glance as he
walked down the short path. 'For God's sake, stay
put. You'll only embarrass him. I'll put him to bed.
Stay in the car and lock the doors. Back soon.'

She sat, grateful to be obedient, conscious of her
own naivete. She shuffled after a minute or two and
wondered, selfishly, how long it took one man to
put another to bed, only aware, from briefer experience than Bailey, that it took one woman quite a
long time, so she settled to wait. Part and parcel of
the life of a policeman's wifely half, waiting.
Bugger Christmas. The half-hearted light of one
street lamp shone directly into Bailey's big car: she
could have read a book if there had been a book to
read. Instead, she turned in her hands the metal hat,
looked at it upside-down and inside-out, thinking,
looking, coming round slowly and regretting the
intake of gin and tonic.

Perry. As in Kimberley Perry. Husband of? Only
connect. In any event possessor of some funny little

item which could pass as the amateur double of that mask Hazel had shown them today. Oh Lord. An anaesthetic mask.

CHAPTER NINE

The phone shrilling in the early morning was so rare for Kimberley Perry she could not believe the sound, woke with that frightful fear of not quite knowing where she was. Back in her mother's house or back with Duncan when calls at all hours were commonplace. In less than seconds, she saw where she was, loathed where she was, struggled a groggy route out of bed with a pounding heart and lifted the receiver. She had no strength to say hello.

'Mrs Perry?'

'Yes, who the . . .'

'Superintendent Bailey. We met, once or twice, I think. I'm sorry to bother you . . .'

Christ, by seven-thirty she should have been up a whole half-hour. What was the matter with her? She dimly remembered getting off the settee and into bed, finding Tom already there, herself so sleepy she had neglected to eat or even brush her teeth.

'You all right?' continued the voice. Such a question. She was asked every day, always replied as she did now.

'Fine.' Then a consciousness of the oddity of this

crept in. 'Yes I do remember you. Duncan's boss. He's not here. What's the matter, what's he done now?'

'No, he's fine. Listen . . .'

So she had listened, promised to phone back, which was why Pip had caught her on his phone in the dispensary while his back was turned. She could have explained to Pip, asked permission first as she had done before when a phone call in working hours was vital, but she did not. She waited until he had gone down the road to buy fruit from Mrs Beale, because none of this was Pip's business. Thus he discovered her, explaining to a senior Superintendent of Police how her son had told her that the metal hat object they were discussing had been given to him by a drug addict in the street and left in his father's car. Describe the drug addict, Bailey said, and she had done that part. Name and pack drill, feeling as if she were giving something away. Kimberley was a jangle of nerves, assailed by emotion. Motherly instincts had told her that Tom, responding so defensively to questions that morning, had lied a little, and duller instincts, half formed and quickly rejected ideas, were making her withdraw from Pip; who had lied about his wife's so-called drug addiction; whose bloody sherry had made her sleep like someone hit on the head; whose eyes were drilling holes in her back as she tried to hurry the telephone conversation to a close.

'You all right?' Bailey was asking again.

'Fine, fine. Look, I've got to go. We get busy after nine.'

'Listen, Mrs Perry, phone me will you? Might help to talk. In confidence, of course. Will you meet your son from school? Yes, I know where. Could we speak then? Here, take my number.' She wrote the number carefully, feeling a flush spread over her shoulders as she scribbled on the back of a packet of paracetamol, crashed down the phone with relief. Yes, it would be nice to talk. About everything. And especially about the fact that Duncan last night must have taken advantage of her profound sleep, sidled indoors with Tom, and stolen half her under-wear. Bras, knickers, gone. Kim rubbed the back of her own neck to postpone the business of turning round, thought of that half-empty drawer in her bedroom and wanted to vomit with a mixture of anxiety and rage. All her cheekiness, her ebullience and jokes in the face of hardship, were gone. She wanted to behave like the tortoise Tom craved and hibernate for the winter.

'Who was that?' Pip asked mildly. She wanted to say, no one, recognised that this would resemble the airy nonsense of Tombo telling a lie, and said, 'Oh nothing. Sorry I had to use the phone. About Tom. School. He was late today. Do you want some tea, before the rush?'

'Please,' said Pip. Kim went for the kettle, passing the door to the back room where Pip had half covered the entrance with piles of boxes. Quickly he looked at the writing on the paracetamol box. Detec Super Bailey, meet school, 471 66, the rest indecipherable. He thought he had seen enough.

'What none of you seems to understand here,' Redwood was shouting, 'is the b-balance of proof.'

Helen thought he might rise and strike the table, the pedagogue incarnate.

'Beyond reasonable doubt. Not beyond the immediate comprehension of the man on the Clapham omnibus: not scientific gobbledygook but straightforward proof. Without flaw.'

'Perhaps a man standing over a dead body with a knife in his hand,' Helen suggested lightly. Redwood glared at her.

'All right, something more like that. Juries are thick. So are magistrates. At least something we could get past the latter. Not a dead drug addict called Daniel Maley who apparently knew all there was to be known about drugs, apparent possessor of an anaesthetic mask which he gave to some child. This wretch has to be suspect number one, dead at the moment. Not some respectable chemist with at least half an alibi and no known motive to murder a perfectly good wife, even if she did like chloroform. You don't convince the Clapham omnibus man with a scientific reconstruction without identikit, provided by a crazy old doctor who should have retired years ago.'

'He's certainly not crazy.' Helen's voice was loudly defensive.

'No,' Redwood admitted, patting the report which was open on his desk. 'Not crazy. He writes like a dream: his thesis is elegant and convincing if only we had a culprit. But he cannot be called as a witness. I'm surprised at you, Helen. I told you to check his background.'

'What?'

Collins shuffled in his seat, coughed apologetically. Redwood leant forward.

'Doctor Hazel's previous convictions, Miss West. Your . . . I mean, I understand Superintendent Bailey did a check. Two for drug abuse, years ago. Suspended by the medical council, temporarily, for sniffing ether, likewise years ago and criticised heavily for anaesthetising, possibly killing his own son. Accident, of course, not deliberate. Do you want any more? The defence would tear that to pieces.'

'Oh.'

Shock fell like a dead weight on her shoulders. She should have guessed with Hazel: there had always been the sense of something hidden. A feeling of conspiracy was growing in this cold room, Bailey, Collins, Redwood, a united front. She rallied, raising her voice, knowing it was useless. 'Since when has there been a rule, house rule or otherwise, that we can't field a witness with previous convictions, especially spent convictions? We call people from prison, don't we? Hazel is the lynchpin. It strikes me we aren't in a position to choose.'

'We are actually. We only call witnesses like that when we don't have a choice. We have a choice here. And I'm exercising it. Anyway I think that's all . . .'

'I'll get someone else,' said Helen. 'Someone else can do Hazel's experiments.'

'As you please. But not in my time and not on my budget. I trust you're fully recovered from your operation having been so busy? I need you to go to court tomorrow and all next week. Mr Collins will continue to investigate.'

Though the sound of a slap did not actually reverberate in the room, she could nevertheless feel the imprint of one in the pink of her face. She knew her reaction bordered on the juvenile, and she was ashamed, but continued. Shrugging with insolent indifference as she walked past his desk to the door, contempt resonant in her footsteps even while she saw the sense in what he said. Like a frustrated child, determined not to agree, she told herself later. Murmuring as she went, 'Fine, absolutely fine, anything you say. By the way, how did Daniel Maley die? If he might have done for Mrs Chemist, they had nothing in common but her husband. See you. Happy Christmas.'

Helen remembered the all-singing, all-dancing bed in hospital. Wanted to lie there and be carried away to some place where wounded pride and the squirming of failure was not visible to any eye, especially her own. There was also the unworthy wish that Bailey had never been born.

Back in her own office, she grabbed the phone. Anger, frustration, a sense of guilt making her fingertips stab at the numbers. Speak to me, nice doctor, please. The one who put needles in my arm, let me sleep, so likeable, so trustworthy, such a good human being. Tell me my judgement of human nature is not as rotten as it seems. And the law which pays my labours not really such an ass.

'I'm sorry I woke you up so early, Duncan. You look as if you could have done with rather longer.'

The faces Bailey encountered at around two o'clock in the afternoon were universally haggard, variously flushed and disorientated, the figures sitting in the CID room slumped in degrees of lethargy depending on their party stamina. A few had been wise, gone home long before the end: they were the ones live enough to joke. There were a few red faces and one or two suspicious silences. Detective Sergeant Perry walked with a pronounced limp: his eyes were swollen, and he had no plans to speak until spoken to, until caught on the wing by bumping into Bailey in the corridor.

'Have a word, Duncan? In my office.'

'Look, I'm sorry, sir. About you having to take me home and all that. I gather I wasn't nice to know.'

'About time you gathered that, Duncan. So far you've confined the worst effects of your drinking to making an exhibition of yourself in front of your wife. Last night you excelled yourself in front of all your colleagues, well done. Might give you some idea of what a bloody fool you look when you hang around Herringbone Parade of an evening. *And* how many uniform coppers there are out there dying to arrest you. Still wondering why she doesn't want to come home?'

Duncan was in a state of fury, taking in each

word, holding himself rigid, looking at the floor between Bailey's well-shone shoes and his own toneless ones. Then he pulled himself upright, gazed at a spot on the yellow wall past Bailey's head, and said again, 'Sir.' He was like a toy soldier, Bailey thought savagely, and himself like a sergeant major.

'Oh for God's sake, man, never mind, getting pissed and pawing a woman isn't the worst thing in the world. But you could have got your bloody head kicked in. Why are you limping? Did you fall over once I'd left you?' Silly question. Duncan would not remember, but Bailey could recall the two of them stumbling at least once on the way upstairs to Duncan's door, also dropping Duncan while he went through his pockets for the key.

'No, sir. I hurt myself yesterday when I was playing football with my boy.'

'And was that when he gave you that thing I was asking you about so unconscionably early this morning? That wire hat thing?'

'He didn't give it me, sir. He showed it me, then left it in the back of the car. I told him he shouldn't collect rubbish. He said it was OK, because it was all clean and wrapped up, but he knows his mother doesn't like it.' Duncan was recovering. 'Tom has a passion for rubbish, sir. He used to bring his mother flowers from the council tip.' A smile flitted across his face and vanished quickly, the grey cells not yet sufficiently alert to do more than wonder why some silly object, favoured by his eccentric child, was the subject of so many questions. Bailey judged that the instinct of the detective, if instinct was the right word for it, would be the last thing to surface in a still stupefied mind. For the moment he was grateful for that.

'I spoke to your wife. She said the boy told her some other lad had given it to him.'

Duncan clearly disliked the thought of such chatting. Bailey reflected he was the sort of man who would resent any man speaking to his wife, while reserving to himself the right to behave like a pig towards the wife of another. A common enough double standard, he supposed, not peculiar to policemen.

'No, sir. I'm sure he told me he'd picked it up from the road, outside where they live. I could be wrong. I'm sorry, sir, why do you need to know?'

'Nothing. Never mind. Nothing.'

Bailey did not know what Tom Perry looked like, but he knew he would be able to detect the mother. Not only from their rare meetings, but also from the photo with the cracked frame on Duncan's bedside table at home. Kimberley Perry had always been discussed: she had the open face of the streetwise girl next door and the figure of a siren, an effortless sexual draw which she did not seem to realise, a swagger which was not ostentatious but nevertheless drew wolf whistles from building sites. A homely body, not beautiful enough to intimidate or slim enough to model; the sort of woman a man might take home to mother and then to bed; likely to be good-humoured on either occasion and an irresistible combination to any officer on night shift.

Bailey himself had noticed her, of course. Since Helen had arrived to save him from cynicism, as well as the succession of affairs which had distinguished his bachelor career after divorce, infidelity had never occurred to Bailey. Other men's needs were their own affair, but such betrayal of trust struck him as the height of bad manners. Nevertheless, he was not blind, still noticed, watched and admired.

The school gates were a mile and a half from Herringbone Parade, and the wind which had dogged the first two weeks of December was still blowing. A small clutch of winter-coated mothers stood gracelessly by the gate, as deferential but eager as those sulky fans outside a theatre waiting for a star who was bound to ignore them. It seemed to Bailey that it was only childless adults who wanted to proclaim their individuality; here, children and parents alike desired nothing more than to be one of the crowd, plead the same backgrounds, the same difficulties, wear the same uniforms to escape envy or scorn, seeking anonymity rather than be noticed. The school matched its scenery: an old-fashioned redbrick school isolated in concrete surroundings, the same vintage as Bailey's own police station, probably furnished with the same thick radiators and gloss paint, the fabric of it as solid as chipped granite. A school where he imagined he might smell cabbage although he did not doubt that meals catering more to contemporary taste were delivered by the carton. And children, he remembered, never did like cabbage.

Cabbage was good when only shown the water, sliced with butter and coriander seed . . . Bailey was hungry and he had become adept at cooking.

Cabbage and the cabbage-like mothers, hidden under those coats, distracted him for a minute or more. There were no waiting men, which did not discomfort him, but he could see why it might have worried Duncan, a man too uneasy with women to stand alone with them.

Then school broke, and it was as if the building were coming apart at the seams with boys and girls shoving out of the main doors, swinging them back deliberately to hit the one behind. The crowd was heralded by one or two and then a great heaving, yelling mass, spilling forth with bravado, dragging coats and bags, and then, having celebrated their own escape, slowed down in the playground, reluctant to leave, shaping into small conspiratorial or sparring groups, full of unintelligible noise. Girls linked arms and walked in whispering pairs, boys circled, swooped, dived and shied away. Bailey could not help the sensation of wonder and jealousy which afflicted him. All that row, that blatant physical perfection not even hidden by the scruffy regularity of school clothes; skinny bodies, fat bodies, blessed with the energy of less than twelve years. His own child might have been thus: he was not contemptuous of the mothers. Found himself looking in that crowd for a girl who might have been his own, instead of looking for Tombo.

He could not imagine how teachers ever distinguished one child from the other, although each walked or gestured differently, pulled faces and wore their hair in different ways. But row on row, he could not have been sure to pick out his own, or anyone else's daughter. Bailey shook himself, concentrated on looking for Mrs Perry. He waited, looking shy by the railings like a man waiting for a date, remembering that too. Waited until every drab mother had disappeared with one or two young, the last posse of fighters fled from the playground, the last promise made before the weekend, and the pavement held nothing but echoes.

Slowly he went into the school building itself. She might have come in here to wait: so might the boy. He found one lone teacher, adjusting a coat in her headlong flight downstairs, comical in her hurry, less than pleased to be stopped.

'You might try the youth club at the back,' she said. 'Some of the kids wait there if their mothers are working.' She had never heard of one Thomas Perry. It was not that kind of school, despite the homely aspect. Watching so closely, he had missed them both.

'Tea?' he said. 'Tea, Kim? You must want a nice cup of charred char by now. Been at least an hour. I'll make it.'

So solicitous today, as if to compensate for yesterday's bossiness, the thin level of reserve covering all tensions like paper over a crack. Kim had recovered from the sleepiness, but not from the tiredness and a slight feeling of wanting to weep. She had been twice to her diary to look at the date and see if the monthly affliction of hormones could provide a reason if not an excuse, but the dates had blurred a little in front of her eyes after the mid-morning coffee which had been such a welcome respite from tea. Besides, when she had reached the handbag and found inside the paracetamol packet with the message, she forgot why she had broached the handbag in the first place. Always a dangerous thing to do: the market place leather contained lists of recriminations. Letters from Duncan, lurking there, the only proof she had he could write.

'Tea?' Pip was saying again. 'I haven't forgotten you're going to meet the little lad from school, plenty of time.'

'Thanks,' she muttered. The toothpaste stack was perfect: the cosmetics were at long last sorted back into place after two weeks' interference from teenagers thinking of Christmas parties and asking about special offers. As well they might, she had been thinking grimly as she kept herself deliberately busy and active in the lull spells outside the dispensary: half this stock is reduced. Wonder if he killed Margaret to get his share? The mere thought made her smile: Pip would not hurt a fly. He would wave a stick at it instead and call it names. Horrified, she had tried to check all such thoughts, stung by the fact that her previous admiration for him had grown to contempt in a matter of days, all without rhyme or reason. Ever since he had put his arm round her and shouted at Duncan. The tea arrived. Purple tea. 'Hibiscus,' said Pip proudly. 'To buck you up.'

'I thought it made you sleep.'

'No, no, only soothes the nerves.' Kim sipped doubtfully.

The door slammed open and shut, admitting one of the regulars from the building site, a recognisable hypochondriac who called in at least twice a week for a different patent remedy every time. He cantered from entrance to counter, looking worried, muttering, 'Jesus, it's cold.' Then stood indecisively, looking round as if expecting pursuit. 'Give us some of those yeller ones,' he croaked. Kim looked at the shelves behind the counter, tea mug in hand, could not quite see what he meant by yellow ones although she was usually quite astute in translating the odder requests.

'No yeller ones? Throat things, then, any kind.'

'You're in a hurry,' Kim remarked, pulling down a packet of pastilles, honey and lemon flavour.

'So will you be soon. All of youse. I'm off all right. Them buggers has found a bomb out there, and I'm not waiting to see how big.' He sped to the door, leaving his change. Kim watched with weary resignation as the toothpaste display toppled. They had their superstitions over there on the site: they were always talking rubbish in that pub. Pip watched her solicitously.

'Kim, you look all in. Why don't you go home and lie down for half an hour? Look, not a customer in sight.'

'Can't,' she mumbled, stifling a yawn. 'Can't. I've got to go and meet Tombo.'

'Don't worry, I'll phone you upstairs, wake you

up in time. Go on, finish that tea and go.' He was gently insistent; so much so she forgot her resentment of his bossiness, thought only of his kindness and got out of the shop without succumbing to the tears which still threatened. The same feeling as yesterday, a not unpleasant drowsiness which turned her hands to sponge and her brain to water. She got as far as the bedroom, took off her overall, and fell on the bed she had not bothered to make. Even the sight of the open drawer, mute witness to last night's petty burglary, did not disturb her.

Tom always knew if there was someone to meet him from school or not. He sensed the presence or absence of either parent or dopey Daniel as soon as he crashed beyond the main door to emerge into the playground, jumping over the flattened flowerbeds which adjoined the building to be trampled daily. On the rare occasions Dad was there, he could be spotted immediately, hanging about with sheepish self-consciousness beyond the wire fence which separated school ground from street, Dad always moving like some kind of warden patrolling a compound. On those occasions, Tom would want to grab the nearest boy, or the largest, any of the casual tormentors who picked on him when there was no other unfair game, and shout, Look, there's my Dad! Point out Duncan's unshakeable six feet, stolid and official and unaware that he would act as a talisman for days to come. No Dad today. Simply some older geezer, a grandad in Tom's eyes standing close to the usual clutch of mothers. Such grandads were a joke: they hung round after the girls for reasons not yet fathomed but faintly disgusting.

Tom's eyes darted quickly. No Daniel, no Mum. You said you'd come today, Mum; you said, you said . . . When she was there, as most days, he approached her with diffidence, shuffling his feet and not indicating welcome, but his heart rising in the acute and hidden pleasure of seeing her, delight disguised in nonchalance. Today, obeying the alternative orders for such occasions, he ran past the throng to the bus stop, attached himself vaguely to some unknown woman and child, and embarked safely for Herringbone Parade.

He never got home. There was a strange sensation about the place, more bustle than usual although there was no market. People gathering in the street, talking and gesturing; Mrs Beale in her shop doorway wearing a coat, smiling as she gripped Tom's arm. "'Lo there, Tom. Where's your shadow, then?' She meant Daniel, he supposed: Mrs Beale always exaggerated. Then she clamped her hand across her mouth. 'Oh, sorry, petal,' she said, looking up the road as she spoke, 'I forgot, he died, poor lad.'

'What?' said Tom, stupidly.

'Your Daniel. Yesterday, I heard. When I was at the doctor's. Oh look!'

Tom looked. There were four policemen moving slowly down the Parade, sweeping people before them with gentle insistence. A motley crowd of people, some of them carrying bags.

'We've all got to go, Tom,' Mrs Beale explained, her voice high with excitement. 'We've got to lock up and go. They've found a bomb left over from the war in those foundations they've been digging. All that time, fancy, lying there. Like being a kid again, this, being evacuated.'

'What did you say about Daniel?'

'Now don't you be worrying about him. Didn't your mum tell you? Come on, love, you'd best get a move on. You come along with us. I bet your mum's already gone, they started that end.' She put a possessive hand on his shoulder, then let go to adjust her coat, enjoying the situation.

Tom slid away and watched. The elderly of Herringbone Parade seemed to agree with Mrs Beale about the fun of the situation. There was cackling laughter, no sign of anxiety and a quite uncustomary obedience to the young constables led by an Inspector whom they addressed as 'Sir', and who seemed to fulfil the role of Pied Piper, leading them away as they emerged and followed, clutching clothes, and, sometimes, cats. The Inspector was enjoying himself too. He raised his megaphone.

'This street to the church hall in Ash Grove, please. All to the church hall. Transport is arriving for non-walkers. There is an unexploded bomb on the building site: I repeat, an unexploded bomb on the site.'

Tom wanted his mother, trod delicately between those moving in the opposite direction until his arm was grabbed yet again. 'Where you going, my lad?'

Born to respect this particular uniform, Tom

answered deferentially. 'My mum, in the chemist up there . . .'

'No she won't be, sonny. She'll have gone to the hall. We started down that end, you'll find her later, promise. Come along now.' So Tom pretended to come along, the bile of fear combining with the burn of panic and deliberate rebellion. At the end of the row of shops, he slipped like a fish from a net and ran into the service road. There were more people there, descending from flats into cars, darkness adding to an orderly confusion. He was not going to go anywhere, not he. Not with Mrs Beale and the kids from the Parade, not without Mum or, at worst, Daniel. Not Daniel: he had hardly comprehended what Mrs Beale had said, but knew it was true, and added to the fear was a leaden weight of guilt, pictures in his mind of Daniel moaning in a huddle. His fault, all his fault, a weight to carry with all this sense of betrayal, and where was Mum? Ducking cleverly from one back yard to the next, shying away from the dark bins, it became clear he would never reach his flat before being collected again, but he found, in the end, that fear of the herd subsumed the fears of these secret places and it was not so difficult to hide. He slid down behind one of the containers he had always envisaged as a coffin, pressed his face against the grubby cold plastic, and settled, heart thumping, to wait for the street to empty.

It was later than normal closing time, but the shops still blazed. Christmas. Decorations suitable for

Regent Street's gracious curve, where Helen sat on the top deck of a red bus, frozen by words. She sat with thirty others, kings of the castle surveying thronged pavements and top windows, contemptuous of crowds and the unaffordable riches of Garrards windows. Hamleys for toys, Aquascutum, Austin Reed for clothes, Liberty for luxuries. A million pieces of china glowed in the crescent while feathered angels twinkled above. I hate this consumer society, Hazel had said. This bloody fixation with shops and goodies. Hate it, although I concede it's an improvement on the war which formed me. And all my dead contemporaries. I was a boy at the end of it, with a son, lucky me. But himself and the wife met a runaway bus when they were out with the ration books, and they brought him home to me on a door. Chloroform, I used then to dull the pain because he was nearly dead and I had some there: ether I used after, for myself. Not for frolics, for oblivion: I've been seeking it ever since. One learns, of course, that there is no such thing. Not even after six years of ritualised conflict in a war and forty-five years' fighting ever since to make a society sick to death. So young you are, you don't know: despair's the real bit. You don't know: you only think you do, you seekers after truth. I'm sorry about your case. You'll find someone else.'

Write it down, she had told him fiercely. Write it down: you can write history, think, read, function. Take this as a start.

'Oh, I may, I may. This has been a shot in the arm, you see. There, Helen West, you've achieved something and people like you always have to be achieving things, do you not? You can never let life alone, can you? And I'll tell you something for free: that woman was murdered, probably deserved it. Not that it matters, you know, not really. Let the poor bastard be. And don't come to me with my raked up past, accusing me with questions. I don't care about your case.'

She looked down at the shops, up at the lights. Consumer society, the long after-effect of war, the antidote to peace. Do not strive so to achieve, he had said: nothing is worth so much. The woman is dead already. Only nurture what you have; learn to protect it.

A nihilist, for all his wit. She had not, after all, made a friend.

CHAPTER TEN

It was only because of Hazel that the short bulletin overheard on the radio at home struck any chord. Unexploded wartime bomb: East End evacuation, reminiscent of wars. Army disposal experts on hand to defuse what may be largest amount of explosive yet discovered. Helen did not really register the area concerned; the East End was a widely ranging definition, loosely used, but in the middle of pondering the events of her day, she also considered the quirkiness of a bomb which did not do its business but remained underground for almost half a century. Maybe a lazy bomb, like a Friday afternoon car, made by the night shift, designed never to work. A soft sort of news item which she ignored until she realised the implications, and even then the news was still bizarre enough to be faintly funny. It was a change from other bombs, Semtex, the IRA, Palestinians and other hell raisers who were not funny at all. And no one was hurt, yet. Like everyone else whose curiosity was faintly aroused, she had blind faith in the experts, some vague admiration for such cold bravery and a belief that everything would be rectified quietly. Revenge from the Luftwaffe at this stage in history seemed absurd, an incident which lacked any element of justice. Even the kind which was purely poetic.

The reality of the thing only impinged further when Bailey rang. Helen had not forgotten his part in making her look an idiot in the little matter of the criminal record of one Dr Hazel. If she and Bailey had joined forces for the night, he was in for some sharp words, to which, of course, he would reply with sour reason, leaving her even more afflicted with futility. Of course he had not been malevolent: Bailey was well able to define the meaning of malice, but it had no part in his makeup, indeed, it was his mildness which sometimes infuriated her, but all the same, the timing was spiteful. As if he had chosen to say, there, I have always known more than you after all; we have our resources, we persons in authority, run away and do your homework. Sharpen the instinct and then try and pretend the law is not really your pet blunt instrument designed to miss the target. Tell me something new, Helen was thinking. Tell me the law is not such an unwieldy instrument that we cannot catch a murderer by legitimate means and we have to stage a trial like a strange musical, with everyone's face painted whiter than white to mirror the cleanliness of their souls. According to Redwood, she would never be able to invite to the witness box anyone who had ever lived hard enough for tragedy, long enough to make mistakes, or fallible enough to command affection. She would look for another dry and blameless doctor. Tomorrow.

When Bailey rang, there was no time for the bone picking, no more suggestion of it than her saying, Oh, it's you, is it?, instead of some more instantly friendly response. She would have thrown off the resentful feeling as being both idiotic and unattractive after a minute or two of this, but news prevailed over the need for such effort.

'Going to be around here, all night, I reckon . . .'

'What?' Helen had not been listening.

'Herringbone Parade, everybody out. They're being very good-natured about it. This bomb, you must have heard. Apparently big enough to devastate a large area. All police hands stand by, etc. I'll probably run a soup kitchen.'

'You don't cover Herringbone Parade. Oh, I see. They need you. Like a riot.'

'No, not like a riot. Peace prevails. But everyone available has to stay. See you tomorrow.'

'Oh, wait a minute. Look out for the chemist, will you?'

Helen still could not confess she had seen him. Remembered those bleached blue eyes.

'Women and children first,' Bailey replied, and that was the end of the conversation. Only later, chewing a sandwich, the sort of sloppy self-provision he detested, dissecting the duplicate papers she had purloined from the office, spreading them out over the living-room floor, statement by statement, in an effort to work out a whole new strategy, did she begin to wonder what Bailey was doing. Looking inside Bailey's mind was a rare privilege, a door opened to an occasional glimpse, like a view into a dim house caught in passing as someone came out or in. Never fully open, not even in summer. Beside him, she could feel garrulous, obvious, rather too talkative, as open as a book. Ah, he had said once. I know why you talk. A disguise, darling: in the end you keep as much secret as I do. Sitting by the fire, Helen could see an element of truth in the observation. She listed the cast of characters in and around the Carlton case, stung by the words of the doctor; conscious of a nagging sensation of danger which had dogged her ever since the first page of the report, wondered long and hard about the motives of men and the dearth of her own instinct.

Many of the refugees had gone to relatives, hence half the Asian population of the square next to the Parade was notably absent from the church halls. Others had been warned not to come home from work, stayed with aunts, uncles and occasionally resentful friends. All had blind faith in the experts, and muttered knowledgeably about steam and explosive, everything perfectly all right by tomorrow, old son. In the centres along with the Red Cross and the St John Ambulance, there were camp beds and blankets, tea and sympathy, laughter and card games with the elderly who never encountered such *esprit de corps* in daily life. Mrs Beale's mother, whom daughter had nurtured crossly for a dozen years, felt herself hugged for the first time in a decade, by a fireman who had lifted her out of her house and called her darling. The thought of that, and the sharp memories of war, made her weep. Amid the organising at which he excelled, Bailey's eyes were everywhere. Five streets and one square had been cleared, or so they'd been told. There was no telling where all of them were. Of Kimberley Perry, and the son he had failed to recognise, there was no sign. In that fact alone there was no cause for concern. She had relatives, she had, albeit reluctantly, Duncan: she need not have come to any of the centres, but her absence, as outside the school gates, worried him. Neither was there any sign of the chemist, which was merely strange without being sinister. On the basis of his reputation, Caring Carlton was unlikely to miss such opportunity for being seen to be charitable to a fault. He could have dispensed the aspirins and the soup, whipped up for himself a round of applause. Ashgrove church hall was stinking warm, fuggy with gas heaters borrowed from a warehouse. The scene inside was reminiscent of an airport lounge full of anxious people subdued into patient behaviour by their belief in authority. Some of them slept. Some of them were a nuisance, talking away anxiety, glad of the holiday. Bailey was a man who seemed to carry his own heat, never more than half wearing a coat, and the atmosphere oppressed him. Then he saw Duncan, huddled into an anorak which had seen better days, walking up and down the rows, checking. Looking for Kimberley. He felt a prickle of alarm, like an itch he could not quite reach.

Herringbone Parade was detached from the world by tapes across each end. From behind, the fairy light crane glowed obscenely, dimmer against the floodlights. A quiet noise, Tom thought: the kind of noise which you could almost touch but without any kind of form to it, like a muttered conversation indicating something important, events out of ear-shot, slightly languid. He wanted to go towards this mysterious noise of industry, but dared not. To do so would be trouble, yells, shouts, pursuit. He wanted to be on top of the crane, looking down and eating sweets, warm above the world, watching. At first, he visualised the bomb as something the size of a hand grenade, something thrown, and could not understand the fuss he had witnessed. Any understanding at all was diminished by the creeping cold and the leg cramp, the sucking of the strap of the satchel, biting his nails, nothing made sense, and the sheer emptiness of the street, the absence of all the familiar sounds, made for disorientation. Like a film on telly about what would happen after the other kind of bomb. A frightening film which he was not supposed to watch, showing a street which might have been desert, nothing in it, like this one, but buildings and drifting wind. The thought struck him that this was the kind of bomb they meant: it had already fallen and apart from the formless noise, he might be the only person alive, anywhere. That particular, whimpering fear made him move. He had to know the worst. Then there was a shout from far beyond him. His eyes, luminous and enor-mous in the dark of the service road, caught sight of a uniformed figure, adjusting the tape which isolated the road and fluttered in the breeze. The figure disappeared. Tom knew then he was not the only one alive, and therefore felt justified in postponing decisions to remain where he was. He resumed his chewing of the satchel strap, sticky and dirty, like a dog worrying a bone. In a minute, just a little minute, he would go home. In the bottom of his pocket, he found the key he had taken illicitly that morning.

At the far end of the service road, a door opened quietly. Philip Carlton stood outside in the tiny yard beyond the hidden entrance to his dark dispensary, looked at the glow of the sky with satisfaction. He was dressed in an overall which was a duplicate of the one he wore in the shop, apart from the colour. In the black cotton of the tunic, buttoned to the neck in the style of Nehru, he was insignificant in the dark, giggling slightly. While Tom crouched back out of sight, dismayed by the emptiness of the street, Pip revelled in it, Lord of all he surveyed. He was higher than the crane, brighter than the stars, glowed with more power than the light which oozed out of the building site. They were digging in there, excavating in the vicinity of a bomb and he did not care. Pip was too young for wars, a man of peaceful memory, bar the screaming of families, the confederacy of women who had brought him to adulthood and ruled him ever after. They spoke of a war he did not know, relived it for his benefit with tales of hardship and ration books, told him how lucky he was, but he knew them all, these aunts, as liars, cheats, persons of manifest ugliness who had held him down for his daily bath, fondling him into screaming, laughing with the laughter which still rang in his ears when he fingered what they had fingered, the echoes of that laughter coming back in his own small giggle of relief. They would tickle, too, oh you like that, don't you, look at him laughing, so comic, the agony of tickling, the hideous humiliation of the whole body squirming out of control. Rearing and arching like a frightened horse, oh please, please, please sto-o-o-p. And now what was he, a man who had only learnt what a man does with a woman with the help of the chloroform, the private ether frolics which made it all possible, but had never yet made him quite understand what he had to know. Such as why the pleasure was great enough to be the cause of wars, the pivot of life in peace. Margaret, poor wrinkled Margaret had not been able to explain the puzzle, but Kimberley Perry, pliant, luscious as fruit would be better than the honeydew melon purloined from Mrs Beale, who had offered other services too. Kimberley would be better than that, or the lonely masturbation of the back room, or the poking of Margaret which had led only to that out of control humiliation which was so similar to the tickling. Kimberley would give him release and she would not even have to participate (oh, if only Margaret had kept still). The girl upstairs had only to remain sleeping, as beautiful and passive as she was, fed with dreams, like a corn-reared chicken, loving without demands. That would do nicely.

Pip had made a new mask. Not new, but old, a replica of the one he had used with Margaret in the days when she had cavorted around the room wearing nothing but. She had raised goose bumps of disgust on him until he breathed the vapour from the duster and at last his penis rose like a flag hoisted at sunrise. Stayed fit for action only as long as it would have taken to whistle three bars of the Last Post, measure itself in supine Margaret, and explode into anticlimax leaving him nothing more than that same helpless sensation of fatigue which had followed the tickles. As for her, she seemed pleased, even if she wept after, unsatisfied, but less than she might have wept if he had never tried at all. She meant to be kind, kept insisting. Until he could bear it no longer.

Pip carried the mask, a duster hidden from sight up one sleeve, and a hip flask. He had plucked the key to Kimberley's flat from the hook where he kept all spare keys to every cupboard and door of his whole domain, enabling him to move from the back dispensary to his own flat, up to Kim's, into the shop; such short journeys, such ease. He staggered slightly. In the piercing cold which threatened frost before dawn, the only visible part of him was the still sweet-smelling vapour that surrounded his mouth, and the bared teeth of his uncontrollable smile.

Upstairs, Kimberley Perry slept the sleep of peace. Knocking on her door had failed to rouse

her, as had the exodus of human life from every
habitation. Drugging Kimberley Perry was easy,
involving no poisons. Really, they had laughed,
Pip, Margaret and she, at this small vulnerability of
his assistant: one soporific cough drop and she
would sleep. He had watched the reaction yesterday,
the glazing of the eyes, the lack of co-ordination
in the lovely limbs, the growing fatigue which had
made her so muzzy today. Each cup of tea, another
capsule of night nurse. Nothing lethal: she would
wake tomorrow, fuzzy but unharmed, imagining
herself ill with flu, perhaps. He did not want to
harm her. What Pip had in mind for a winter afternoon, after she had left the shop to sleep and he had
shut up the doors to follow, was something he had
also had in mind to repeat. A very quiet impreg-
nation, a coupling with one of them conscious, not
too fast, but not slow either. But the bomb was a
blessing: Pip had never imagined there would be a
time quite as perfect as this, so free from prying
eyes. That part was sheer fluke and when the warnings came, he had been thinking fast, pretending to
obey, lock his doors and follow the crowd which
departed in bus and car. Then he had stopped and
smiled, retreated beyond his boxed-in door and
stayed almost still; playing, thinking, smiling, putting against his face the smooth silky touch of Kim's
stolen negligée, the brassières, knickers and slips as
yet untouched.

Kim Perry had woken once. To be sick in one
sleepy stagger to the lavatory, trailing back,

confused by the sounds from outside but not caring, shrugging out of the nylon blouse which made her sweat in bed, not quite remembering where she was. She called for Tom, thought she heard him reply. There had been a knock on the door which might have been someone bringing him home. Then she slept, half-dressed, her feet growing cold, her generous body half covered, one arm under her head, the other outflung in an attitude of open abandonment. Her hair was wild, spread on the pillow, and her half-open mouth suggested invitation. When Pip came into her room on his soft-shod feet, she looked like some picture he had seen, some Victorian depiction of a woman lost. He smiled, catching his breath, unable to stop smiling. Paused for a long moment, watching her.

Duncan Perry was following Bailey round the room, like a dog at a master's heels, three steps behind with a kind of urgent dignity, not quite plucking at his sleeve or tripping over his shoes, but almost. Bailey had noticed that Duncan smelled slightly of drink, not enough to cause offence or even be noticed by anyone less observant, and not enough to impair his performance. Only the residue of lunchtime or early evening when Duncan would seek the solace of a pub as soon as possible after darkness. Already they seemed to be swimming in the middle of the night, an impression extended by the dozing evacuees, but the hour was early, no more than seven in the evening, black as pitch. The winter solstice, mid December, drawing everyone away from the moon and into despair. Bailey no longer believed such thoughts were fanciful. His mouth was downturned, his spirits too: he wanted away from the irritation of Duncan's presence, a man with less to recommend him than many of the others who came looking, mildly worried, for their grannies.

'Sir,' Duncan was saying insistently, the way he did whenever Bailey paused. 'Sir, I can't find them anywhere. I thought she might come to me when they all had to get out: they had time to phone and make arrangements after all, why didn't she come to me?'

'Look, Duncan, she could have gone anywhere. Friends, relatives, anywhere. We don't know where half the people have gone.'

'She hasn't gone to her relatives. There's only her mother and she doesn't get on with her mother. She goes to her sister, but she didn't, I rang. I know. I want to go and see if she's still in the flat.'

'Don't be silly. We've moved all the uniform to the edge of the area. This bloody thing is for real. Why the hell would she stay?'

'I don't know,' Duncan mumbled.

'No, neither do I,' said Bailey briskly. 'I should go home. She may be trying to ring you. They won't let you anywhere near, so don't try. Go home, man, where you might actually be useful.'

Duncan gave him a look such as a man might give to one who had betrayed him, a look expressing plea and contempt.

'That's my woman you're talking about.'

'I wasn't talking about her, not as such.' Bailey's irritation took the form of pedantry. 'Listen, I'll go out there in a little while and look. Where's Tom?'

'That's what I've been saying. No Tom either. Tom would have been coming home from school . . .' The light of hope appeared in Duncan's eyes as he talked more to himself than his audience. 'Oh, I get it now. Kim would have gone to meet him, so they would never have got back into the flat, the timing . . . She must have gone off with someone else from the Parade. They would have been coming back just as everyone was leaving.' The anorak slipped further off one shoulder. 'I wish she'd phoned, though. Might've known I'd worry. Women. I phoned that bloody flat of hers, to make sure she'd gone, but there was no reply.' The smile which broke through on to his face illuminated his features into something human, even likeable. For one brief moment, seeing the mischief behind the smile, Bailey could understand why a woman might once have adored him.

'Well,' he said uncomfortably. 'Give her a chance. To get wherever she was going. She's probably been ringing you while you've been wasting your time here. Go on home. I'll check in with you later.'

There was a mocking, cheerful quality to Duncan's salute.

Bailey wondered as he often did about the true parameters of responsibility. Or, more precisely, whether he should have told his sergeant that Kimberley Perry had not met her son outside school: they had not gone home to be turned away from the street where they lived, herded to safety with the rest. The nagging unease which had afflicted him ever since he had waited outside the school gates, grew into alarm, and he wished he could trust Duncan enough to tell him he had made an assignation of sorts with his wife, without provoking hostility and suspicion. Duncan, if he thought at all, had long since concluded there was little enough reason to preserve his own safety; he was brave at the worst of times, and running into a street threatened by a bomb would not have troubled him in the slightest. Bravery. Duncan had always been content to act as the battering ram because he never foresaw that anything untoward might follow. Life was a joke to Duncan, the man who laughed until he cried, nothing between the extremes, but still he deserved to know something that might affect his family. There was no time for these considerations. Bailey knew he might regret what he said or did: he felt the prospect of regret like a breath on his face, and all the same, kept silent.

'Go home,' he repeated. 'I'm sure she's safe as houses.' And realised as he spoke what a bad analogy this was in the face of a ton of explosive poised to destroy whole streets. Duncan, who knew nothing of such subtleties, went, and in watching his progress out into the dark, Bailey's irritation was greater than his conscience. Duncan had nothing else to do with his evening. He could have stayed to help with the other volunteers: they needed people simply to talk, could have done with a troupe of entertainers. Thinking of one of Helen's opinions, Bailey smiled to himself. Not all policemen are born philanthropists, while those who are get it driven out of them.

'Scuse me, sir.' A voice at his elbow, literally from that level, the woman behind the voice tiny and bent, plucking his sleeve like a child, gentle but insistent. 'Scuse me, but where can I make a phone call? Got to tell my daughter . . .' He used his portable phone for her, watching the colour rise in the excitement of yet more novelty. Then, as an afterthought, he dialled Kimberley Perry's number. Bailey logged almost any phone number he had used in the last week into the bank of his memory, and pressed out the numbers without the slightest trouble. The line was engaged. He stood still, ignoring another plucking at the sleeve, his mind distracted but clinging to words. What did a man mean when he said there was no reply? Did he mean the phone rang without response, or did he mean the phone was engaged? What would a literal man like Duncan have meant? A man of Duncan's ilk would have meant what he said; no reply meant no reply, not any other sort of signal, however innocent. Bailey ran from the hall to see if Duncan might have delayed his departure, failed to start his damned car. The road outside was full, parked vans, well-meaning people, but no Duncan.

Kimberley Perry was not aware of having knocked the bedside phone to the floor in that last removal of her reluctant body back to bed, might not have cared if she had known. The shining eyes of Philip

Carlton, so at ease with the interior of this place he could function in the semi-dark, raked the half-covered body from one exposed foot to the tip of the head, failing to notice the cream receiver on the old carpet below within touching distance of two outstretched fingers. There was sufficient light in the room from the window: Kimberley liked daylight: she was overlooked by nothing other than the crane and her curtains were rarely drawn. In some token gesture to her mother's principles, there were nets, saving nothing from anyone's gaze, but obscuring her own view very slightly, as if she cared. Kimberley kept her place clean and that was all she did. Tom kept his room cluttered to make his home there. Philip Carlton looked at his assistant's tidy room, sighed for no reason at all. Play your cards right, girl, and I'll see you do better. Don't wake, let me look at you.

He pulled back the duvet, dropped it as if the material were red hot as she stirred, then opened and closed her mouth, silent words forming in sleep. Her head moved restlessly from one side to the other and with one abrupt heave, she turned on to her back, one arm protectively across her breast, fingers splayed over the nipple, an ineffective covering. Then she lay as still as before, but although he knew how much any human being will move in sleep, he had not bargained for the shock. Pip's store of scientific knowledge intervened into his mesmerised mind, posing questions and answers. Does a woman partially anaesthetised turn or toss? Had she neglected any of the tea her politeness had obliged her to drink? Could she, in the meantime, have been sick, discharging with the vomit that which made her sleep deeper? He removed himself to the door of the room, came back inside noisily, walking with the businesslike step of an innocent man in case she should wake. Kimberley remained as she was. A slight snore escaped from her perfectly receptive throat. He considered that.

All the impedimenta were in the same kind of white polythene bag they used for heavier prescriptions. So prosaic, he had always thought, to sniff the stuff of dreams from a household duster kept in a polythene bag. He withdrew a bottle labelled dry cleaning fluid from the bag, unscrewed the top and poured a little on to the folded duster which glowed bright in the dim room. There was no other colour apart from the reflected glory of the Christmas crane. Pip did not notice the tiny buzzing sound from the phone, tempted as he was to raise the chloroform cloth to his own nostrils. Instead he bore the cloth towards her face, kept it there for her to breathe. Then paused again, lost in a kind of wonder, put the cloth on the coverlet, squatted by the side of the bed and began to stroke her. A tentative stroking at first, his hand hovering above the warmth of her belly, the palm skimming skin, his fingertips amazed by the texture. Then he inserted his whole hand between her thighs, shocked at the heat of her, stunned into the awareness of where he was and why. A little more on to the cloth, held above her face, not touching such a perfect face with the cheeks as flushed as if she had come in from the cold. Deep sleep, my lovely, and quiet breathing.

Something in the scent afflicted her; the young body warned her sleeping brain not to ignore it, waking her in time for a brief but terrifying protest. The hand which had lain on one breast joined the other to push away the smell, fluttering weakly while her back arched in a spasm of disgust, her knees bent to raise themselves so that her feet were inches from her torso and trembling. Futile protest. Pip adjusted himself on the bed, held her firmly by the hair and kept the duster over her mouth.

'Shhhh, darling, shhhhh. Sweet sleep, sleep tight.' Strange murmurings emerged from his own throat, reminding him of Margaret, their various stores of non-consequential words and revolting endearments. Kim's automatic protest faded as abruptly as it had begun. One hand fell on the pillow alongside her hair: the other jerked back towards the floor. Her legs flopped open with the heels still close. Pip sniffed the cloth. With automatic care, he placed it on top of the polythene bag, felt the rising of manhood in his trousers, touched himself briefly, looked down at Kimberley and at himself with enormous pride. He thanked God there was time to contemplate the wonder of both. Silence and time. Sweet sleep, my lovely. There is more of this.

Tombo's legs were numb. The gravel embedded in the one knee that was slightly less frozen than the other was a relic of an earlier playground struggle which had not hurt at the time. The silence was even more profound: he felt he could lean out and cut the darkness with a knife. The comforting mumble of traffic on the distant Whitechapel Road was so much a part of his breathing as to offer nothing. Quite suddenly, out of the emptiness came the bravery of desperation, because all the things which had seemed to matter in the halcyon late afternoon did not matter now. Such as being caught. Such as being the only person left alive. Such as Mum clutching the bomb or having gone somewhere else, or Dad never coming to look for him. Piglets, bums, bastards, shit shit shit: There did not seem anything to lose. Tom expressed his contempt for his own immobile cowardice by standing straight and directing the stream of his urine on to the bin which had sheltered him. Amazing how far the flow travelled: he could have won any competition with that and impressed many eyes, yes he surely could, and the sound was amazing too, like a steaming waterfall which fell to earth with a hiss. No one came near. No one could bear to come near a performance like that, but apart from manifold other needs, he needed to do the big stuff too. Nothing urgent, but his own fastidious habits forbade him to relieve himself here. Even in the privacy of a clean toilet equipped with copious quantities of paper, he could not bear the evidence of his own crude digestion.

Well, go home then, silly billy. You've got a key, all you have to do is wait. If anyone else is alive, they'll phone, but I hope Uncle Pip is dead. Why anyone as remote and disliked as Uncle Pip should swim into his mind was beyond him. There were a few others whose disappearance from the scene would not have disturbed a night's sleep either: Pip was simply the one whose demise was most devoutly wished. Even against large Larry of the playground, Mrs Beale and the Parade mob, and quite a gang otherwise, Pip was foremost as an object of hate. Tombo wished he had been pissing on Pip, dismissed that thought as more than faintly shameful, the joke better than the doing, stood even straighter and emerged from his hiding place. He tried to shout, but the shout refused to arrive. He looked up at the crane and dimly remembered some story about a star in the east, Christmas legends watered down at school because of his Pakistani contemporaries' lack of interest. He wondered if he should behave like the three kings and follow the crane on to the building site which he and Daniel had so admired. He would have company there. He went into the middle of the service road instead and tried to whistle in the dim hope that something, even a dog, would emerge and claim him. There was a cat, Mrs Kennel's mangy moggy, which emerged in a distinct black and white streak, howling in abandonment. For the first time in their few encounters, Tom knew what the cat meant and wanted to embrace it. She sat for a moment, distant from him, level with his own house, gesturing contempt from forty paces, and, using her as his guide, he walked towards home. The satchel with the frayed strap was carried across his chest, red satchel, plain as a pikestaff, but nobody saw. At both ends of the road, tapes flickered neon yellow. Not all of the windows were dark: some rooms had been left lit. Tom was grateful for the lights: he had not known they were there or he might have looked sooner for that stray comfort, but he knew the rooms behind those benign electric eyes were as empty as his pockets. The steps he took were solid and slow: he felt for the handrail announcing the stairs to the flat, paused to kick a stone under his foot. The flat was dark as pitch, but, from indoors, he imagined he could see the flickering light of a torch.

CHAPTER ELEVEN

Helen was aware of becoming a nuisance, and did not care. The operation scar gave small stabs of recrimination for being ignored, nothing important. She had decided on the way across the city that being a nuisance, even being branded 'interfering cow', was better than the guilt which always attended indifference and felt like cowardice. Bailey's caution was another matter: he would often advocate doing nothing; if in doubt, do not buy, or move: impetuosity makes a good target for a sniper. You do not always achieve much by your addiction to movement. But in movement was comfort; in self-restraint, none.

It was not, of course, quite as unpremeditated as that. She had phoned the number given on the news, found out where some of the refugees from Herringbone Parade might possibly be and in another injudicious call where she had been content for once, to pose as Mrs Bailey, gained some clue from a sergeant as to Bailey's whereabouts. He was with the men, three St John Ambulance, two of his own, loading tins of soup from a van into the kitchen of a new community hall ugly enough for this patched part of the world. Helen slung her bag across her chest and joined the queue, so inconspicuous that Bailey had passed her a box before he noticed. He sighed in exasperation, relieved her of the burden, and walked into the hall without a word. She followed him.

'Anything I can do?' A careless invitation with a shrug of the shoulders. Take it or leave it.

'Probably. Quite a few things other than carrying heavy stuff three weeks after your operation. Why did you come?'

'I don't know. What a pointless question. Because it was Herringbone Parade. Because you were here. Coincidentally, because of that damn chemist and doctor talking about war. Is this the only shelter?' She was looking round, alert and interested. He usually responded better if she was very casual and she liked to pretend he could be fooled.

'Nope, just the largest. Most of them have gone to relatives. No sign of the chemist. Or his assistant or her son.'

'And the bomb?'

'Very dangerous indeed, possibly the biggest ever. Crazy, after forty-five years. Area isolated, no patrol cars, no uniform, no nothing at the moment. I'd like to go and look for Kimberley Perry. It doesn't make sense.' He was talking half to himself and Helen recognised the symptoms. Signs of unease, that reserve before action she so loathed but still admired. Fretful signs of involvement in a Bailey more familiar than the manager he had become.

'What doesn't make sense?'

'Kimberley Perry. She didn't answer her phone to Duncan soon after they'd all been herded out. When I tried half an hour ago, the phone was engaged.'

'What will you do?'

'Go and look, as soon as I'm allowed. Got to wait: I'm not in charge. In a minute or two.'

'No,' said Helen. 'You will not, do you hear me? You'll do no such thing.'

'Helen . . .'

'No. You'd make a lovely corpse, but no, not that kind of corpse. All smashed up. Don't go.'

'I'll think about it. I can't immediately. Listen, if you want to be useful, go on. The practical angles are all covered here, enough food, etcetera. Go and talk to some of these old ones. Tell them their cats and dogs are going to be all right. That's what we need, someone to chat, reassure. Lie as much as you like.'

'Don't go.'

'We'll see.'

There was a clear division of labour then. Men did the practical things, providing beds, blankets and food; women offered the succour. No one was dying. There was a sense in the hall of absolute safety while Helen, the easy talker, joined the women and did as she was told. Warmth seeped in and out of old bones and into the air. Once in a while, she stepped out into the cold in order to remember what cold was and to check, like an anxious hen, for Bailey. Heard with her sharp ears what the evacuees were not supposed to hear. About steam being used on a bomb, and no one, but no one being allowed to move.

Pip was aware of a faint hissing sound from outside. Half an ear registering some unfamiliar sound which was neither threatening nor any more alien then the kettle boiling in the dispensary for yet another cup of tea. His hands were still playing and he had no sense of time. Winter nights stretched from the middle of the afternoon until the morning beyond, a time of almost unbroachable darkness, making all thought of time irrelevant. Nothing moved but the bosom of his beloved, rising and falling, insensitive to his touch as he stroked her nipples and felt them harden, a sensation beneath his hands which made him laugh. So strange, so shaming: a woman would remain on heat even in the grave. This part of them never died, and something in this made him think of her as animal. So different from the wizened, black-dressed mother he had buried with such relief, hoping the interment was a route to freedom. Sweet dreams and quiet breathing, and then, dear God, she moved again. Pip was so shocked this time at Kimberley's violent stirring, he did not know for a moment whether what lay before him was indeed a sleeping beauty or a corpse. He leapt up from his knees where he had been praying by the bed, and swore softly and obscenely in a manner which would have made his mother faint. Then he seized the duster in a trembling hand, draped it over the wire mask, placed the whole ensemble over Kim's

237

head, and held it there while he dripped more chloroform from the bottle. She had stopped moving before these manoeuvres were complete; the heave had been no more than an aberration, nothing real; no indication of intolerance. After a minute or two, Pip removed the mask and placed it on the floor. His trembling ceased and his smiling resumed. He began to stroke her hair, crooning to himself, stopped for a moment and raised the yellow duster to his face. He had come to love this perfume, breathed deep, fondled himself inside the unzipped trousers, gasped. A roaring in his ears, now, now, now. This is the time to discover. Now. Oh, my love.

Tom had intended to let himself into the flat with as much noise as possible, whistling, singing and banging to make himself heard, ensuring that he would be greeted if there was anyone there, detected if there was anyone nearby, and, in any event, make himself bold by striking back at the weird silence. But the stillness had defeated him: more complete a silence than he had ever known, even with the hissing; an awesome stillness which demanded a respect which he had found himself unable to defy with his clattering footsteps. Instead he had tiptoed up the steps, holding his breath, and stood on the balconette under the light of the crane. He paused to see what he could see in the building site and found there was nothing but the glow, a shh-ing sound, the generator which was always alive. There were no voices, no indication of human life, as if someone had left the machinery and run away. Tom turned from the light in disappointment, put the key in the lock and entered his own house like a careful thief. Put his satchel down on the kitchen floor, stood for a minute, feeling foolish. The flat was small: kitchen merged into living-room, their own rooms fanning away. Both bedroom doors were open. Mummy's white overall glowed on the sofa, visible in the light from the Parade which let him see since his eyes, used to the greater dark, adjusted easily.

He knew immediately there was someone there, someone alien and dangerous. The freezing of his movements was temporary: a great stirring of anger displaced fear as he stepped towards Mum's bed-room, following the sound, then stopped at the door, paralysed.

A tableau of two figures, one obscuring the other. Tom knew his mother lying on the bed: who else would lie on that bed? No one, except, hopefully his father. But the man leaning over the bed was not his father. Daddy was big, running to flab. These bare buttocks, with trousers obscenely lowered, were small and neat, the lights from the crane colouring them pink in the curves, unearthly blue in the hollows, and the black clothes glimpsed above the skin were never his father's clothes. A duster was on the floor and next to it was his metal hat, the one he had left in Dad's car. A little dirty man touching his mother, a sound of heavy, grunting breathing which filled him so full of disgust he wanted to retch. With a howl of rage, Tom launched himself forward in one massive leap into the room. He picked up the metal hat and struck blindly towards the back of the frightful head: he wanted to kick, bite and scratch at the same time, did not know he was yelling, 'You-you-you bastard, bastard, bastard . . .' struggling for the memory of every dirty word he had ever heard. The hat was heavier, infinitely more solid than he remembered: the metal was smoother, the rim sharper, so that in between blows he was aware of the unfamiliarity. Then the man turned, the eyes so intense, Tom could not meet them, sparkling eyes, hateful Pip, wafting the same smells he had known from the other cold night when he had trespassed downstairs. A smell of glue, deodorised sweat, and a sweet, sweet smell which was clamped over his mouth while his muffled shouting changed to desperation and his arms clawed the skin of the man's back. 'Daddy, Daddy, Mummy, Mummy . . .' His skin was burning, his face twisting and turning: he was on the bed, half off the bed, grasping at flesh and cotton, his heels drumming without sound.

'Daddy, Daddy, Dad . . .' And then, no shouting.

It was so easy.

Pip remained, holding the duster with liquid trickling between his fingers, pressing gently. C'mon, lad, c'mon, don't really want to hurt, don't want to hurt anyone. Please, please. The rage, the bitter disappointment, died quickly as he watched, silent and fascinated as one small fist clenched and unclenched against the dark carpet, finally remaining open with the fingers spread. Alongside that pale hand lay the cream receiver for the telephone. True to his meticulous self, begging time before making decisions, Pip replaced the receiver on to the cradle. Immediately, the phone rang and the eyes, Kim's eyes from the white pillow of the bed, opened wide. Pip ducked below the level of her sight, a gesture of sudden shame. The eyes widened further in puzzlement, then, slowly, closed.

Hot bath, warm bed, hot bath, warm bed, both of these dreams. The phone plucked in one hand, two rings, then silence. Duncan came to, looking at his watch, dismayed to find he had snoozed at all, but grumpy to see he had only snoozed for so short a time. Shouldn't have had the whisky. Not a tumblerful anyway, followed by another, without an ounce of grace to the whole proceeding. Get bottle out of pocket: open and pour straight into something which resembled a tooth mug, drink without aid of H_2O in the same way another might drink the water after a run, without any sensation of taste. Half awake now, he repeated the dose. A small dribble of whisky hit his chin: the slow drip on to his shirt made him feel ashamed. Trying to shake away the dream, he dialled Kim's number. Engaged. Duncan went into his bathroom, and saw with the acuteness of vision which was not a blessing, what a mess he was. It was salutary to see his own image in a glass so dirty. The spots on the glass horrified him more than the reflection; the surface was covered with what might have been smashed insect, white drops for toothpaste, grey bits for shaving foam, little speckles of something which may have been blood, the whole effect like a fly-blown windscreen. He had put out his hand, felt the surface of the mirror, felt through his fingertips how it was encrusted. No wonder, then, she did not want him, clean Kim.

Back in the living-room, suddenly aware of the musty smell, he dialled her number again. Remembered what he had dreamt; that hideous vision of his wife in the arms of another man. Forgot his coat, forgot being over the limit and fitter to walk than drive. Remembered the dream and the sound of the dialling tone. Ran.

Into the car with the still bent fender and the engine which roared. Not a single logical thought in his head, the man who was used by others to smash down doors, motivated by a delayed reaction to being stopped, a bad dream and a nascent rebellion. Someone had been lying to him, Bailey, Kimberley, something about that silly hat and a succession of days and nights like the party where he had existed only to be fooled and humiliated. Forbidden the touch of any woman. A certain cunning as well as the memory of bombs and officialdom made him slow down. At midnight, the tall buildings of the commercial city were empty, deep glass façades blank to everything but lamps and headlights, no sign of midnight oil, nothing stirring but hidden security guards drowsing behind doors, and in the distance, one, two, three cranes, lit for Christmas, bowing at the moon.

Beyond the confines of the city, where the ambience of prosperity ended, he saw the first yellow tape across the road. Drove through, snapping the tape, heard a voice yell and saw a fist raised, drove further. Got out and ran again.

Only when he ran this time, blindly in the direction of the Parade and feeling his pockets as he went, did he see in his mind's eye the bedside table where all useful but never used items lingered for months. He stopped, cursed, ran on. He had forgotten to bring the vital key to Kim's flat.

There was a strange law of diminishing returns in talking to people this late at night. Like a priest giving a winter sermon in the church Helen remembered as a child, heated with a stove in the centre so that the congregation was ever thickest in the middle, his voice and message no competition for warmth; everyone wanting to be home, but quite content to postpone movement, complainers subdued into silence long since. There was that dormitory air, like a hospital ward. Helen was aware she had assisted just a little in the pacification process, and felt that for what it was, a dull task, helpful rather than vital. Like most of her daily tasks. She, too, wanted to go home. Not because her store of philanthropy was wearing thin, but because she was redundant. She turned to find Bailey. An old woman called Mrs Beale, who was telling her all about previous occupants of Herringbone Parade and its environs, was enough to distract her attention. Somehow gossip was better if you did not know any of the protagonists and there was no guilt in the listening.

'There was the Carlton sisters of course. Lived next door to me. He died in the war, and the three of 'em joined up under one roof. Big mistake if you ask me. All them women and one little lad. Didn't seem to do him no harm, though. A good boy that, very good. Still is. Got the chemist's shop now, after his ma died . . .'

'The chemist's shop in the Parade? Must have been a clever boy, then. Where else did he work?'

'Yes. Clever boy. His ma said she wasn't going to have him a wastrel, brought him up nice, she did. He went to the Polytechnic, then he worked in a big chemist's at Limehouse for years. Funny, he married so late. Must be forty-five, still looks a lad. She put paid to the girlfriends, though, his mother, she was like that. And he couldn't go far: she'd have him back, what with her being so poorly and everything. Mind, there was some said she was never as ill as all that. And then when she's gone, he goes and marries, just like that. Another one the same. Bossy, that Margaret, and always at the doctor's. Sort of woman drives a man to it, if you see what I mean.'

'Drives them to what?'

'Oh, I don't know. Things. Funny man, Pip Carlton. I could have told them coppers a thing or two lately, only they didn't ask. Like how he's always fiddling in his back room. Doesn't need to do that. And what does he do with all that stuff he gets back?'

'Sorry, what stuff?'

'Stuff we return. People my age who look after other people. Mr Ahmed, they're nice these darkies really, they look after their own. Anything you've got left, always bring it back, Pip says. Specially the worst stuff. He must have enough in there to poison the whole district.' She laughed, looked round at her sleeping neighbours, her eyes narrowing. Tiredness and spite. 'Mind some of them would be better off . . .'

Helen crossed the arms of old Mrs Beale, so that she sat like a pyramid, feet firmly planted, a blanket on her knees, the edifice narrowing to a small and pointed head bedecked with regulation grey curls. The product of Sylvie's in the Parade, perhaps, half price to pensioners on Thursdays only. A fund of knowledge, Sylvie's, specially on Thursdays; the kind of knowledge which only the faintly malicious or the idle found time to accumulate. Helen was angry now. The curiosity, her conviction about the Carlton case was no longer dimmed by Hazel's defeatism, the criticisms of the day, the accusations of interference, restlessness, of being so bent on achievement she missed some vital point. Were common sense and energy really in such short supply she could afford to stay still and would it really have been absurd for someone in the local police to sit in the local hairdresser for a while? Women would make so much better detectives for local crime. Better chemists, better neighbours, better at just about everything. On such chauvinistic, irritated thoughts, she looked again for Bailey. Gone without word or whisper.

On second thoughts, she added to herself, men are better at subterfuge and avoiding embarrassment. Also regard themselves as better at the rough stuff. Little women don't interfere. She shut her eyes and tried to imagine Herringbone Parade in darkness. A comprehensive street, a good street, a tribute to life where everyone watched everyone else without watching for them, as secretive as any neighbourhood with the city on the doorstep. She had known the modern sham of real villages, liked that less. Crime, like blindness, was not a matter of diet or environment. Go on, then, Bailey, like a dog off a leash, Go on. Be a policeman, but I wish you could have let me go with you.

Bailey thought of nothing when he turned his back on the community hall, except a vague thought as he got in a car about how little community halls had to do with communities. They replaced churches, he supposed, and had little to do with those either. His mother, older than Mrs Beale to whom he had spoken at such length long before Helen arrived, had no truck with churches. She had pre-empted social workers in the East End, a woman of such conspicuous virtue she had driven her neighbours mad with kindness and earned their pity for having a husband who was always in the pub.

Mothers. Bailey could recall the power of mother, especially an East End mother. Mother and smother worked the same, post-war women with more than half their men lost to some sodding battle they did not understand, left with their infants, legitimate or otherwise. Mrs Carlton and her two sisters. He wondered about Pip Carlton, the caring chemist, such a lad, such a jolly lad, Mrs Beale had said, you should have seen him. Always the scientist, playing with stink bombs even as a boy, always collecting old muck and going on about history and being a doctor. Nothing alters, you know. People are like time. They are time. But he never got to be a doctor. Something happened, Mum was ill. He could have got a grant. Tell me, Mr Policeman Bailey, what did he do with all those drugs he kept?

I don't know, Bailey had said with his best humility, thinking as he drove how odd it was he was only let near the scene of this bomb because of reports of some lone lunatic racing the streets. A man who had missed a bus: such things drove people mad in central London, but this one had left a car and, what's more, he had known who it was. You will let me in there, he had wanted to say, to look for this lone man, whom I think I know, although I will not say so, but you would not allow me to when I wanted to check if everyone was out. Strange priorities, better say nothing. If only I could act on instinct and be furious at the imposition of other people's rules, other people's orders which I have been taught to respect even when they are ludicrous. I might have an ounce of Helen's anxiety, her fury with the formalities of law which get in the way of what is perfectly obvious. Something I seem to have lost, and I lecture her so she might lose it too. She knew she had a murderer: I did not. She knew what Mrs Beale knew; something odd about that boy. I have been in these streets for forty years, and I did not. If I have the instinct, I no longer trust it.

He had known when he held Daniel Maley in his arms that the man was not only dying, but dying murdered. It had awoken interest, but he had not moved mountains to pursue his belief. Bailey was glad he wasn't a woman. No man in his right mind would ever wish to be a woman apart from a moment like this when he would have liked their instincts, their sheer, bloody-minded scent for blood.

But he was trusting to instinct now, looking for whoever it was who had abandoned his car and run through the lines. Maverick Duncan, inevitably going in the same direction as he was going himself which somehow lessened the need for speed. Say what one would about Duncan, he was good at beating down doors. And whatever else was inevitable about Duncan, if he got there first, he would not understand.

For the first time in a long time, Duncan was afraid. If he had been pursued in the last two hundred yards since he lost the car, he was not aware of it, nor did he care, but he cared about the silence which was terrifying. Streets were never silent like this; the dreadful stillness of desertion which allowed him to hear his own thumping breath. At the far end of the Parade he almost stopped, thought the hissing sound which filled his ears was a sound· from inside his own head, his heart on the verge of explosion. Which end . . . where? He became confused: there was nothing, no one. He wanted no interference, but when Bailey's car caught him in the lights and he heard that despised voice of authority, cool where he was hot, the savagery of his expression softened. The phone, he began to say, the bloody phone . . .

'Yes, I know. Looks like someone at home.'

'You knew? Why didn't you do something, you cunt?'

He sprinted up the steps to Kim's door, rattled the handle, grunting with frustration. Glanced grimly at Bailey, their faces weird in the light, their voices raised against the hissing steam in the cavern beyond.

'Do you have a key?' Bailey shouted. Duncan patted his pockets, shook his head, sizing the door with his eyes. There was a plant, dead, by the side: Bailey picked up the pot and smashed the glass in the door neatly, put his hand inside for the latch, as couth as a burglar. A fragment of glass grazed the back of his hand, the brief pain a reminder. Duncan charged indoors, shouting, Kim, Kim, Kim. Bailey followed delicately.

Kimberley Perry lay in the bed, sleeping. Both men stood at the door of the room, looking at her half in awe, half exasperation. She lay curled, demurely covered, her breathing noisy, her head to one side and her hands beneath the pillow like a depiction of innocence. 'Kim, wake up,' Duncan shouted. Relief was turning to anger, concern curdling the face of such peace. 'I'll bloody wake her . . . What the hell does she think she's doing?'

'No. Wait.' Something in the way she lay arrested Bailey: something in the smell of the room with the windows firmly closed. Something he had read or heard somewhere of how Margaret Carlton had been found without being photographed, with her head on one side, body curled like a foetus. Surely women did not copy each other in sleep as in other things: the peace was deceptive. 'Wait,' he said, 'don't touch.'

'Wake up, Kim,' Duncan shouted, obedient all the same. Bailey turned on the bedside light, saw the phone in the cradle, out of arm's reach from the bed; noticed a faint red mark on her forehead. The sickly smell, sweet and cloying, was denser nearer the floor and pillow.

'She's just asleep!' Duncan was fuming, relief still finding outlet in anger. 'She's bloody irresponsible, that's what she is. What's she done with Tom? And where's that fucking chemist who's supposed to be so good to them all the time? Kim, Kim . . .' He shook her shoulder, pulled down the cover, shielding his wife from Bailey's gaze.

'Get her up gently, Duncan,' Bailey said quietly. He was thinking fast. Such a deep sleep and unquiet breathing: she could not naturally have slept so long. They could not get a doctor in here with men steaming explosive from a bomb within a hundred yards: they must treat as they found. Rely on instinct. Phone Helen, get the number of that old doctor, ask what you should do with chloroform overdose. Quick quick. Slowly, slowly, Kimberley Perry responded to the shakings, surfaced into the light of the room, the sixty-watt bulb beneath the cheap shade, the colours from the window. Her eyes focused reluctantly, the pupils tiny: her mouth rounded to release a scream and she was suddenly, violently sick.

'Christ. Jesus H. Christ. Where's Tom, where's Tom?' The first words, noises rather, the sense slurred.

'All right, all right,' Duncan murmured, arms round her shoulders, immune to the coloured mess now on the pillow, the greenish skin, the wild eyes. 'He's safe somewhere, don't worry.'

'No,' she was mumbling. 'He was here. I saw. Asleep, on the floor. God, I feel sick.'

'You've been dreaming, sweetheart. Only dreaming. What the hell did you take?' Duncan's voice became harsh. 'You fucking whore.' On one of her rounded thighs, carelessly revealed as she struggled upright, he could see a fantail of fingerprints. 'What you been taking, you silly cow, and while you were at it, who took you?'

She looked at him, her eyes widening in horror, looked at the direction of his gaze, uttered a small cry subdued in a rising tide of fresh nausea, looked at Bailey in plea. 'Sir, Mr . . .' He was crouched, feeling the surface of the nylon carpet with delicate fingertips. Clinging to the tough surface were

251

yellow threads, fluff, and, in spots, a stickiness he knew to be blood, that viscous texture horribly familiar. Far beneath the bed, in an otherwise tidy room, he could see a child's training shoe, adorned with dim red flashes on the side.

'Tom was here all right,' Bailey said slowly. 'His satchel's in the kitchen. He was here, with someone else. Duncan, you have to get her to hospital. Now.'

'It was that fucking chemist, wasn't it? Him, he did this, didn't he? He fucking did. You slope off to be with your fucking boyfriend. Where is he, where is the bastard?'

'Duncan, can it. You've got to get her to hospital . . .'

Kim began to cry, a retching cry, graceless in agony. Something terrible, a threat, a touch of clammy hands was crowding at her memory, making her whimper, wanting touch, but despising it.

'She can walk,' Duncan said brutally, relinquishing his hold on her like an abandoned toy. 'If she can go to bed with him, she can walk. I got things to do. I'll get that bastard.'

'There's the bomb. First things first. You're a sod, Duncan.'

Bailey was aware that his voice was high, his temper dangerous and all his diplomacy gone.

'Screw the bomb,' said Duncan. 'It's a con. Get out of my way.'

The rain had begun in earnest. An icy rain which

fell in soft, cold sheets, straight lines of moisture unmoved by wind. Pip could not distinguish between what was rain on his face and what was tears, but the latter flowed with the same relentless ease, salty in his mouth, dribbling down his chin: tears flowing without sobbing or heaving, well behaved, very silent tears. Symptoms of despair, and more, the sadness of loss. Never to plant his seed without disgust, never know what it was like to be carried beyond himself on a tide of passion. Never, oh, my love; only the same feeling of rage when he struck Tom as the rage he had felt when Margaret had said, Shut the window please, it's cold in here.

'You all right, Tombo?'

There was silence. Oh Christ, such silence with the rain falling over them both. Tom and he were covered in a plastic sheet, the boy on his lap, sleeping trustfully, a sensation of warmth against Pip's chest he felt he almost enjoyed. Perhaps this would have been some substitute, a child of his own. Pip looked down at Tom's dark, wet head with something approaching affection. Something in him could never have liked any child, particularly this skinny little boy, a nervous, pansyish creature who reminded him of himself. A fretful boy who either asked too many questions or remained speechless, his whole attitude one of profound suspicion. The creation of such a large and brutish father, the kind of man women loved. Hateful, both of them, but for now, the boy was warm, and in his own arms, almost loving.

'I hope I didn't give you too much,' Pip murmured to no one. In his mind's eye was the bottle: impossible to say how much was too much: you could only tell when they stopped breathing and Tom had not stopped breathing. He presumed Daniel had stopped breathing on thrice the daily dose of pyseptone, bullet pills of poison only to be swallowed by someone made unwary by a big, heavy blow. Mother had stopped breathing and Margaret; Tom did not. As if it mattered, but it did. The plan was clearly for Tom to stop breathing, but preferably not with some lethal overdose in his frenetic bloodstream.

'You all right, Tom, boy?' He said it louder. The silence was reassuring, but curiously dissatisfying. He shook the boy. Small feet, one without a shoe, looked sad as they protruded from beneath the blanket of clear plastic grabbed from the back dispensary as they left. Pip did a last mental check, wishing the tears were less blinding than the rain.

'Right. Kim never saw anything. Asleep. Will wake up feeling sick. Too much Night Nurse in her tea, doubt they'll test blood, you can always depend on ignorance. They'll only find alcohol. All signs, duster, white poly bag, removed into bin. Through dispensary, no muddy feet. Careful, careful. Not more than a few milligrammes of stuff in this boy either, not by the time they find him in the morning or whenever this stupid bomb business is over. Meanwhile, everyone, this is what happened. Little Tom ran away over the building site because he is frightened of crowds, never was a kid who could stand crowds, couldn't even take a Christmas party, Mrs Beale told me. Fell into one of the holes. An accident. Like all of this, really. Not my fault. Little bastard; you shouldn't have come home, you hear? You shouldn't . . .'

Pip felt in his pocket. On their way downstairs, gasping under Tom's weight, he had collected some of the worst stuff from his back room. Methadone, a little morphine. One vague plan was to give some to the boy, another half-formed plan to chuck it away in the same way he could hide the child. This plan was messier. Logical plans always avoided mess.

They were sitting below the hoardings at one end of the building site which both of them had explored, one with feet, the other with eyes, fascinated in different ways by the subterranean domain of mud which made for this strange series of vaults below the level of the earth. Pip remembered hating Tom most when Tom had begun excavating for Australia, from the yard. Not because of his proximity to the back dispensary, which Tom would find anyway, but for the similarity with something he had done himself. People like Tom and he were always excavating for a hiding place and it had always seemed as if the builders were doing no more than the same. Useful, said Pip to himself, trying to harden his own features, breathe hard, think hard. Concentrate, to survive. And this little one will go in one of those pits. Only a small fall into one of those dark graves called foundations. I'm sorry, boy.

The hissing of the steam persisted fifty yards away. Pip could not guess if the sound itself had increased or if they were simply closer to the awning erected against the rain. Arc lights and vehicles shrouded the sound like Quatermass and the Pit. Men busy in an island of light, leaving all the rest a pool of darkness, the noise fit to mask all footsteps over the mud. Move soon: put this boy down, he won't sleep for ever even with these cuts on the head, inflicted in revenge with the smooth rim of the anaesthetic mask. Soon. Any minute now. If only the child were not so warm: if only he could stop crying. Never, never, never. Oh, my love.

CHAPTER TWELVE

'Do not deliver an emetic if there is any chance of chloroform. She'll be nauseous anyway. If she's conscious, nothing but air; sit upright, keep airways open. Avoid excitement. If young and healthy, she's already past the risk of heart failure. Just let her gulp oxygen. Liquids, fruit juice if she can take it.' Hazel paused for breath, listened.

'Methadone? Narcan, intravenously. A lot. Not a stomach pump, for God's sake. Plenty of narcan, always brings them round.'

'Thank you,' said Helen hesitantly. Then, 'Are you all right?' Dr Hazel had poured acid on both their endeavours, but she never relinquished a friendship easily. She wondered as she spoke why she had mentioned methadone, as if the thought of Daniel Maley had provoked it.

'Am I all right? A greatly overused query, but yes. Phone any time you need. A bomb, you say? And not left by the Irish? We like a good bomb.'

'You need a new job.'

'Find me one, then.'

'I shall.'

Another phone call. Bailey's voice with a coughing in the background.

'Helen, can you come here, now? They'll let you through: I said you were a nurse. Only I can't really expect anyone else to volunteer. If you see what I mean, not fair, only . . .'

'Yes. Yes of course.'

'And you know·the way.'

'Do I?'

'Yes of course you do. You left a bag full of things from that chemist's shop. In the kitchen, a few days since. I recognised the labels.'

She might have known her own inability to keep a secret and the thought of his quiet but unfailing observation made her smile. The distance was barely three-quarters of a mile, the sensation of movement and cold faintly enjoyable. The car made Helen feel slower, a person carried without volition with all her reflections as varied and vivid as the lights from the crane which no longer promised celebration. There were visions of dancing hospital beds, masks, small, fleeing boys and the inconsequential thought of how infrequent were the opportunities in life for someone like herself to be brave. Bravery was the stuff of dreams, the lot of police officers and soldiers. Her few acts of courage seemed to have been merely accidental and this was no exception. Someone removed a tape from across the road and waved her on like royalty, making her feel foolish as well as wishing that all driving were as easy as this. Queen of the road: the only thing moving in half a square mile.

Finding the right flat in Herringbone Parade posed no problem since the environs of the place were etched in her mind. She passed the chemist's and jolted to a halt. The window in Carlton's Caring Chemist was smashed, leaving a jagged hole, eloquently violent. She tried to ignore that, stopped in the road beyond where the dark hissing made her shiver, mounted the steps towards where the chemist's balcony fitted snugly against that of its neighbour. Such cosy passage from one to the other: no one had thought of that. There was suddenly no reason for speed: she paused again for a backward look at the building site; found the size and depth of the foundations faintly shocking. To live here must be like living next to a mine. Such large excavations, sites for future houses, looking like graves for giants. The rain glistened in the depths: the contours of the ground were uneven: all of it seemed to move with strange shadow and she believed she could see figures. Only here did this hidden and massive quantity of explosive become real, like a primeval monster about to rise. Helen shivered, and went through the door left open by Bailey.

He stood in a drab kitchen where every dish was clean, every scuffed surface polished beneath the unsympathetic strip light of the ceiling. On the lino floor there was a small, sinister patch of blood. Bailey's skin looked yellow.

'Stay with her, will you? Tell her I've gone to find Tom.'

'I wish you'd explain. The son? Here?'

'Yes, I'm sure he was. Also the chemist. You were right about him, I think, but this is no time for apologies. One of them's been cut, don't know which. Worse still, Duncan's gone in pursuit.'

'Oh. Duncan the destroyer of evidence.'

Bailey looked towards the bedroom. 'If only that were all.' He disappeared down the steps, soundless in the rubber-soled shoes.

'Bailey!' she shouted after him, her voice lost in the rain. 'The building site . . . Careful. Look at the shop, window broken . . .'

He might not have heard. She sounded like a fishwife in the silence: she felt absurdly like a woman leaning from a tenement window and shouting at the kids to bring home fags.

Kimberley Perry looked at the new visitor with the sourness of anxiety.

'Hallo.'

'Hallo.'

'He said you weren't a nurse, but you'd know what to do. Shoot me, I would. I don't know what I've done or what the fuck's happened. I don't know why I feel like shit, and I'm a bloody pharmacist. What the hell did I take? Tell me. Please. Nothing much more than a dozen bloody cups of tea. Where's Tom? He's all right, isn't he, and who are you anyway?'

'His friend. Bailey's, I mean. I don't suppose he told you much.'

'Not exactly. Not much, not anything.'

'He's like that. Aren't they all? They think we're stupid.'

Slowly, reluctantly, they smiled at each other. Even in this state of sick distress, Helen thought Kimberley Perry looked strangely magnificent, like a vision of some *déshabillé* dancer from the Folies Bergère in the days when it was fashion to be large. She had been making a half-hearted attempt to dress, one stocking half up to the knee, the blouse half on, thick hair all over, all sense of modesty gone, but, even in distress, embarrassed to be found thus. The smell in the room was putrefying.

'Out of here, I think,' said Helen. 'Shut the door on it, wash your face and nothing else. Windows open, all over . . .'

'I didn't shut it. I never have the window shut . . .'

'Never mind. Clean clothes, but don't touch anything. And then . . .'

'Not tea. Not bloody tea. That bastard put something in my tea.'

Light was beginning to dawn in Kim's dull eyes.

'Coffee then,' said Helen. Again, they smiled.

'Men,' said Kimberley Perry with a touch of her old asperity. 'What a load of arseholes. Where's my son? Where's my Tom?'

Duncan had never known how close his wife lived to her would-be lover. Even Tom, wary of Dad's temper, had never said how Uncle Pip lived right next door at the domestic level as well as working cheek by jowl, to say nothing of bum to bum, in that overcrowded shop. Duncan, ever woolly about details, never quite imagined the proximity, although if he had thought, he would have known it. Somehow he never visualised neat little Pip, so precise in answering the phone and the parking of his car, to be quite as near as that in those depressing little flats. On that account he did not leg it over the balcony in search of the man who had abused his wife: he ran downstairs, and round the corner to the shop front where he had peered surreptitiously on so many occasions, picked up a plastic bread crate abandoned by the baker, and hurled it through the window. The sound of smashing glass did not diminish his rage, a rage made worse by the knowledge of his own injustice, his inability to do anything else but react. Duncan followed the hole he had made into the shop itself. There was a stand of toothpaste en route to a night light at the back, illuminating the written wish that all customers would have a happy Xmas. Heavy breathing at the counter was enough to move the tinsel strands in yellow and gold which drifted down towards Duncan's face. Pip's thumb tacks into the ceiling were inefficient and the tin foil drooped. Duncan seized it in one fist and tore it down.

'Come out, you randy little bastard, where are you . . .'

He did not expect a reply, nor was there one. Duncan stepped into the dispensary, marginally calmer. A slight breeze caught him from the jagged window and one large shard of glass fell with a delayed crash. He was legs, arms, underused muscle, sweeping away with one hand the contents of a shelf. Prepackaged goods, impossibly bound in cellophane and cardboard, fell to the floor. He squinted in the dim night light to read the label of a carton which fell against his head on the way down. Take three times a day. Towards the back of the room were more piled boxes, neat, obscuring a door under which shone a light. Duncan paused, smelt the familiar challenge of a door locked. He measured the length of the small corridor in which he stood, kicked the handle twice, winced as pain shot up into his knee, then cannoned against the wood. A flimsy door, easy Yale lock: the frame hung crooked as he went inside. A skill of his, to shoulder a door without propelling himself forward into the arms of enemy or dog, recovering soon enough to come to a breathy halt, with his hands over his groin, to protect what heavyweight denim could not. Silence. The place, empty, tiny, cramped and neat, enough to still all momentum, drown all sensation. The smell alone was one of aggressive innocence, the antiseptic smell of the hospital ward. Of righteousness and helplessness, persons in white coats saying they knew better, swallow this poison, and expecting obedience. Books ranged in neat lines, laboratory equipment, cupboards open. Duncan paused, awed by a sense of learning. Remembered instead the sense of revenge inflamed by a warmth and light in here. He caught sight of a small but uncongealed spot of blood on the floor.

Duncan cannoned through the second door, somehow expecting a succession of rooms, only to find beyond a deserted yard and the steps back upwards, the reverse of the route he had just followed in blind anger. In such anger, Duncan had only ever gone wherever he was led, directionless without guidance. He was essentially quite lawless: like a police dog which followed scents without landmarks, baying with excitement, protected later for its indiscretions. Part of him knew this, none of him cared. Get the bastard. The scent propelled him through a hole in the hoardings the other side of the road. Rapidly, hideously downhill in the rain, a sliding slippery slope like a sledge run, a trap. Stones and bricks fell against him: the bricks from some old cellar kept back by mud. He sat there, soaking and panting. Duncan had always needed a team.

Tom had never had a team, not even a quorum. He had been awake for a few seconds, which felt like minutes or hours, hugged as he was to this damp, muscular chest. Only when the man moved, rising with a sigh, did Tom's drugged mind begin to function, surfacing into fear with a swelling of nausea. But he was clasped tight in iron arms, large hands forming a cradle beneath his own buttocks, round his head polythene rustled with deafening sound. The chest was warm, but Tom had no sensation in his feet. His arms were folded against his chest and for a moment, he wanted to close his eyes again. He submitted to the temptation, but they refused to stay shut although he squeezed tight. Peering sideways, he began, in a series of blinks, to see where he might be and with whom. Then he opened his mouth to scream, but his throat, nose and ears were full of the sweaty scent of Pip's shirt and Pip's distinctive, lavender-flavoured, antiseptic smell. Tom's arms moved in compulsive disgust. Pip stopped abruptly.

'You awake, Tom, boy? Are you?'

Tom slumped. The voice was ominous, full of sedulous concern, the voice he knew and recalled hanging over him as his lungs filled with fumes: the same voice, now a loud whisper echoing against his head. There was silence all round them. Tom maintained it and Pip sighed again, adjusting the weight he carried by hoiking Tom further towards his shoulder as he walked. Footsteps squelched in the mud, slow, ponderous and purposeful, the rain easing down Tom's neck behind the cover. They were walking on a ridge between the foundations, Pip beginning to move slightly faster.

Urgency carried him forward to the destination he could see from the upstairs window. The foundations between which he trod had been mere scrapings of the earth when he had noticed them first on the night Margaret died, but now, below where the crane stood like a cross in the sky, and furthest away from the service road, was the largest excavation of all. Water below, only a few inches, but black water, ready to freeze before morning. He reached the edge. A mere sixteen feet of digging, plenty deep enough. Pip looked down, slightly giddy. If he threw Tom in here, he would hit the bottom via the side, revive perhaps for a minute or two, and perish quietly. In his mind's eye, Pip could hear the splash, the possible breaking of bone, the ensuing silence. No, not thrown: too brutal and the strength was draining from his numbing arms. The boy must merely be dropped, after a fashion. He walked carefully to the crumbling brink, leant right over carefully, Tom's foot swinging into view. Abruptly Pip heaved upright. The sight of that foot, a human piece of what he carried and held in this embrace, was unbearably pathetic, and the tears which had blinded him before were ceaseless still, blurring that spectacle of lethal black water. Feet without shoes. He hauled himself upright, panting.

'I can't, I can't, I can't . . .' Out loud, a voice he did not recognise as his own, a howl of despair. 'God help me, I can't do this . . .' Like the flash in the eyes of the drowning man he saw his orchestrated life, the love, the popularity, the carefully won respect, crumbling to nothing in the face of discovery. He could not move. The crane's lights shot daggers into his own, fragmenting tears. Tom's eyes, head lolling from sudden movement, caught the glimmer of water and the grave below their feet. He kicked, jerked, jackknifed his small body convulsively, and fell to earth. He curled where he fell, grasping the edge at Pip's feet, grovelling for the ankles to hold, an attitude of terrible, unconscious supplication. Then he heard, over and beyond another crescendo of sound bursting in his head, the banshee yell of his father, saw the mud-splattered legs of Uncle Pip vanish, heard a thin, fading scream.

Bailey saw them. Others, running from the workmen's shed, but not in pursuit, saw them. Boy and man, stumbling across the mud, Duncan in their clumsy footsteps, following. Watched the boy drop and Pip raise his hands in the air, gesturing to heaven. Duncan's renewed howling as he reached them both and dealt Pip a massive blow to the small of his back. Running, running, far too slowly through the weight of the mud, Bailey saw Pip catapult from sight, Duncan upright, and himself still seconds away. Bailey slipped, fell, ran again. Their growls carried on the air like the piercing shriek of a woman, Duncan again, a dark silhouette, standing mammoth as Bailey drew within feet of him, a gorilla of a man holding aloft a massive stone, raised above his head to fling on the recumbent form of Pip which lay below. Bailey cannoned into him, dragged both of them to earth in snarling, spitting fury, Duncan fighting him, fighting mad, pressing his face into mud. And then the heavens opened in one almighty crash, even the earth trembled and the world was full of the sound of smashing glass, rending metal. With his head jerked forward, Bailey could see the crane wobble before everything round them fell into complete and eerie silence. From a great distance, translated through his own, thunderous heartbeat, there came the sound of cheering.

In the early hours of dawn, the population of Herringbone Parade began to filter back. They came in staggered groups of cars, coach or ambulance, hollow-eyed, suspicious and relieved. As well as slightly disappointed by all this damp normality, the sad minimum of mess, some expecting to find a miraculous change. Such a fuss about nothing. Mrs Beale junior was enraged. The windows facing the service road and a mere few at the front were smashed, a crumbling of glass which left fragments inside as well as out, a sort of implosion. 'Bloody looters,' she howled. 'Where was those police boys then, shifting us all over the place. They should have bin here, watching.'

'They should've been keeping out of the bloody way,' Mrs Beale senior snorted with superior sense, clutching to the banister leading to her prison upstairs. 'What do you want? Young lads risking their balls to guard apples and rubbish?' She cackled. 'Besides, it's not looters, only the detonator. Same in the war, when they defused them. You don't know nothing.' Her daughter-in-law reflected how nimble she had become, as if the sudden change of scene had been a tonic: no talk of ulcers or heart attacks until she remembered the benefits of invalidity.

'Oh, dear, I need my prescription . . . Oh dear, oh dear . . . Having a turn . . .'

'Well you'll have to do without. Chemist's shut. Window boarded, police in there. See? Someone was robbed.'

Only Carlton's seemed to have been burgled, and the off-licence video, swift action perhaps by returning children, the one shop abruptly sealed by police, the video man left to seal his own. He was disgruntled by this unfair division of labour, ceased grumbling when told Mr Caring was in hospital. Poor Mr Pip, hope he's better soon. The bastards.

They seemed to like one another, Bailey sensed. Not, perhaps, destined to survive this particular emergency, but an easy attachment nevertheless, an exception to that strange and awkward shyness which seemed to afflict Helen amongst police officers' wives, the same defensiveness which crippled him with most of her peers of either sex. Two independent women, not surprising: they had probably spent half the anxious night talking. The fact that Helen liked Kimberley and Kimberley liked Helen enough for them to remain with each other was perfectly satisfactory for present purposes. Standing against the wall of the white hospital room, he wished he could summon half an ounce of affection for Duncan.

'I don't need to be in bed,' Kim said. 'For Christ's sake, they've taken samples of everything already. I don't even feel sick, specially now I know . . . well, he didn't quite get there, did he? I would have known that.' Flashes of the old bravado, desperately returning in search of itself. 'I've done a few things, but I've never been known to sleep through it. Have they finished with Tom?'

'Soon.'

All present fell silent. Tom, carried back to the flat, had been strangely withdrawn. My ears hurt, Mummy, they hurt, feeling sick. Nothing else, just that again and again like a litany. Sick as a dog. You and me both, said his mother, unable to prise away either her arms from his or his from hers, his face hidden in her chest like a suckling baby. Don't go, don't go, the same as he was ushered into the room in the light of mid-morning and placed himself immediately as close as he could get, only just becoming self-conscious about this need for touch. The skin was pinker, the eyes brighter, the attitude returning to some approximation of normal, enough for the enormous bandage round his head to be an obvious subject of pride. Half of him wished to show this dramatic badge to the world: the other half wanted to stay still and never, ever go back to Herringbone Parade.

'Do you want to tell us what happened?' Kim asked, her voice gentle but with an edge like sandpaper. His own version of roughly known or guessed facts was vital, but he shook his head. Helen held back any prompt, hating herself for thinking, I need this child as a witness: of course a ten-year-old boy can take an oath and doesn't even need corroboration. For seeing his mother prostrate, naked under the satyr-like figure of Uncle Pip, Tom had not quite forgiven her. For the rest, distortion was rife. He looked at them all. That woman, that man and Mummy. He was perfectly sure what he wanted to believe: there was a measure of hope in his voice.

'Daddy rescued me, Mum. He did, Mum, honestly. He rescued me, he was brave. It was Daddy brought me back. He was great.' The eyes held a challenge, a desperate dare, sliding away from Bailey's distant gaze, expecting, and prepared for, denial. Helen met Bailey's face across the tableau of the other two, noticed how no muscle moved, except to smile reassurance. 'Daddy's a big strong man,' Bailey murmured, and again Helen felt the treachery of other thoughts. If this boy lies here like this, will he lie elsewhere in a statement? If I know his evidence is tainted or embroidered to suit his own memory, could I ever present him as a witness of truth if the time comes? Thinking like Redwood. Kim was watching closely, feeling the silence through tired limbs. Continued simply to embrace her boy and, on the subject of Daddy's bravery, said nothing at all. Stretched instead. 'Where's you know who?' she asked after an interval. 'Getting better, is he? Only I am a pharmacist, and I'm worried about the shop. You know who can roast in hell, but I do care about the shop. Someone must watch it.'

Someone must watch, Pip thought. Someone is watching me now. Narcan, intravenously, dripping into his veins, the antidote for the methadone he had found in his muddy pockets and swallowed at the bottom of the pit, that damp hell where he had lain, weeping, listening to the world roar round him. In the moment of his own redemption, there had been that cataclysm of sound, like the thunderous voice of God, visiting revenge. He had lain there, staring upwards, his face half in water, proof against his own instinct to stand, watching the lights of the crane rock above him as if about to fall and crush his misery in one grande finale. He hauled himself to his knees in the pool, and his hands, not quite numb, fished in his pockets for some of the incrimination he carried. Returns from the shop, the same source of methadone he had given in that massive dose to Daniel the watcher, when Daniel was bemused by the blow. Raised and preserved in gentility, Pip the man had been almost proud of that blow. A step on the way to manhood, when no one was watching, a gesture disallowed in childhood when he was always watched. As he was watched now.

Someone watching him, someone always watching him, for ever and ever, amen. A life like this, no manhood, no privacy. When the nurse left him behind the screens, beyond which sat a man, Pip tried to pull the drip out of his arm. It was clumsily done, hurt with the dull insistence of toothache, but the plaster held it firm and he was weak. He did not want this antidote: he had not wanted to be alive. They knew more than he expected. Narcan, intravenously, not a stomach pump which would have hastened the end, and he cursed them for their knowledge.

He turned in the hard bed. With the one detached hand, he drew the sheet round his chin and shut his eyes. So he would tell them. Everything, why not? About how she would not have the window open, dear, darling Margaret. How Mama had tickled him to death. He would tell them all about chloroform kicks, write it down for them, and he would be watched all the time, never ever knowing what it was to exorcise passion. They would understand:

he hoped they would understand what was, to him, perfectly obvious. Prison. More and more watching. Until, with his knowledge of pills, he could find another route to oblivion.

Please, please, would someone open the window?

'It's stuffy in here. Smells. Is that dead dry cleaning in the back? Why do you always forget it? Shall I open the window?'

'If you like. Cold, though. You look terrible. Open it, I don't mind either way. Better than hospital air.'

'Sure you don't mind?'

Helen stopped pulling at the elusive seat belt of her car, a tangled piece of webbing which either spun enough belt to cover three fat persons at a time, or refused to budge without a series of savage pulls, and laughed in sudden, uproarious amusement.

'What's so funny?' Bailey was slightly injured to be the object of her infectious bark.

'You. You ask me three times if I mind about the window being open: you dither about something so small. I can see you looking at the handle, absolutely indecisive about whether to touch it or not, I'll watch you frown all the way home, wondering if you've done the right thing. Well, it is funny from a man who never thinks for a second about anything important. Leap into a pit of rattlesnakes, chase the devil barefoot over a minefield, juggle with bombs, no problem. Wind down the window, problem insoluble. Takes a good half hour to decide.'

He had the grace to smile, a full smile, reaching the eyes.

'Are you, by any chance, angry with me?' he asked.

'Nope. Never for long. Frequently puzzled. I'm well endowed with confusion, badly off for anger.' Her words, he noticed, always gathered speed and obscurity when she was tired. She started her car, which coughed into its own reluctant version of life. Bailey disliked being driven, hated the steam on the windows, wished she would consider a decent car for once. Then he opened the window.

'She's a great girl, Kimberley Perry. Will she go back to crazy Duncan?'

Bailey remembered the raging animal in the dark, ready to throw the stone which could murder, action without checks, strength without discrimination, love without analysis. 'I sincerely hope not,' he said.

'I was thinking,' Helen said, driving slowly, conscious of Bailey's discomfort and the ice on the road. 'I was thinking how it isn't all Duncan's fault. What he is, I mean. Somewhat abused. You told me he's always used because of the width of his shoulders, like a fearless animal. The person you send into the fray, the portable battering ram. Programmed, psyched up in advance. Then when he breaks down the door or brings another gorilla to earth, everyone fêtes him, buys him drinks, says, great lad, Dunc, yeah. Bit like being some sort of soft porn pin-up. Feed booze to the animal door breaker, don't encourage him to think, he's so useful as he is. As subtle with women as he is with doors. Until suddenly, it all goes wrong on him and he doesn't know how to change and being Mr Big Guy doesn't work. If he's got any finesse, he's been taught to suppress it. Sorry, if I'm not being very clear.'

Again, he noticed the speeding up of words. Remembered Duncan by the bedside, caring less for the wife than the despoiling of his property. Caring less for his son than he did for revenge.

'You're quite astute and very forgiving,' Bailey remarked, fishing for the cigarette which would shorten the journey, 'but I doubt if Kimberley will see it quite like that.'

'Oh I don't know. I really don't. He did come out, didn't he? Stopped Carlton. Got you there? Christ, the law's stupid. And slow. We mess round with statements and meetings and decisions and proof and personalities, while Hell freezes.' There was a hard edge of bitterness to her voice. 'And then it takes a drunken bum to do what we couldn't. It makes me ashamed to be what I am.' Angry tears were standing in her eyes, never to fall. They drove on in silence.

'Nice little boy,' Helen added, apropos of nothing, a very slight undertone of wistfulness in her voice.

'Yes he is. Wouldn't you like one?'

Helen was silent, thinking on another tangent. Changing from woman to lawyer.

'Will he tell the truth, though? I want him to forget it all for his own sake, remember it for a

275

statement,' was all she said. Then, 'I want to see what the chemist has to say. Why? Why did he do all this? What festers with him? What's the background? He's talking to Collins. Collins says he won't stop. Good. We need confessions.'

The heater in Helen's car was always slow. She was right: it was cold, inside and out. Bailey wiped the side window with the back of his hand, feeling as he did so the cold of the moisture and an indefinable sensation of sadness.

She was better frail.